THE
ULTIMATE,
ILLUSTRATED
beats
CHRONOLOGY

THE ULTIMATE, ILLUSTRATED *beats* CHRONOLOGY

Robert Niemi

Soft Skull Press

2011

Library of Congress Cataloging-in-Publication Data
is available.

ISBN 13: 978-1-59376-411-1

Cover design by Alvaro Villanueva
Cover photograph by John Hopkins
Interior design by Domini Dragoone
Printed in the United States of America

Soft Skull Press
An Imprint of Counterpoint LLC
1919 Fifth Street
Berkeley, CA 94710

www.softskull.com
www.counterpointpress.com
Distributed by Publishers Group West
10 9 8 7 6 5 4 3 2 1

TO
CONNIE
DUFOUR,
THE
hippest
CHICK
OF THEM
ALL

AND FOR
STEVE
SOITOS,
WHO
GAVE ME
shelter
FROM THE
STORM

THE ULTIMATE, ILLUSTRATED *beats* CHRONOLOGY

CONTENTS

INTRODUCTION

NO OTHER MODERN LITERARY-CULTURAL phenomenon has been so maligned, so over-praised, so caricatured, or so misunderstood as that of the Beats. Progenitors of a coun-tercultural revolution that has transformed the world since the mid-1950s, Jack Kerouac, Allen Ginsberg, William S. Burroughs, Gregory Corso, Lawrence Ferlinghetti, Gary Snyder, John Clellon Holmes, Herbert Huncke, Bob Kauf-man, and many others expressed an anarchic, ecstatically existentialist sensibility—one that affirmed fellow feeling over indifference, non-violence over militarism, creative spontaneity over drudgery, sexual and emotional freedom and candor over repression, raw experience over social status, simple joy in life over political

1

paranoia and emotional sclerosis. In the years after World War II, when America was inexorably morphing into a permanent garrison state dedicated to worshiping money and power, the Beat writers merrily wandered off the reservation in search of something—anything—more meaningful than accumulating capital or settling for a steady job, a starter house, a La-Z-Boy recliner, and a droning TV set.

Not surprisingly, in their rebellion against the hegemony of materialism, the Beats earned the undying enmity of corporatist lackeys, Cold Warriors, conservative religionists, professional moral scolds, and decency cops of all stripes. The Beats also earned the often-valid criticism of more temperate intellectuals who found their work sketchy and their lives and values even sketchier. Indeed, as expressive of a freewheeling, restlessly experimental aesthetic, the literary quality of Beat writing varies widely, from the sublime to the banal and the sometimes ridiculous. The Beats were, by any reasonable measure, a very motley crew in terms of personal deportment. Righteous citizens need not look far to find damning examples of aberrant or atrociously irresponsible behavior and misogynist tendencies. William S. Burroughs, a longtime heroin addict, shot and killed his wife, Joan, in a drunken game of William Tell in Mexico City—and avoided prison by fleeing to Morocco. Kerouac was a world champion wastrel, anti-Semite, and mama's boy who quite literally drank himself to death by the age of 47. Allen Ginsberg, Carl Solomon, and Seymour Krim were alumni of mental institutions. Ginsberg's long-term partner, Peter Orlovsky, was a sometimes-violent drug addict and an all-around loose cannon. Ex-con Neal Cassady—whom Kerouac used as his model for the hero of *On the Road*—was probably a sociopath, certainly a womanizing con man who, whenever it became expedient, abandoned his wives, girlfriends, and children, as did Burroughs and Kerouac. Gregory Corso was a convicted felon, drug addict, and freeloader, as were Herbert Huncke, Alexander Trocchi, and many other writers of that period. Beat fellow traveler Lucien Carr stabbed and killed his gay stalker, David Kammerer, and spent a year in prison for manslaughter. Norman Mailer, another Beat fellow traveler, stabbed and almost killed his second wife, Adele. Among the major Beat writers, perhaps only Ferlinghetti, Snyder, and Holmes could be deemed relatively "normal" and reliable.[1]

Yet ad hominem attacks on the Beats' artistic bona fides or personal ethics ultimately miss the point of the Beat movement. It's not who they were exactly or what they achieved or didn't achieve—it's all about the instinctual spirit of rebellion they embodied, an unashamedly individualistic spirit that hearkens back to America's frontier origins. In essence, the Beats were party crashers par excellence. They demanded the unthinkable in a modern, technocratic, and tightly controlled class-based society: the freedom to live the sorts of emotionally, spiritually, and culturally rich lives exclusively reserved for members of the leisure class—a demand understandably met with horror and outrage by guardians of the status quo because it flew in the face of capitalist modernity's master equation: that money equals life and that those without money must resign themselves to boredom, anonymity, and dull toil. Much is made of the Beats as cultural rebels; more needs to be said about them as social class rebels.

Now that American-style business civilization, in ideology and practice, has finally conquered the world, imposing its crushing imperatives of debt, worry, and helplessness on most every hapless citizen of the planet, the Beat ethos looks surprisingly sane and increasingly appealing. Though no one would have predicted it fifty years ago, the

Beat phenomenon has exhibited amazing staying power, as demonstrated by the chronology you are about to peruse. Consider the scope of the time frame. Kerouac, Ginsberg, and Burroughs met in New York City in the early 1940s. They did their best work and achieved their greatest notoriety in the 1950s. Since then, international interest in the Beats has grown steadily, almost exponentially, and it shows no sign of abating. As you will see in the final pages of this chronology, a new book, film, or public event relating to the Beats seems to surface every month or two—poignant evidence that the perennial human need to be free, creative, expressive, and at home in the world is as alive and persistent as it ever was.

WHY PRODUCE AN EXHAUSTIVELY DETAILED and thickly contextualized Beats chronology? Many other Beats chronologies exist, either in omnibus form or on individual Beat writers. True enough, but a really comprehensive, precise, and richly detailed chronology that affords an instant overview of all the major and minor Beat figures has never been attempted until now. A number of related insights emerge from the myriad juxtapositions and convergences set out here. Particularly striking is the immense scope of the

Beat phenomenon in terms of the time frame, the number of people involved, and the amount of work produced. More specifically, a cursory survey of the "prehistory" of the Beats suggests that, apart from Kenneth Rexroth, William S. Burroughs, Lawrence Ferlinghetti, and a few others, most of the first generation of Beat writers were born in the 1920s and were thus children of the Jazz Age and still very young during the first flowering of modernism. These young people were growing up just as the country plunged into the Great Depression. This traumatic expulsion from a halcyon time into a dystopian world of wounded nostalgia, defeated idealism, and an enduringly tragic sense of life was a psychohistorical catastrophe for a whole generation.

From a sociological standpoint one also notices the sheer diversity of origins, geographically and demographically, though some patterns quickly emerge. Most of the first-generation Beats hailed either from the northeast megalopolis (especially from Massachusetts, New York City, and New Jersey) or from the West Coast (with the notable exceptions of William S. Burroughs, who was from Saint Louis, and Neal Cassady, from Salt Lake City). No surprise here; the coastal areas have always been more densely populated and more culturally active than other parts of the country, thus providing more fertile ground for the cultivation of restless, intellectually inquisitive sensibilities.[2] The other thing one notices about the Beats is the sheer diversity of their social and class backgrounds, from fairly affluent (Paul Bowles, the son of a dentist; Henri Cru, the son of a French professor; William S. Burroughs, from a family of means) to bourgeois (Allen Ginsberg, the son of a schoolteacher and poet; Jack Kerouac, the son of a printer) to working class (Bob Kaufman, the son of a merchant seaman; John Wieners, the son of a janitor) to lumpen (Neal Cassady, the son of a Denver drunk; Gregory Corso, an abandoned child who grew up on the streets). Place of origin and family circumstances clearly helped shape the Beats but not in any predictable way. One might therefore attribute the emergence of the Beat sensibility to the cultural zeitgeist of the 1940s, but that would be an exercise in pop-cult mysticism. There is no zeitgeist per se, no ontological world spirit that infiltrates the age like a psychic fog. There are, instead, specific and concrete influences and events that shape the consciousness of unusually perceptive individuals. What the Beats saw and felt in the 1940s was a world beyond crisis, a world that had ruptured and spilled all its putative meaning and legitimacy into an obscenely violent quotidian that did not deserve and could not support the credulity or emotional loyalty of any thinking human being. Even a casual study of the first-generation Beats shows that—contrary to the persistent, derogatory stereotype of them as dilettantes—almost all were incredibly well-read intellectuals but intellectuals of a particular stripe. While Ezra Pound and T.S. Eliot cited classical Eastern and Western literary and religious texts as their inspiration, the Beats were moved by grittier, more contemporary fare: for example, the fascinating memoirs of career criminal Jack Black, the nightmare picaresque novels of Louis-Ferdinand Céline, the dark prophecies of Oswald Spengler. More deeply and fundamentally alienated, the Beats and their fellow travelers had the street smarts and experiences to make a virtue of spontaneity and improvisation (which they learned from jazz) and thus avoid the plodding, fey intellectual elitism that characterized the high modernists and their epigones in academe. In short, the Beats were better equipped to push life and art much closer to the Nietzschean abyss and to plumb its mysteries for better or worse. The

Beats still survive and flourish as a cultural phenomenon because they were and are sexy, dangerous, irreverent spiritual anarchists in a tame world. As Joyce Johnson aptly put it, "repression breeds intensity."

NOTES

1. It may be worth pointing out, however, that many modern American writers who appeared more conventional were hardly paragons of mental health. Ernest Hemingway, Sylvia Plath, John Berryman, and Anne Sexton were all people with chronic depression who eventually committed suicide. Scores of other writers not associated with the Beats were maladjusted and had medical conditions, including alcoholism, drug addiction, bipolar disorder, and schizophrenia.

2. Interestingly, not a single Beat was from the South, unless one considers Hunter S. Thompson, a third-generation quasi-Beat writer who was enamored of guns and fireworks.

CHAPTER ONE

PREHISTORY 1903– 1942

1903

NOV. 29: **Myron Reed "Slim" Brundage** is born at Idaho State Hospital, an insane asylum in Blackfoot, Idaho, where his mother is employed. [DEC. 17: THE WRIGHT BROTHERS MAKE THE FIRST POWERED AIR-PLANE FLIGHT AT KITTY HAWK, NORTH CAROLINA.]

1905

DEC. 22: **Kenneth Rexroth**, a prime force behind the post–World War II San Francisco poetry renaissance, is born in South Bend, Indiana, the son of Charles Rexroth, a pharmaceuticals salesman, and Delia Reed, a homemaker.

1906

APRIL 5: **Richard Myrle Buckley** (later known as hip comic-monologist **Lord Buckley**) is born in Tuolumne, a remote Californian mining village on the western edge of Yosemite National Park.

1910

DEC. 19: **Jean Genet** is born to a young prostitute in Paris (who puts him up for adoption after a year);
DEC. 30: **Paul Bowles** is born in Long Island, New York, the son of a dentist; DEC. 27: **Charles Olson** is born in Worcester, Massachusetts, the son of a mailman.

1911

DEC. 13: **Kenneth Patchen**, the son of a Youngstown, Ohio steelworker, is born in Niles, Ohio; he later becomes a poet-artist and a precursor to the Beats.

1912

[APRIL 15: DURING ITS MAIDEN VOYAGE FROM SOUTH-AMPTON TO NEW YORK, THE "UNSINKABLE" RMS TITANIC SINKS WITHIN THREE HOURS AFTER HITTING AN ICEBERG; 1,517 DROWN IN THE FRIGID WATERS OF THE NORTH ATLANTIC; 705 SURVIVE IN LIFEBOATS.]
SEPT. 10: **William Oliver Everson** (later known as **Brother Antoninus**) is born in Sacramento, California, to Christian Scientist parents.

1913

[FEB. 17—MARCH 15: THE INTERNATIONAL EXHIBITION

OF MODERN ART (I.E., "THE ARMORY SHOW") IS HELD AT THE SIXTY-NINTH REGIMENT ARMORY, LEXINGTON AVENUE, BETWEEN TWENTY-FIFTH AND TWENTY-SIXTH STREETS, NEW YORK CITY.] **Kells Elvins** is born in Saint Louis, Missouri.

1914

FEB. 5: **William Seward Burroughs Jr.** is born into a wealthy family in Saint Louis, Missouri; [JUNE 28: WORLD WAR I BEGINS.] SEPT. 28: **Miriam Oikemus** is born in Belmont, Massachusetts, to Finnish socialist parents.

1915

JAN. 6: **Alan Wilson Watts** is born in Chislchurst, Kent, England; OCT. 15: **Gabrielle Levesque** and **Leo Kerouac** are married at the Saint Louis de Gonzague Catholic Church, 38 W. Hollis Street, Nashua, New Hampshire; DEC. 9: **Herbert Edwin Huncke** is born in Greenfield, Massachusetts, the son of Herbert Spencer Huncke and Marguerite Bell Huncke.

1916

JAN. 19: **John Clifford Brion Gysin** is born in Taplow, England, eight months after his father's death in action in World War I; MAY 26: **Louis Thomas Hardin** is born in Marysville, Kansas; he later becomes the

blind street musician and composer **"Moondog"**;
JULY 16: **Harold Rosen (Harold Norse)** is born to an
unmarried Lithuanian Jewish immigrant in Brooklyn,
New York City; AUG. 23: **Jack Kerouac's** older brother,
Gerard Kerouac, is born in Lowell, Massachusetts.

1917

FEB. 22: **Jane Sydney Auer (Jane Bowles)** is born in
New York City; [APRIL 6: THE U.S. ENTERS WORLD WAR I
AFTER THE SINKING OF THE *LUSITANIA*.] NOV. 2: **George
Alexander Legman (Gershon Legman)** is born in
Scranton, Pennsylvania, the son of a kosher butcher.

1918

THIS YEAR: **William S. Burroughs** is allegedly sexually molested by a male friend of a beloved nanny, an
incident that leaves deep psychosexual scars; JAN. 17:
Shirley Burns Brennan, later known as **Sheri Martinelli**, is born in Philadelphia; OCT. 25: **Jack Kerouac's**
sister, **Carolyn "Nin" Kerouac**, is born in Lowell, Massachusetts. [NOV. 11: ARMISTICE DAY—WORLD WAR
I ENDS AFTER FOUR AND A HALF YEARS OF FIGHTING;
TEN MILLION PEOPLE HAVE BEEN KILLED, AND MIL-
LIONS MORE HAVE BEEN WOUNDED OR DISPLACED.]

1919

JAN. 7: **Edward Howard Duncan Jr.** (later known

as **Robert Duncan**) is born in Oakland, California; his mother dies in childbirth; MARCH 24: **Lawrence Ferlinghetti** is born in Yonkers, New York; his father, **Carlo Ferlinghetti**, had died six months before, and his mother, née **Clemence Albertine Mendes-Monsanto**, is committed to an insane asylum shortly after his birth; he is raised by an aunt. [DEC.: ATTORNEY GENERAL A. MITCHELL PALMER (1872–1936) ORDERS A SERIES OF RAIDS ON SUSPECTED "SUBVERSIVES" (E.G. LEFTISTS, UNION ACTIVISTS, PROGRESSIVE INTELLECTUALS).]

1920

AUG. 16: **Heinrich Karl "Charles" Bukowski** is born in Andernach, Germany; OCT. 22: **Timothy Leary** is born in Springfield, Massachusetts, the only child of an Irish American dentist; **Edward H. Duncan Jr.** is adopted by **Edwin** and **Minnehaha Symmes**, a prominent pair of devout Theosophists; they rename him **Robert Edward Symmes**.

1921

APRIL 2: **Henri Cru** is born in eastern Massachusetts to an English mother; his father, Albert L. Cru, is a French professor.

1922

JAN. 23: **Alan Aisenstein (Alan Ansen)** is born in

Brooklyn, New York, the son of a New York watch importer; [FEB. 2: SYLVIA BEACH PUBLISHES *ULYSSES* BY JAMES JOYCE.] MARCH 12: **Jean-Louis "Jack" Kerouac** is born in Lowell, Massachusetts, the son of a self-employed printer and a homemaker; MAY 11: **Seymour Krim** is born in New York City; MAY 22: **Kerouac's** childhood friend, **Sebastian G. Sampatacacus (Sammy Sampas)** is born in Lowell, Massachusetts; SEPT. 20: **Frankie Edie Parker** is born in Detroit, Michigan; [OCT. 28: BENITO MUSSOLINI COMES TO POWER IN ITALY; NOV.: *THE DIAL* MAGAZINE PUBLISHES THE *WASTELAND* BY T.S. ELIOT.] **William S. Burroughs**, 8, begins writing his own stories, such as "The Autobiography of a Wolf"; DEC. 24: **Jonas Mekas** is born in Semenikiai, a small village near Birai, Lithuania; DEC. 29: **William Gaddis** is born in New York City; **William "Bill" Cannastra** is born in Schenectady, New York; **William S. Burroughs** is introduced to firearms by his father.

1923

JAN. 21: **Norman Kingsley Mailer** is born in Long Branch, New Jersey; FEB. 4: **Joan Vollmer** is born in Loudonville (an affluent suburb of Albany, New York); APRIL 28: **Carolyn Elizabeth Robinson** is born in Lansing, Michigan; SEPT. 28: **Tuli Kupferberg** is born in New York City; OCT. 20: **Philip Whalen** is born in Portland, Oregon; **Kenneth Rexroth**, 18, serves a prison term in Chicago for part ownership of a brothel; **Haldon "Hal" Chase** is born in Colorado; **Herbert Huncke**, 8, has his first homosexual encounter, with a man about twenty years old, in Chicago.

1924

MARCH 9: **Herbert Gold** is born in Cleveland, Ohio; **Allan Temko** is born in New York City; **Joan Vollmer** is born in Loudonville, New York (just north of Albany); [SEPT. 10: JUDGE JOHN R. CAVERLY SENTENCES NATHAN LOEB, 19, AND RICHARD LEOPOLD, 19, TO "LIFE PLUS 99 YEARS" FOR THE "THRILL KILL" SLAYING OF BOBBY FRANKS, 14, IN CHICAGO.] **Kenneth Rexroth**, 19, hitchhikes across the U.S.; NOV. 9: **Robert Frank** is born in Zurich, Switzerland; DEC. 31: **Taylor Mead** is born in Grosse Pointe, Michigan.

1925

JAN. 30: **John Lester "Jack" Spicer** is born in Los Angeles; MARCH 1: **Lucien Carr** is born in New York City; [APRIL 10: SCRIBNER'S PUBLISHES F. SCOTT FITZGERALD'S THE *GREAT GATSBY*.] APRIL 18: **Robert Garnell "Bob" Kaufman** is born in New Orleans; MAY 18: **Robin Blaser** is born in Denver, Colorado; [JULY 10–21: THE SCOPES "MONKEY TRIAL" IS HELD IN DAYTON, TENNESSEE.] JULY 30: **Alexander Whitelaw**

Robertson Trocchi is born in Glasgow, Scotland; SEPT. 1: Future jazz great **Arthur "Art" Edward Pepper Jr.** is born in Gardena, California; OCT. 13: **Leonard Alfred Schneider** (later known as **Lenny Bruce**) is born in Mineola (Long Island), New York.

1926

FEB. 8: **Neal Leon Cassady** is born in Salt Lake City, Utah; MARCH 12: **John Clellon Holmes** is born in Holyoke, Massachusetts; MAY 21: **Robert Creeley** is born in Arlington, Massachusetts; JUNE 2: **Jack Kerouac's** older brother **Gerard**, 9, dies of rheumatic fever; JUNE 3: **Irwin Allen Ginsberg** is born in Newark, New Jersey; AUG. 26: **Lewis Barrett "Lew" Welch Jr.** is born in Phoenix, Arizona; SEPT. 2: **Jean Genet**, 15, begins serving a thirty-one-month sentence at the Mettray Penal Colony (near Tours, France) for various crimes and misdemeanors. [OCT. 22: SCRIBNER'S PUBLISHES ERNEST HEMINGWAY'S "LOST GENERATION" NOVEL *THE SUN ALSO RISES*.]

1927

JAN. 23: **Anton Rosenberg** is born in Brooklyn, New York, the son of a wealthy industrialist; [MAY 20–21: CHARLES A. LINDBERGH FLIES SOLO ACROSS THE ATLANTIC OCEAN, NEW YORK TO PARIS, AND BECOMES AN INTERNATIONAL CELEBRITY.] JULY 30: **Victor Wong**

(Huáng Zìqiáng) is born in San Francisco; OCT. 23:

Philip Lamantia is born in San Francisco; **William**

S. Burroughs, 13, reads **Jack Black's** underground

autobiography *You Can't Win* (Macmillan, 1926)

and is deeply impressed; [AUG. 23: TWO ITALIAN

ANARCHISTS—NICOLA SACCO, 36, AND BARTOLOMEO

VANZETTI, 39—ARE EXECUTED FOR THE MURDER OF

A BROCKTON PAYROLL CLERK IN MASSACHUSETTS

AMIDST MASS PROTESTS; DEC. 28: **WALTER BENJA-**

MIN, 35, TAKES HASHISH AND LATER EXPERIMENTS

WITH OPIUM AND MESCALINE.] **Kenneth Rexroth**, 22,

marries **Andrée Schafer**, 25, an artist, in Chicago; the

newlyweds hitchhike to Seattle for their honeymoon

and then move to San Francisco (where **Rexroth** will

remain for the next forty years); **Herbert Huncke**, 12,

begins smoking marijuana and travels to New York City

from Chicago but the police return him to New York.

1928

MARCH 30: **Carl Wolfe Solomon** is born in the Bronx,

New York; MAY 5: **Albert Gilbert "Al" Aronowitz** is

born in Bordentown, New Jersey; MAY 8: **Richard**

William "Dick" McBride is born in Washington, Indi-

ana; JUNE 23: **Hubert Selby Jr.** is born in Brooklyn,

New York; his father is a merchant seaman; JULY 4:

Theodore "Ted" Joans is born on a riverboat in Cairo,

Illinois; AUG. 6: **Andrew Warhola (Andy Warhol)** is

born in Pittsburgh, Pennsylvania; **Robert Creeley**, 2, loses his left eye as the result of a car accident; [SMITH, KLINE & FRENCH BEGIN MARKETING AN OVER-THE-COUNTER BENZEDRINE INHALER.] **Will Petersen** is born in Chicago to German immigrant parents, Robert Petersen and Minni Eder.

1929

[FEB 14: SAINT VALENTINE'S DAY MASSACRE: FOUR OF AL CAPONE'S HENCHMEN MURDER SIX MEMBERS OF A RIVAL GANG IN CHICAGO.] APRIL 2: **Edward Merton "Ed" Dorn** is born in Villa Grove, Illinois; MARCH 1: **Jean Genet**, 18, is released from prison; he joins the French Foreign Legion but is soon discharged as unfit; APRIL 27: **Paul Bowles**, 18, sails to France; JULY 24: After three months in Europe, **Bowles** returns to New York; [OCT. 24: BLACK THURSDAY—THE STOCK MARKET CRASHES.] NOV. 6: **Harvey Martin Silver (Jack Micheline)** is born in the Bronx, New York; **William S. Burroughs**, 15, afflicted with sinus troubles, is sent to the arid atmosphere of New Mexico (in the 1940s, a primary site of the Manhattan Project), where he enters a boy's academy, Los Alamos Ranch School, and publishes his first essay, "Personal Magnetism," in the *John Burroughs Review*; **Harriet Sohmers (Harriet Zwerling)** is born in New York City; **William Mossman (Bill Heine)** is born in New York City.

1930

MARCH 26: **Gregory Nunzio Corso** is born in New York City; APRIL: **Corso's** sixteen-year-old mother, **Michelina Corso**, abandons him; Corso spends the next eleven years in foster care; MAY 8: **Gary Sherman Snyder** is born in San Francisco; NOV. 17: **David Amram** is born in Philadelphia, Pennsylvania; DEC. 31: **John Thomas Idlet** is born in Baltimore, Maryland.

1931

[MARCH 30: AN ALL-WHITE JURY IN GEORGIA INDICTS THE "SCOTTSBORO BOYS" FOR ALLEGEDLY RAPING TWO WHITE WOMEN.] SEPT: **Brion Gysin**, 15, is sent to Downside School (in Stratton-on-the-Fosse, near Bath in England), a prestigious college known as "the Eton of Catholic public schools" run by the Benedictines; **Joan Haverty** is born in Los Angeles; **Carolyn Robinson's** family moves from Lansing, Michigan, to Nashville, Tennessee; she attends the Ward-Belmont Preparatory School for Girls.

1932

JAN. 14: **Lenore Kandel** is born in New York City; [JULY 28: U.S. ARMY TROOPS LED BY **DOUGLAS MACARTHUR** AND **GEORGE PATTON** ROUT THE "BONUS ARMY" IN WASHINGTON, D.C.] APRIL 9: **Paul Krassner** is born in New York City; JUNE: **Charles Olson** graduates from

Wesleyan University with a BA in English; SUMMER: **William S. Burroughs**, 18, loses his virginity in an East Saint Louis brothel; SEPT.: **William Everson**, 18, begins college at California State University, Fresno; OCT. 20: **Michael McClure** is born in Marysville, Kansas; [NOV. 5: FRANKLIN DELANO ROOSEVELT IS ELECTED PRESIDENT OVER INCUMBENT HERBERT HOOVER.] NOV. 27: **Stanton "Kirby" Doyle** is born in San Francisco; **Slim Brundage**, 29, opens the first "College of Complexes," a forum for radical intellectuals at 1317 N. Clark Street, Chicago, but the establishment closes after a few months; **Edward Marshall** is born in Chichester, New Hampshire; **Herbert Huncke**, 16, meets **Elsie John**, a hermaphrodite, pot smoker, and heroin addict, in a Chicago midway freak show; **Huncke** becomes **John's** drug courier for a time.

1933

[JAN. 30: ADOLF HITLER BECOMES CHANCELLOR OF GERMANY; MARCH 4: FRANKLIN DELANO ROOSEVELT TAKES OFFICE.] MAY: **Charles Olson** earns an MA in English from Wesleyan University; JULY 8: **Peter Orlovsky** is born on the Lower East Side, New York City; **William S. Burroughs**, 19, and **David Kammerer**, 22, spend the summer in Paris and London; SUMMER: **William Everson**, 21, drops out of California State University, Fresno to join the Civilian Conservation

Corps (CCC); [SEPT.: CLASSICS SCHOLAR JOHN ANDREWS RICE (1888–1968) AND COLLEAGUES WHO RECENTLY WERE FIRED OR HAD RESIGNED FROM ROLLINS COLLEGE, WINTER PARK, FLORIDA, ESTABLISH BLACK MOUNTAIN COLLEGE, AN EXPERIMENTAL LIVING-LEARNING COLLEGE NEAR ASHEVILLE, NORTH CAROLINA.] **Jack Kerouac**, 11, begins writing fiction; **Elise Nada Cowen** is born to a wealthy Jewish family on Long Island; DEC. 31: The Modern Editions Press publishes **Paul Bowles's** "Two Poems."

1934

JAN. 6: **John Wieners** is born in Milton, Massachusetts, the son of a Boston maintenance worker; FEB. 22: **Ray Bremser** is born in Jersey City, New Jersey; APRIL: Little, Brown publishes the first U.S. edition of **Louis-Ferdinand Céline's** 1932 novel *Voyage au bout de la nuit (Journey to the End of the Night)*, translated from the French by **John H.P. Marks**; JUNE 28: **Kenneth Patchen**, 22, and **Miriam Oikemus**, 19, marry in Sharon, Pennsylvania; AUG. 6: **Diane di Prima** is born in Brooklyn, New York; [AUG. 19: HITLER MERGES THE OFFICES OF PRESIDENT AND CHANCELLOR TO BECOME GERMANY'S FÜHRER.] SEPT. 21: **Leonard Norman Cohen** is born to a wealthy Jewish family in Montreal, Quebec, Canada; OCT. 7: **Everett LeRoi Jones (Amiri Baraka)** is born in Newark, New Jersey;

His father, Gerald Roi Jones, works as a postal supervisor and lift operator; his mother, Anna Lois (née Russ) Jones, is a social worker; [OCT. 23–24: THE FINAL, DELIRIOUS WORDS (SOME 2,000 OF THEM) OF DYING GANGSTER DUTCH SCHULTZ (ARTHUR FLEGEN-HEIMER) ARE RECORDED BY A POLICE STENOGRAPHER; THIS DOCUMENT WILL LATER FASCINATE WILLIAM S. BURROUGHS.] NOV. 15: **Ted Berrigan** is born in Providence, Rhode Island; NOV. 19: **Joanne Kyger** is born in Long Beach, California; **Hettie Cohen** is born in Brooklyn, New York; Obelisk Press (Paris) publishes **Henry Miller's** *Tropic of Cancer*; **Neal Cassady**, 8, has his first sexual experience; **Brion Gysin**, 18, moves to Paris, falls in with members of the surrealist movement; **Jane Auer**, 17, meets **Louis-Ferdinand Céline**, 44, on a trans-Atlantic voyage to New York; she decides to become a writer.

1935

JAN. 30: **Richard Brautigan** is born in Tacoma, Washington; FEB. 3: **Ira Cohen** is born in New York City; FEB.: **Jean-Paul Sartre** experiments with mescaline; JUNE 20: **William S. Burroughs's** friend **Kells Elvins** graduates from Harvard University cum laude; SEPT. 17: **Kenneth Elton "Ken" Kesey** is born in La Junta, Colorado; **Joyce Glassman** is born in New York City; Obelisk Press (Paris) publishes **Henry Miller's** *Aller*

HENRY MILLER'S
TROPIC OF CANCER, 1934

Retour; **Charles "Charley" Plymell** is born in a converted chicken shed outside of Holcomb, Kansas; DEC. 13: After initially including some of **Brion Gysin's** artwork in a major group exhibition of surrealist drawings at the Galerie aux Quatre Chemins, **André Breton** changes his mind and excludes **Gysin**; **Carolyn Robinson**, 12, joins the Nashville Community Playhouse, where she later wins awards for set designs.

1936

JAN. 14: **Ken Babbs** is born in Columbus, Ohio; MARCH 30: **Kenneth Patchen** is awarded a Guggenheim Fellowship; JUNE: **Burroughs** graduates from Harvard University with an AB in English literature; he goes to Vienna to study medicine but does not complete his studies; Obelisk Press (Paris) publishes **Henry Miller's** *Black Spring*; [JULY 17: THE SPANISH CIVIL WAR BEGINS; SEPT: WALTER J. FREEMAN AND JAMES WATTS PERFORM THE FIRST LOBOTOMY; THE

PATIENT IS A SIXTY-THREE-YEAR-OLD WOMAN NAMED ALICE HAMMATT.] OCT. 3: **Nancy Joyce Peters** is born in Seattle, Washington; NOV. 10: **Ann Danberg (Ann Charters)** is born in Bridgeport, Connecticut; NOV. 11: **Michael John Fles** is born in London to a British mother, Pearl Rimel; his father, George Fles (1908–1939), a Dutch communist, is imprisoned in a Russian gulag during **Stalin's** Great Purge; [DEC.: 30: IN FLINT, MICHIGAN, MEMBERS OF THE UNITED AUTO WORKERS BEGIN A "SIT-DOWN STRIKE" AGAINST GENERAL MOTORS; THE STRIKE LEADS TO THE UNIONIZATION OF THE U.S. AUTO INDUSTRY.] **Maude Jean Scheuer Cassady**, 44, **Neal Cassady's** mother, dies; his alcoholic father raises Cassady thereafter.

1937

MARCH 8: **Richard Fariña** is born in Brooklyn, New York; APRIL 15: **Dan Propper** is born in Coney Island, Brooklyn, New York; JUNE 24: **Allen Ginsberg's** mother, **Naomi (Levy) Ginsberg**, 43, attempts suicide; JUNE: **Allen Ginsberg**, 11, begins to keep a journal; [JULY 2: FAMED AVIATOR AMELIA EARHART, 39, GOES MISSING OVER THE PACIFIC WHILE ATTEMPTING AN AROUND-THE-WORLD FLIGHT.] JULY 18: **Hunter S. Thompson** is born in Louisville, Kentucky; [AUG. 2: MARIHUANA TAX ACT, CRIMINALIZING MARIJUANA, IS PASSED BY CONGRESS.] **Kenneth Patchen**, 26, is per-

MARY CARNEY, 1921-1993

manently disabled by a back injury while attempting to repair a friend's car; AUG. 2: At the U.S. consulate in Athens, Greece, **William S. Burroughs**, 23, marries **Ilse Herzfeld Klapper**, 37, a wealthy German Jew, so she could immigrate to the U.S. and avoid Nazi persecution; **Burroughs** and **Klapper** see each other socially in New York until **Klapper** returns to Europe in 1945; **Burroughs** obtains a divorce in 1946; AUG. 21: **Robert Stone** is born in Brooklyn, New York; **Stone's** father soon abandons him and his mother, a grammar school teacher whose schizophrenia often leads to her hospitalization, while **Stone** is still an infant; SEPT. 10: **Antony Balch** is born in London.

1938

JAN. 1: **Jack Kerouac**, 16, begins his first love affair, with a Lowell girl named **Mary Carney**; FEB. 21: **Jane Auer** and **Paul Bowles** marry; MAY: **Harold Norse**, 22, graduates from Brooklyn College and meets **Chester Kallman**; SUMMER: **Brion Gysin** meets **Jane** and **Paul**

Bowles in Paris; **Bob Kaufman**, 13, joins the merchant marine; Gallimard (Paris) publishes **Jean-Paul Sartre's** *La Nausée (Nausea)*; Little, Brown publishes the first U.S. edition of **Louis-Ferdinand Céline's** *Mort a Credit (Death on the Installment Plan)*, translated from the French by **Ralph Manheim**; **William S. Burroughs** and **Kells Elvins** write a comedy sketch entitled "Twilight's Last Gleamings," which features the first appearance of Dr. Benway; **Burroughs** submits the piece to *Esquire* magazine, but it is rejected as "too screwy, and not effectively so for us."

1939

[JAN.: CHRISTOPHER ISHERWOOD AND W.H. AUDEN SAIL TO THE U.S. FROM BRITAIN; APRIL 1: AFTER ALMOST THREE YEARS OF FIGHTING, THE FASCISTS WIN THE SPANISH CIVIL WAR.] JUNE 28: **Jack Kerouac**, 18, graduates from Lowell High School; JULY 29: **Brenda Frazer** is born in Washington, D.C.; AUG.: **Burroughs** attends **Alfred Korzybski's** weeklong seminar on general semantics in Chicago and is strongly influenced by **Korzybski's** theories of language; AUG. 17: **Edward "Ed" Sanders** is born in Kansas City, Missouri; [AUG. 23: NAZI-SOVIET NONAGRESSION PACT IS SIGNED; SEPT. 1: GERMANY INVADES POLAND; WORLD WAR II BEGINS.] SEPT.: **Sheri Brennan**, 21, and **Ezio Martinelli**, 26, marry in Philadelphia; **Brion**

Gysin, 24, leaves France for Portugal; SEPT.: **Charles Bukowski**, 20, enrolls at Los Angeles City College; **Herbert Huncke**, 24, arrives in New York City and begins to haunt the Times Square area as a street hustler; SEPT. 22: **Jack Kerouac** begins a year at Horace Mann, a prep school at 231 W. 246th Street, Riverdale, New York; [OCT. 6: POLAND SURRENDERS TO NAZI GERMANY FIVE WEEKS AFTER BEING INVADED.] DEC.: **Jack Kerouac**, 17, loses his virginity to a Times Square prostitute; **Burroughs's** friend, **David Kammerer**, 28, meets fourteen-year-old **Lucien Carr** at a Saint Louis youth group and begins an obsession that ultimately leads to **Kammerer's** death in August, 1944; **Barbara Moraff** is born in Paterson, New Jersey; **Carl Solomon**, 11, is devastated by the death of his father.

1940

APRIL: **William S. Burroughs**, 26, uses shears to cut off the tip of the little finger of his left hand, perhaps to impress an unfaithful boyfriend, to achieve full "transference" with his psychiatrist, **Herbert A. Wiggers** (1907–1953), to emulate the Crow Indians' vision-quest rites, or to prove to himself that his yoga techniques give him power to ignore pain; he is admitted to Payne Whitney Psychiatric Clinic (525 E. Sixty-Eighth Street, New York City) through late MAY upon release **Burroughs** returns to Saint Louis;[1] [APRIL–MAY: SOVIET SECRET POLICE (NKVD) MURDER AND SECRETLY BURY 21,768 CAPTURED POLISH OFFICERS IN THE KATYN FOREST, APPROXIMATELY 20 KILOMETERS (12 MILES) TO THE WEST OF SMOLENSK, RUSSIA; APRIL–MAY: NAZI GERMANY INVADES THE LOW COUNTRIES AND FRANCE; MAY 26–JUNE 4: EVACUATION OF DUNKIRK, FRANCE; JUNE 22: FRANCE CAPITULATES.] JUNE: **Brion Gysin**, 24, arrives in New York; [JULY 10: BATTLE OF BRITAIN BEGINS.] SEPT.: **Jack Kerouac** starts his freshman year at Columbia University on a football scholarship; **Seymour Krim** starts his freshman year at the University of North Carolina at Chapel Hill; **Carolyn Robinson**, 17, matriculates to Bennington College, Vermont, on scholarship; [SEPT. 7: THE LONDON BLITZ BEGINS; SEPT. 17: HITLER CALLS OFF OPERATION SEA LION, THE PLANNED INVASION OF BRITAIN.] OCT.: **Kenneth Rexroth's** wife, **Andrée Schafer Rexroth**, 38, dies during an epileptic seizure; **William Everson**, 28, registers with his draft board as an anarchist and a pacifist; OCT. 19: **Kerouac** breaks his leg in a football game against Benedict Prep.; **Wilhelm Reich** constructs the first orgone energy accumulator (i.e., an "orgone box"); [OCT. 31: AFTER FIFTEEN WEEKS OF AERIAL COMBAT, THE BATTLE OF BRITAIN ENDS WITH BRITISH VICTORY.] **Burroughs** spends most of the year in Saint Louis, living with his parents and working for their gift shop as a delivery man; through musician-writer friend **John Treville Latouche** (1914–1956), **Brion Gysin** finds work as an assistant to **Irene Sharaff** (1910–1993), designing costumes for seven Broadway musicals between 1940 and 1943; Roger-Maxe de la Glannege (pseudonym for **Gershon Legman)** self-publishes *Oragenitalism: An Encyclopaedic Outline of Oral Technique in Genital Excitation; Part I, Cunnilinctus*; the U.S. Postal Service seizes and destroys every copy it can find.

1941

JAN.: **Jack Kerouac**, 18, joins the Phi Gamma Delta fraternity at Columbia; MAY: **Kerouac** is elected vice president of the sophomore class; [FEB.: WILHELM REICH VISITS ALBERT EINSTEIN AT EINSTEIN'S HOME IN PRINCETON, NEW JERSEY.] MAY 24: **Robert Allen Zimmerman (Bob Dylan)** is born in Duluth, Minnesota; JUNE 4: **Kerouac** reads **Walt Whitman's** epic poem *Song of Myself*; JUNE: **Hal Chase** graduates from Eastside High School; **Lawrence Ferlinghetti**, 22, graduates from the University of North Carolina at Chapel Hill with a BA in journalism; he spends the summer living with two college friends on Little Whaleboat Island in Casco Bay, Maine, lobster fishing and raking moss from rocks to be sold in Portland,

THE JOURNAL OF THE ALBION MOONLIGHT, 1941

Maine, for pharmaceutical use; SUMMER: **Kerouac**, 19, is in Lowell with his friends **Sammy Sampas** and **G.J. Apostolos**; he reads **James Joyce's** 1916 novel, *Portrait of the Artist as a Young Man*; [JUNE 22: *UNTERNEHMEN BARBAROSSA:* HITLER'S ARMIES, NUMBERING 3.3 MILLION MEN, INVADE THE SOVIET UNION ALONG AN EIGHTEEN-HUNDRED-MILE FRONT.] AUG.: New Directions publishes **Kenneth Patchen's** *The Journal of Albion Moonlight*; SEPT.: **Allen Ginsberg** enters Eastside High School (150 Park Avenue, Paterson, New Jersey) and is introduced to the poetry of **Walt Whitman** by his English teacher, **Frances Durbin**; **Hal Chase** begins his freshman year at Columbia University; **William Gaddis**, 18, starts college at Harvard University; OCT.: **Kerouac** quits Columbia and returns to Lowell; OCT. 10: **Robert Peter Cohon (Peter Coyote)**, is born in New York City; [DEC. 5: SOVIETS LAUNCH A COUNTEROFFENSIVE THAT PUSHES THE *WEHRMACHT* AWAY FROM MOSCOW; DEC. 7: JAPANESE CARRIER-BASED PLANES ATTACK

JUSTIN W. BRIERLY, 1905-1985

DEC.: **Lawrence Ferlinghetti**, 22, enrolls in midshipmen's school in Chicago; **Neal Cassady**, 15, meets his future mentor (and first homosexual lover), **Justin Brierly**, 36, grandson of Denver pioneer **John Walters** and a prominent educator; **Naomi Ginsberg** takes her son, **Allen Ginsberg**, 15, with her as she roams rural New Jersey by bus in search of a rest home; **Allen's** father retrieves him the next day; [DEC. 12: WILHELM REICH IS ARRESTED BY THE FBI AND JAILED AT ELLIS ISLAND FOR THREE WEEKS AS AN IMMIGRANT WITH A COM- MUNIST BACKGROUND.] **Charles Olson**, 31, moves to New York City to live with **Constance Wilcock**, 20, in a common-law marriage; **Olson** becomes the publicity director for American Civil Liberties Union (ACLU).

1942

FEB. 5: **Janine Pommy**, part Polish, part Prussian, is born to Joseph P. and Irene Telkowski Pommy in Union City, New Jersey; MAY 31: WBBM (Chicago) broadcasts "The City Wears a Slouch Hat: Incidental Music for the Radio Play" by **Kenneth Patchen**, with music composed by **John Cage** and performed by **Xenia Cage**, **Cilia Amidon**, **Stuart Lloyd**, **Ruth Hartman**, **Claire Oppenheim**, with **John Cage** conducting; [JUNE 4–7: BATTLE OF MIDWAY: JAPAN SUFFERS ITS FIRST MAJOR DEFEAT IN THE PACIFIC.] JUNE: **Leonard Schneider**, 17, joins the U.S. Navy and takes a three-week training course in Newport, Rhode Island; JULY 21: **Jack Kerouac** joins the merchant marine and sails to Greenland on the SS *Dorchester*, an ocean liner converted into a troop transport ship (sunk by a U-boat on FEB. 3, 1943); SUMMER: **Seymour Krim**, 20, joins the United States Office of War Information (OWI); **William S. Burroughs** works for two weeks as a reporter for the *St. Louis Post-Dispatch*; **Burroughs** joins the U.S. Army but is soon discharged for psychological reasons; **Burroughs** moves to Chicago and takes a job with A.J. Cohen as an exterminator; [AUG. 2: THE MURDER OF **JOSE DIAZ**, WHOSE BODY IS FOUND AT THE SLEEPY LAGOON RESERVOIR IN SOUTHEAST LOS ANGELES, LEADS TO THE ARREST OF SIX HUNDRED LATINO YOUTHS AND THE CRIMINAL TRIAL OF TWENTY-ONE OF THEM (THEIR CONVICTIONS ARE REVERSED ON APPEAL IN 1944); THE SLEEPY LAGOON MURDER CASE IS CONSIDERED A PRECURSOR TO THE ZOOT SUIT RIOTS OF 1943.] OCT. 5: **Jack Kerouac** is discharged from the merchant marines in New York; OCT 6: **William Everson** is classified as IV-E (conscientious objector) by the Fresno draft board; OCT. 24: **Leonard Schneider**, aboard the USS *Brooklyn*, a light cruiser, sails for North Africa; [NOV. 5: BRITISH FORCES UNDER BERNARD MONTGOMERY DEFEAT ERWIN ROMMEL'S AFRIKA KORPS AT EL ALAMEIN; NOV. 28: FIRE SWEEPS THROUGH THE COCOANUT GROVE NIGHTCLUB IN BOSTON; 492 ARE KILLED, HUNDREDS MORE ARE INJURED.] DEC.: **Kerouac** meets **Edie Parker** through **Henri Cru**; DEC. 31: **Kerouac** moves in with **Edie Parker** and **Joan Vollmer Adams** at their apartment on W. 119th Street, New York City.

NOTES

1. Cited from "The Life of William S. Burroughs: A Timeline" by Phil Cauthon, http://www.lawrence.com/news/2007/jul/30/timeline/.

CHAPTER TWO

THE WILD PERIOD
1943–1951

1943

JAN.: **Jack Kerouac** reads **Thorstein Veblen's**
The Theory of the Leisure Class (1899); [FEB. 2:
WORLD WAR II IS EFFECTIVELY DECIDED WHEN THE
SURROUNDED GERMAN SIXTH ARMY SURRENDERS
AT STALINGRAD.] JAN. 21: **William Everson** arrives at
Camp Angel, a Civilian Public Service (CPS) camp
in Waldport, Oregon, to do alternative service as a
conscientious objector; MARCH 22: **Jack Kerouac**
reports for duty at the U.S. Naval Training Station,
Newport, Rhode Island; MARCH 30: After only eight
days of active duty, **Kerouac** experiences a mental
breakdown and goes on the sick list; MARCH: **Edie
Parker** and **Joan Vollmer Adams** move from W. 119th
Street into an apartment at 421 W. 118th Street,
New York City; APRIL 2: **Kerouac** is transferred from
the NTS to the Newport Naval Hospital; MAY 14:

Kerouac is transferred to Bethesda Naval Hospital in Maryland; **Kerouac** is given an IQ test and scores 128 ("superior intelligence"); [JUNE 6–12: ZOOT SUIT RIOTS OCCUR IN LOS ANGELES.] JUNE 28: **Kerouac** is discharged from the Navy; his condition is classified as "Constitutional Psychopathic State, Schizoid Personality"; he moves in with his parents at 133-01 Cross Bay Boulevard in Ozone Park, Queens, New York; [APRIL 16: ALBERT HOFMANN, A RESEARCH CHEMIST AT SANDOZ LABS, ACCIDENTALLY TAKES THE FIRST "ACID TRIP" IN BASIL, SWITZERLAND; APRIL 19: HOFMANN TAKES LSD INTENTIONALLY FOR THE FIRST TIME.] JUNE: Soon after his release from the Navy, **Kerouac** signs aboard the Liberty ship USS *George Weems* as a merchant seaman; **Carl Solomon**, 15, graduates from Townsend Harris High School (for gifted students), 149–11 Melbourne Avenue, Queens, New York; [JUNE: ALBERT CAMUS MEETS JEAN-PAUL SARTRE IN PARIS.] **Jack Spicer** graduates from Fairfax High School, Los Angeles; **Jean Genet** is arrested (his thirteenth arrest), tried, and convicted for stealing a deluxe edition of **Paul Verlaine's** poetry; he serves three months in prison; JUNE 23: **Allen Ginsberg** graduates from Eastside High School, Paterson, New Jersey; [JULY 12: HITLER CALLS OFF OPERATION CITADEL; THE BATTLE OF KURSK ENDS IN SOVIET VICTORY.] AUG. 18: **Jack Kerouac**, onboard the Liberty ship USS *George Weems*, leaves New York for Liverpool, England; while on bow watch, **Kerouac** spots a mine and alerts the bridge; SEPT.: **Jack Spicer** begins college at the University of Redlands, California; he also works as a private detective; **Ginsberg** begins his freshman year at Columbia University; **Carl Solomon**, 15, begins college at City College of New York (but soon drops out); OCT.: **Ginsberg** starts his first journal; **William S. Burroughs** moves to New York City from Chicago; DEC.: While staying in the same deserted Columbia dorm over Christmas break, **Allen Ginsberg** meets **Lucien Carr** (starting at Columbia as a second-semester freshman); **Carr** introduces **Ginsberg** to **William S. Burroughs** and **David Kammerer**, who has followed **Lucien Carr** to New York; **Burroughs** takes a small apartment at 69 Bedford Street in the West Village and becomes addicted to heroin, an addiction that will last until 1956; **Gregory Corso**, 13 and homeless, is arrested for petty larceny and sent to Manhattan Detention Complex ("The Tombs"); Marc Barbezat's "little press," L'Arbalete, publishes **Jean Genet's** first novel, *Notre Dame des Fleurs (Our Lady of the Flowers)*, a book that will have great influence on the Beats; although he is only fifteen years old, **Hubert Selby Jr.** is allowed to join the merchant marines; **Herbert Gold** meets **Allen Ginsberg** and

Jack Kerouac at Columbia; Gold, sensing Kerouac's anti-Semitism, takes an instant dislike to him; JULY–DEC.: Carolyn Robinson spends half the year in New York City; until she and her roommate can find an apartment of their own, they are hosted by Robert Sherwood (1896–1955), playwright and author of FDR's speeches; by day she works for Dazian Fabrics, by night she studies at Traphagen School of Fashion, 1680 Broadway; on weekends she browses the Metropolitan Museum and the Museum of Modern Art for little-known prints of period dress; Robinson also attends Broadway stage productions, witnesses the beginning of the American Ballet Theater, and takes in performances of the biggest swing bands of the era; both she and her roommate become air raid wardens, serving as auxiliary members of the NYPD; Knopf publishes *Two Serious Ladies* by Jane Bowles.

1944

[JAN. 27: THE NAZIS LIFT THEIR SIEGE OF LENINGRAD 872 DAYS AFTER IT BEGAN.] FEB.: Jack Kerouac, 21, meets William S. Burroughs and Lucien Carr; MARCH 2: Kerouac's close friend, Sebastian G. Sampatacacus (Sammy Sampas), 22, dies from wounds sustained in combat at Anzio, Italy; FEB.: Herbert Huncke and Joan Vollmer meet Burroughs; Huncke's use of the word *beat* (i.e., tired, defeated,

JACK KEROUAC
AND LUCIEN CARR
AT COLUMBIA
UNIVERSITY, 1944

strung out) first comes to **Burroughs's** attention;
MARCH 4: **Brion Gysin**, 28, is inducted into the U.S.
Army; MARCH: **Burroughs** begins psychoanalysis
with Austrian psychoanalyst and disciple of Freud,
Paul Federn (1871–1950); MARCH/APRIL issue of
Story magazine contains an early **Charles Bukowski**
publication, "Aftermath of a Lengthy Rejection Slip";
MAY: **Jean-Paul Sartre** and **Simone de Beauvoir**
meet **Jean Genet** at the Café de Flore, 172 Boulevard
Saint-Germain, Paris; JUNE: **Neal Cassady**, 18, is
arrested in Denver for possession of stolen goods; he
spends ten months in Colorado State Reformatory,
Buena Vista, Colorado; **Ginsberg** meets **Burroughs**
and **Kerouac**; [JUNE 6: D-DAY: ALLIED FORCES INVADE
NAZI-OCCUPIED EUROPE AT NORMANDY, FRANCE.]
JUNE 6: As commander of subchaser USS *SC-1308*,
Lawrence Ferlinghetti witnesses D-Day; **Alan Ansen**,

22, graduates from Harvard with both a BA and an MA in English literature; **John Clellon Holmes**, 18, enters the U.S. Navy Hospital Corps; **Carolyn Robinson**, 21, graduates from Bennington College (Vermont) with a BA in Stanislavsky drama; she becomes an occupational therapist for the U.S. Army at the sixteen-hundred-bed Torney General Hospital, 1150 N. Indian Canyon Drive, Palm Springs, California (formerly the El Mirador Hotel); **Tuli Kupferberg**, 20, graduates, cum laude, from Brooklyn College; **Henry Miller** settles near Big Sur, California; [JULY 3: THE CONFIRMED EXISTENCE OF NAZI DEATH CAMPS IS FIRST MADE PUBLIC; JULY 20: HITLER IS SLIGHTLY WOUNDED WHEN A BOMB GOES OFF IN HIS EAST PRUSSIA HEADQUARTERS IN A FAILED ASSASSINATION AND COUP ATTEMPT BY NAZI MILITARY OFFICERS.] JULY: **Jonas Mekas** and his brother **Adolfas Mekas** leave Lithuania because of the war; en route, their train is stopped in Germany and the Mekas brothers are imprisoned in a labor camp in Elmshorn, a suburb of Hamburg, for eight months; **Allen Ginsberg** moves into room 6Q at the Warren Hall Residence Club, 404 W. 115th Street, New York City (**Lucien Carr** is living in room 6V); JULY 22: **Charles Bukowski**, 23, is arrested for draft dodging and incarcerated for seventeen days at Moyamensing Prison, 1400 S. Tenth Street, South Philadelphia; [AUG. 1: THE

AUG.: August issue of *Politics* (edited by **Dwight Macdonald**) contains "The Homosexual in Society," a pioneering progay article by **Robert Duncan**; **Joan Vollmer Adams** gives birth to a daughter, **Julie Adams**; AUG. 14: **Lucien Carr**, 19, stabs and kills his thirty-three-year-old gay stalker, **David Eames Kammerer**, in Riverside Park at W. 115th Street, New York City, with a Boy Scout knife; **Kerouac** helps **Carr** dispose of the murder weapon and is jailed as a material witness; **Burroughs** is also arrested for not reporting the crime; [AUG. 19: ALLIED FORCES LIBERATE PARIS FROM NAZI OCCUPATION.] AUG. 19: **Lucien Carr** is arraigned on murder charges; Magistrate **Anna M. Kross** orders **Carr** held without bail; AUG. 22: **Kerouac** is temporarily allowed out of jail to marry **Edie Parker**; AUG. 24: **Charles Bukowski**, 24, fails his psychological exam for military service; he is classified as 4-F (unfit); AUG. 30: **Kerouac** is released on $2,500 bond— supplied by **Edie Parker's** parents—after spending two weeks in jail; SEPT.: **Joan Vollmer Adams**, a student at Columbia's School of Journalism, moves into apartment 51 at 419 W. 115th Street, New York City; **Kerouac** and **Edie Parker** move in to share the rent; they introduce **Joan Vollmer Adams** to **William S. Burroughs**; **Jack Spicer**, 20, transfers from Redlands to the University of California, Berkeley for his senior year; he meets **Robin Blaser** and **Robert Duncan**; **Kerouac** and **Edie Parker** take a train from New York City to Detroit to live with Edie's parents on Somerset Street in Grosse Pointe Park; **Kerouac** takes a factory job at the Fruehauf Trailer Company in Detroit; SEPT. 16: **Lucien Carr** pleads guilty to first-degree manslaughter; [OCT. 2: AFTER SIXTY-THREE DAYS OF FIGHTING, THE WARSAW UPRISING IS FINALLY CRUSHED.] OCT.: **Ginsberg** moves into a dorm at 627 W. 115th Street; **Ginsberg** is classified 4-F for admitting to homosexual tendencies; **Kerouac** returns to New York City; **Edie Parker** soon follows; OCT. 6: **Lucien Carr** is sentenced to serve one to twenty years at the Elmira Reformatory for the "honor slaying" manslaughter of **David Kammerer**; OCT. 9: Carr begins serving his sentence; OCT.: **Jack Kerouac** sails on the Liberty ship USS *Robert Treat Paine* from New York; he jumps ship in Norfolk, Virginia, and returns to New York City; NOV.: **Edie Parker** is in a car accident in Detroit; thrown through the windshield, she sustains injuries that require fifty-two stitches; **Kerouac**, upon hearing of **Edie's** accident, takes the train back to Detroit; NOV. 27: **Brion Gysin**, 28, receives an honorable discharge from the U.S. Army in order to enlist in the Canadian Army; he subsequently meets **Cleland "Tex" Henson**, the great-grandson of Rev. Josiah Henson, the model for

THE KEROUAC FAMILY PAYING HOMAGE TO
ALCOHOL, NEW YORK CITY, 1944

Uncle Tom in Harriet Beecher Stowe's *Uncle Tom's Cabin* (1852); NOV. 28: **Eugene Leo Michael Emmett Grogan** is born in Brooklyn, New York; DEC.: At **Kerouac's** request, **Edie Parker** joins him in New York City; **Kerouac** and **Parker** move back into apartment 51 with **Joan Vollmer Adams** at 419 W. 115th Street; **Kerouac** starts using Benzedrine (a habit probably acquired from **Adams**); **Edie Parker**, 23, works as a cigarette girl at Club Zanzibar, 1614 Broadway (at W. Forty-Ninth Street); [DEC. 16: HITLER'S ARDENNES OFFENSIVE (THE BATTLE OF THE BULGE) BEGINS.] **William Gaddis**, 23, is ejected from Harvard for rowdy behavior; he moves to New York City and takes a job as a fact-checker for *The New Yorker*.

1945

JAN.: **Robert Creeley**, in the American Field Service, arrives in Bombay, India, after a month at sea;

Lew Welch, 17, enters the U.S. Army Air Forces;
Burroughs, 30, meets **Herbert Huncke**, 30, while
trying to dispose of syringes and a submachine
gun; JAN.: **Edie Parker** and **Jack Kerouac** split up;
Parker returns to Grosse Pointe, Michigan; [JAN. 25:
AFTER FIVE WEEKS OF FIERCE COMBAT AND HEAVY
CASUALTIES, THE BATTLE OF THE BULGE ENDS IN
ALLIED VICTORY; FEB. 13–15: ALLIED AIR FORCES
FIREBOMB DRESDEN, GERMANY, KILLING TENS OF
THOUSANDS OF CIVILIANS; FEB 19–MARCH 26: BATTLE
OF IWO JIMA: THE U.S. VICTORY COMES AT THE COST
OF MORE THAN TWENTY-SIX THOUSAND CASUALTIES,
INCLUDING ALMOST SEVEN THOUSAND DEAD.] MARCH
16: **Allen Ginsberg**, 18, is suspended from Columbia
for a year for not only allowing **Jack Kerouac**—who
had been banned from campus in connection with
the **Kammerer** slaying—to sleep in his dorm room
but also for drawing an obscene cartoon and writing
"Fuck the Jews" and "Butler [Columbia's president]
has no balls" in the dust on his dorm room window
in an attempt to get the cleaning lady to do her job;
after a short stay at his father's house, **Ginsberg**
moves into **Joan Vollmer Adams's** apartment with
Burroughs and **Kerouac**; APRIL 2: **Anne Waldman** is
born in Millville, New Jersey; **John Clellon Holmes**,
19, is discharged from the U.S. Navy Medical Corps;
he enters Columbia University on the GI Bill;

[APRIL 12: **FRANKLIN DELANO ROOSEVELT**, 63, DIES OF A CEREBRAL HEMORRHAGE IN WARM SPRINGS, GEORGIA; **HARRY S. TRUMAN** BECOMES PRESIDENT; APRIL 28: ITALIAN PARTISANS CAPTURE AND KILL **BENITO MUSSOLINI**, FORMER FASCIST DICTATOR OF ITALY; APRIL 30: **ADOLF HITLER** COMMITS SUICIDE IN HIS BERLIN BUNKER TO AVOID CAPTURE BY THE RUSSIANS; MAY 5: **EZRA POUND** IS ARRESTED NEAR GENOA, ITALY AND IS CHARGED WITH TREASON; MAY 7: NAZI GERMANY SURRENDERS UNCONDITIONALLY.] JUNE 23: **Neal Cassady** is released from Colorado State Reformatory after serving eleven months and ten days of hard labor. [JULY 16: THE U.S. SUCCESSFULLY DETONATES AN ATOMIC BOMB AT A SITE CODE-NAMED "TRINITY" IN THE WHITE SANDS PROVING GROUND, THIRTY-FIVE MILES SOUTHEAST OF SOCORRO, NEW MEXICO—THE NUCLEAR AGE BEGINS; SUMMER: **RALPH ELLISON**, 38, STARTS WRITING *INVISIBLE MAN* (PUBLISHED IN 1952) IN A BARN IN WAITSFIELD, VERMONT WHERE HE IS ON SICK LEAVE FROM THE MERCHANT MARINES.] AUG. 1: **Neal Cassady**, 19, meets and almost immediately marries **LuAnne Henderson**, 15, in Denver, Colorado; **Ginsberg** joins the merchant marines in Brooklyn; **Burroughs** returns to New York City from Saint Louis; **Carl Solomon**, 17, joins the United States Maritime Service; [AUG. 6 AND 9: B-29S DROP

NEAL CASSADY'S
FIRST WIFE, LUANNE
HENDERSON

ATOMIC BOMBS ON HIROSHIMA AND NAGASAKI;
BOTH CITIES ARE LEVELED; AUG. 15: VICTORY OVER
JAPAN DAY (V-J DAY)—WORLD WAR II ENDS AFTER
MORE THAN SIX YEARS OF CONFLICT THAT TOOK
THE LIVES OF MORE THAN FIFTY MILLION PEOPLE.]
SEPT.: **Joan Vollmer's** husband, **Paul Adams**, returns
home from the war; appalled by her drug use and
decadent friends, he divorces her; OCT.: **Lucien Carr**
is released from prison after serving one year; [OCT.
29: JEAN-PAUL SARTRE DELIVERS A LECTURE IN PARIS
ENTITLED "EXISTENTIALISM IS A HUMANISM"; THE
LECTURE BECOMES A DEFINING STATEMENT OF THE
EXISTENTIALIST MOVEMENT.] NOV.: After six weeks'
training, **Allen Ginsberg** graduates from Merchant
Seaman's Training School (MSTS) at Sheepshead
Bay, the Bronx, and ships out as a messman on the
Kearny-to-Norfolk run; NOV. 19: **Robert Creeley's**

ship, returning from the Burma campaign, docks in Halifax, Nova Scotia; DEC.: **Jack Kerouac** begins to develop thrombophlebitis (clots and inflammation) in his legs from Benzedrine use; he starts to write *The Town and the City*; DEC. 19: New Directions publishes *The Air-Conditioned Nightmare* by **Henry Miller**; [DEC. 21: EZRA POUND IS ADJUDGED INSANE AND MENTALLY UNFIT FOR TRIAL; HE IS SENT TO SAINT ELIZABETH'S HOSPITAL, A GOVERNMENT PSYCHIATRIC FACILITY AT 1100 ALABAMA AVENUE, WASHINGTON, D.C.] DEC.: **Kerouac** and **Burroughs** collaborate on a fictionalized account of the **David Kammerer** killing titled "And the Hippos Were Boiled in Their Tanks" (finally published sixty-three years later); **Neeli Cherkovski** is born in Santa Monica, California.

1946

[JAN. 17: WALTER FREEMAN PERFORMS THE FIRST TRANSORBITAL (OR "ICE PICK") LOBOTOMY IN WASHINGTON, D.C.] JAN.: **William S. Burroughs** moves into the 115th Street apartment; [MARCH 26: THE TERM *BEBOP* ENTERS THE MAINSTREAM VIA AN ARTICLE IN *TIME* MAGAZINE ON DIZZY GILLESPIE.] APRIL: **Burroughs** is arrested for forging drug prescriptions (an alert pharmacist notices that the word *Dilaudid* is misspelled); JUNE: **Burroughs** is brought to trial and given a four-month suspended sentence; by court mandate he returns to his father's home in Saint Louis and lives there for three months; SPRING: **Sheri Martinelli** joins **Anaïs Nin**, **Gore Vidal**, and others to act in **Maya Deren's** fifteen-minute silent art film *Ritual in Transfigured Time*; **Martinelli** appears in the party scene in the middle of the film and in the park scene at the end; JUNE–NOV.: **Burroughs** visits **Kells Elvins** in Pharr, Texas (one hundred forty miles southwest of Corpus Christi); MAY 17: **Leo Kerouac** (**Jack Kerouac's** father), 49, dies of stomach cancer; JUNE: **Gabrielle Kerouac** goes to Rocky Mount, North Carolina to live with her daughter, **Nin Adams**; [JUNE 5: DUELL, SLOAN & PEARCE PUBLISH *THE COMMON SENSE BOOK OF BABY AND CHILD CARE* BY BENJAMIN SPOCK; IT SOON BECOMES THE POSTWAR AMERICAN CHILD-REARING BIBLE.] JUNE: **Will Petersen**, 18, graduates from Steinmetz High School, Chicago; upon graduating, **Petersen** goes to live with his grandparents and soon enrolls at Wright Junior College in Chicago; JUNE 24: Padell publishes **Kenneth Patchen's** surrealist novel *Sleepers Awake*; [JULY 1: U.S. DETONATES A TWENTY-THREE-KILOTON NUCLEAR WEAPON IN BIKINI ATOLL, MARSHALL ISLANDS] AUG.: An incoherent and disoriented **Joan Vollmer Adams** and her two-year-old daughter, **Julie**, are picked up by police; **Joan** is hospitalized at Bellevue (462 First Avenue, New York)

JOAN VOLLMER
ADAMS BURROUGHS,
1923-1951

for acute Benzedrine psychosis; **Ginsberg** closes down the Morningside Heights apartment and moves back in with his father; **Carolyn Robinson**, 23, moves to Denver to pursue a masters degree in fine arts and theater arts at the University of Denver; SEPT. 18: **Edie Parker** files with the Archdiocese of Detroit for an annulment of her brief marriage to **Jack Kerouac**; OCT.: **Allen Ginsberg** moves into apartment 2W at 200 W. Ninety-Second Street (at Amsterdam Avenue), New York City; [OCT. 16: TEN HIGH-RANKING NAZI OFFICIALS, CONVICTED OF WAR CRIMES AT THE NUREMBERG TRIALS, ARE HANGED; HERMANN GÖRING ESCAPES HANGING BY COMMITTING SUICIDE.] OCT. 31: **Joan Vollmer** is released from Bellevue; **Vollmer** and **Burroughs** rent a cheap hotel room off

Times Square, where they conceive a child (**Billy Burroughs**), who will be born on JULY 21, 1947; NOV. 1946–MAY, 1947: **Alan Ansen** is **W.H. Auden's** student at the New School; he then serves as **Auden's** secretary and amanuensis; NOV.: **Burroughs** goes to Texas with **Joan Vollmer** and her daughter, **Julie**; NOV. 23: **Burroughs** purchases ninety-nine acres near New Waverly (in Walker County, Texas); DEC.: **Hal Chase** introduces **Neal Cassady** to **Allen Ginsberg** and **Jack Kerouac**; **Gregory Corso**, 16, is sent to prison on a robbery charge; DEC. 16: **Brion Gysin** is made a U.S. citizen; DEC. 30: **Patricia Lee Smith** (punk rock singer-composer **Patti Smith**) is born in Chicago; **Philip Lamantia's** first collection, *Erotic Poems*, is published by Bern Porter (Berkeley, California); Creative Age Press publishes **Brion Gysin's** biography of Josiah "Uncle Tom" Henson entitled, *To Master—a Long Goodnight: The Story of Uncle Tom, A Historical Narrative*.

1947

JAN.: **William S. Burroughs, Joan Burroughs,** and **Herbert Huncke** move to a dilapidated farm outside New Waverly, Texas (forty miles northwest of Houston) to evade police and grow marijuana; **Herbert Huncke** lives and works with them until OCT.; JAN. 10: **Ginsberg** and **Cassady** begin a short,

HEBERT HUNCKE, AGE 32, AT WILLIAM S. BURROUGHS'S FARM IN NEW WAVERLY, TEXAS, 1947

intense love affair; [JAN. 15: ELIZABETH SHORT, 22, A HOLLYWOOD ASPIRANT, IS MURDERED AND NEATLY CUT IN HALF AT THE WAIST; HER BODY PARTS ARE DUMPED ADJACENT TO EACH OTHER IN AN EMPTY LOT IN LOS ANGELES; THE PRESS DUBS HER "THE BLACK DAHLIA"; THE HORRIFIC CRIME IS NEVER SOLVED.] MARCH 4: **Neal Cassady**, 21, leaves New York City for Denver by bus; days later in Denver, **Cassady** meets and begins an affair with **Carolyn Robinson**, 23; APRIL: **Madeline Gleason** inaugurates the San Francisco Poetry Renaissance by organizing the First Festival of Modern Poetry at the Lucien Labaudt Gallery (1407 Gough Street); Reynal & Hitchcock publishes **Charles Olson's** *Call Me Ishmael*; "The New Cult of Sex and Anarchy," by consumer advocate and freelance writer **Mildred Edie Brady**, appears in *Harper's Magazine*; the article excoriates **Henry Miller** and California bohemianism; [APRIL 15: JACKIE ROBINSON BREAKS THE COLOR BARRIER IN MAJOR LEAGUE BASEBALL BY STARTING FOR THE BROOKLYN DODGERS; APRIL 16: IN SOUTH CAROLINA, BERNARD BARUCH DELIVERS A SPEECH WRITTEN BY JOURNALIST HERBERT BAYARD SWOPE THAT OFFICIALLY INAUGURATES THE COLD WAR: "LET US NOT BE DECEIVED: WE ARE TODAY IN THE MIDST OF A COLD WAR"] MAY 26: "The Strange Case of **Wilhelm Reich**," a damning article by **Mildred Edie Brady**, appears in *The New Republic* magazine and precipitates **Reich's** downfall by attracting the attention of the FBI; [JUNE 5: IN THE COMMENCEMENT ADDRESS TO THE HARVARD CLASS OF 1947, SECRETARY OF STATE GEORGE C. MARSHALL PROPOSES AN AMBITIOUS PLAN TO REBUILD EUROPE (THE MARSHALL PLAN); JUNE 23: CONGRESS PASSES THE ANTI-LABOR TAFT-HARTLEY ACT.] JUNE: **Lawrence Ferlinghetti**, 28, earns a masters degree in English literature from Columbia University; JULY 17: **Jack Kerouac**, 25, begins his first cross-country trip from his mother's apartment at 133-01 Cross Bay Boulevard in Ozone Park, Queens, New York; JULY 21: **William S. "Billy" Burroughs Jr.** is born—amphetamine addicted—in Conroe, Texas; JULY 24: **Kerouac** reaches Cheyenne,

Wyoming; JULY 28: **Kerouac** arrives in Denver, Colorado; AUG.: **William S. Burroughs's** parents—**Laura** and **Mortimer Burroughs**—travel to Texas to see their infant grandson; **Ginsberg** visits **Neal Cassady** in Denver but must compete with **LuAnne Henderson** and **Carolyn Robinson** for his attentions; AUG. 10: **Kerouac** arrives in San Francisco; AUG.: While boarding a bus to Los Angeles, **Kerouac** meets a beautiful young Mexican woman named **Bea Franco** (fictionalized as "Terry"); while working as migrant laborers in Selma, California (twenty miles southeast of Fresno), the two have a brief affair, recounted in "The Mexican Girl," *The Paris Review*, no. 11 (Winter 1955) and in *On the Road* (1957); AUG. 29: After hitchhiking 985 miles from Denver, **Ginsberg** and **Cassady** arrive in New Waverly, Texas, to visit **Burroughs**; SEPT. 1: **Ginsberg**, lovelorn, finally accepts the fact that **Neal Cassady** is not homosexual; SEPT.: **Jack Spicer** begins graduate studies in English literature at Berkeley; **Gary Snyder**, 17, enters Reed College (Portland, Oregon) on scholarship; SEPT. 7: Dejected over his failed love affair with **Neal Cassady**, **Ginsberg**, 21, ships out from Galveston, Texas, on the Liberty ship USS *John Blair* bound for Dakar, Senegal; the trip ends in New York in October; SEPT. 30: **Burroughs**, **Huncke**, and **Cassady** drive a trunk load of uncured, homegrown marijuana packed in mason jars from Texas to New York City to sell, but the venture is a total failure; OCT.: **Kerouac** returns to New York City; [OCT.: THE HOUSE UN-AMERICAN ACTIVITIES COMMITTEE HOLDS HEARINGS ON "ALLEGED COMMUNIST INFLUENCE AND INFILTRATION" OF HOLLYWOOD.] NOV.: **Ginsberg** signs the forms authorizing doctors to perform a lobotomy on his mother, **Naomi Ginsberg**, a decision that will haunt him the rest of his life; **Ginsburg**, fearing for his own sanity, begins biweekly therapy sessions with Reichian analyst **A. Allan Cott** (1910–1993) in Newark, New Jersey; [DEC. 3: TENNESSEE WILLIAMS'S *A STREETCAR NAMED DESIRE* (ORIGINAL CAST: MARLON BRANDO, JESSICA TANDY, KIM HUNTER, AND KARL MALDEN) OPENS A CELEBRATED TWO-YEAR RUN ON BROADWAY.] **Henri Cru** moves to San Francisco; **Hubert Selby Jr.**, 19, is diagnosed with advanced tuberculosis while at sea; **Selby** is taken off a ship in Bremen, Germany, and returned to the United States for prolonged medical treatment; **Robert Frank**, 22, moves to the U.S. from his native Switzerland and secures a job as a fashion photographer at *Harper's Bazaar*.

1948

JAN. 1: Saunders (Philadelphia) publishes **Alfred Kinsey's** groundbreaking study *Sexual Behavior in the Human Male*; he obtains some of his data from interviews with **Herbert Huncke** and other Beats; JAN. 14: **William S. Burroughs** has himself committed to the Federal Narcotics Farm in Lexington, Kentucky for two weeks in a determined but ultimately failed attempt to rid himself of his heroin addiction; JAN.: **Ginsberg** takes a small room at 536 W. 114th Street, New York City; [JAN. 30: MOHANDAS K. GANDHI IS ASSASSINATED; FEB. 2: PRESIDENT HARRY S. TRUMAN ORDERS THE DESEGREGATION OF THE U.S. MILITARY.] FEB.: **Burroughs** is back in East Texas; SPRING: **Jay Landesman**, a Saint Louis art gallery owner, starts publishing *Neurotica*, a short-lived journal described as "a literary exposition, defense, and correlation of the problems and personalities that in our culture are defined as 'neurotic'"; APRIL 1: **Neal Cassady**, his marriage to **LuAnne Henderson** annulled, marries **Carolyn Robinson** (who is already three months pregnant with **Cassady's** baby); APRIL 16: "Nature Boy," **eden ahbez's** protohippie song, tops the pop charts (**Kerouac** later mentions **ahbez** in *On the Road*); MAY: **Kerouac** completes *The Town and the City*; MAY 6: **Burroughs** buys forty acres in Hidalgo County (at the southern tip of Texas); Bee County Sheriff **Robert Vail Ennis**—notorious for having shot and killed seven people in the "line of duty"—arrests **Burroughs** and **Joan Vollmer** in Beeville, Texas (fifty miles northwest of Corpus Christi) for drunkenness

EDEN AHBEZ, 1908-1995

and "public indecency" (i.e., for having sex by the side of the road while their two young children—**Julie**, 3, and **Billy**, 10 months—wait in the car); the state of Texas suspends **Burroughs's** driver's license and fines him (**Burroughs's** parents wire $173 to pay the fine); [MAY 14: THE STATE OF ISRAEL IS ESTABLISHED.] JUNE: Deeming Texas "very uncool," **Burroughs** and **Joan Vollmer** move to New Orleans and take up residence in a rooming house at 111 Transcontinental Drive, Metairie, Louisiana (a suburb west of New Orleans); JUNE: **Burroughs** begins reading **Wilhelm Reich** and becomes interested in orgone boxes; JUNE: **Anatole Broyard's** scathing "A Portrait of the Hipster" appears in *Partisan Review*; JUNE 10: **Paul Blake Jr.**, **Jack Kerouac's** nephew, is born in Rocky Mount, North Carolina; [JUNE 27: THE BERLIN AIRLIFT BEGINS AFTER THE SOVIETS BLOCKADE THE

CITY.] JUNE 23: While in New Orleans, **Burroughs** signs the deed to sell his East Texas farm; JULY 4: **Kerouac** first meets **John Clellon Holmes** at a party at **Ginsberg's** Harlem apartment; JULY 18: **Allen Ginsberg**, now in a sixth-floor sublet apartment at 321 E. 121st Street, East Harlem, New York City, has a profound mystical experience triggered by an auditory hallucination (i.e., he hears the voice of **William Blake** reciting **Blake's** poems "The Sick Rose" and "The Sunflower"); AUG. 2: **Burroughs** buys a "shotgun shack" (his residence for the next 13 months) at 509 Wagner Street, in the fifteenth ward of New Orleans, Louisiana; AUG. 23: **Kerouac** comes up with the title *On the Road*; [SEPT. 1: HOLLYWOOD MOVIE STAR ROBERT MITCHUM IS ARRESTED FOR POSSESSION OF MARIJUANA; HE SUBSEQUENTLY SERVES A FORTY-THREE-DAY JAIL SENTENCE.] SEPT.: **Will Petersen** transfers to Michigan State University, East Lansing, Michigan where he studies lithography with **John S. deMartelly** and painting with **Charles Pollock**, **Jackson Pollock's** older brother; **Lew Welch**, 22, moves to Portland, Oregon to attend Reed College on the GI Bill; he rooms with **Gary Snyder** and **Philip Whalen**; **Lenore Kandel**, 16, enters Los Angeles City College; SEPT. 6: **Carolyn Cassady** gives birth to a daughter, **Cathleen Joanne Cassady**; OCT. 8: **Kerouac** registers for The Twentieth-Century Novel in American Literature, a course taught by **Elbert Lenrow** (1903–1993) at the New School for Social Research in Greenwich Village, New York City; OCT. 14: **Burroughs** contracts to buy a plot of land in Kenner, Louisiana (west of Metairie); DEC. 1: **Allen Ginsberg** moves into an apartment at 1401 York Avenue (between E. Seventy-Forth and E. Seventy-Fifth Streets), New York City; NOV.: **Kerouac** begins writing an early version of *On the Road* (originally entitled "Beat Generation"); DEC. 15: **Neal Cassady** abandons his wife, **Carolyn Cassady**, and his three-month-old daughter, **Cathleen**, in San Francisco and expropriates the family savings to buy a '49 Hudson to travel to New York with ex-wife **LuAnne Henderson**; they pick up **Kerouac** and drive back to San Francisco for a three-day visit; DEC. 18: **Al** and **Helen Hinkle** marry; **Al** sends **Helen** on to New Orleans to stay with **Burroughs** and await his arrival; DEC. 26: **William Everson**, 36, has a religious experience during midnight mass at Saint Mary's Cathedral, 1111 Gough Street, San Francisco; he later becomes a Dominican lay monk and adopts the name **Brother Antoninus**; DEC. 29: **Neal Cassady**, **LuAnne Henderson**, and **Al Hinkle** arrive at the home of **Kerouac's** sister in Rocky Mount, North Carolina, where **Kerouac** and his mother are living; **Kerouac** joins them on the road.

1949

JAN. 28: **Kerouac**, **Cassady**, **LuAnne Henderson**, and **Al Hinkle** leave New York City for New Orleans to visit **Burroughs** (for a week), pick up **Helen Hinkle**, and then proceed on to San Francisco; FEB.: **Neal Cassady** abandons **Kerouac** and **LuAnne Henderson** in San Francisco; **Kerouac** returns home to his mother; **Ginsberg** reluctantly allows **Herbert Huncke**, **Vickie Russell** (a prostitute known as "the Detroit Redhead"), and **"Little Jack" Melody** to move in with him and use his apartment at 1401 York Avenue, New York City, to stash stolen property; FEB. or MARCH: **Burroughs** buys a house containing two side-by-side apartments—one to live in and one to rent—at 1128–1130 Burgundy Street, French Quarter, New Orleans; MARCH 15: **Neal Cassady** breaks the thumb of his left hand when he strikes **LuAnne Henderson** on the head; it remains in a cast for several months; MARCH 29: Harcourt, Brace & World accepts **Kerouac's** first novel, *The Town and the City*, and advances him $1,000; MARCH 30: **Carl Solomon**, on his twenty-first birthday, voluntarily commits himself to the Psychiatric Institute of New York and demands a lobotomy but receives a series of electroshock treatments instead; APRIL 5: **William S. Burroughs** and three other friends—**Joseph M. "Pat" Ricks**, 40, **Horace M. Guidry**, 41, and **Alan Cowie**, 21—are arrested on marijuana charges at the 1800 block of Calliope Street, New Orleans, after a police chase; **Burroughs** spends two days in jail—withdrawing from heroin "cold turkey"—before making the $1,500 bail, which his parents provide; **Burroughs** is taken straight to DePaul Sanitarium, 1040 Calhoun Street, New Orleans, for treatment; [APRIL 15: KPFA, PACIFICA RADIO (94.1, BERKELEY, CALIFORNIA), THE FIRST PUBLIC (I.E., LISTENER-SUPPORTED, NONCOMMERCIAL) RADIO STATION, IS FOUNDED BY PACIFIST LEWIS HILL (1919–1957).] APRIL 15: **Joan Vollmer** takes **Burroughs** out of DePaul against medical advice; APRIL–OCT.: **Burroughs**, **Joan Vollmer**, and children **Julie** and **Billy Burroughs** stay with **Kells Elvins** in Pharr, Texas (on the U.S.–Mexico border, just north of Reynosa, Mexico); APRIL 21: **Allen Ginsberg** is involved in a police chase and car accident in Queens, New York, with **Huncke**, **Russell**, and **Melody**; all four are arrested for possession of stolen property; [MAY 12: THE BERLIN AIRLIFT ENDS; THE SOVIET BLOCKADE OF BERLIN IS DEFEATED.] JUNE 1: **Neal Cassady** begins work curing recapped tires as a mold man at Goodyear (San Francisco); [JUNE 8: SECKER AND WARBURG (LONDON) PUBLISHES *1984* BY GEORGE ORWELL; HARCOURT, BRACE PUBLISH A U.S. EDITION A FEW MONTHS LATER.] JUNE–JULY: With proceeds from *The Town and the City*, **Jack**

DUST JACKET FOR THE FIRST EDITION OF *THE TOWN AND THE CITY*

Kerouac, 27, buys a house at 6100 W. Center Street, Lakewood, Colorado (a suburb west of Denver) but lives there with his mother, **Gabrielle Kerouac**, for only two months; JUNE 29: At a court hearing, accompanied by two of his Columbia professors of English—**Lionel Trilling** (1905–1975) and **Mark Van Doren** (1894–1972)—his therapist, **A. Allan Cott**, and Lionel's wife, **Diana Trilling** (1905–1996), **Ginsberg** agrees to commit himself to the Columbia Presbyterian Psychiatric Institute to avoid prison; he subsequently meets fellow mental patient **Carl Solomon** at the institute; JULY 29: **William Everson** is baptized Catholic; AUG. 1: **James Dennis "Jim" Carroll** is born in New York City; AUG.: **Kerouac** and his mother return to New York City to live at 94-21 134th Street in Richmond Hill, Queens (**Kerouac's** primary home until 1954); **Jack Kerouac** introduces

CARL SOLOMON
(1928-1993), TO WHOM
ALLEN GINSBERG
DEDICATED "HOWL"

Neal Cassady to **Diana Hansen**; AUG.: **Cassady** and **Kerouac** make a series of road trips together from the East Coast to San Francisco via New Orleans, from San Francisco to New York (stopping in Detroit for several days to visit **Edie Parker**), and from New York to Mexico City—all recounted in *On the Road*; [AUG. 29: THE SOVIET UNION EXPLODES ITS FIRST NUCLEAR BOMB.] SEPT.: With a trial set for October and with the looming prospect of a two- to five-year sentence at the Louisiana State Penitentiary in Angola, **Burroughs** resolves to move to Mexico City; in preparation he ventures there alone, rents an apartment at 26 Rio Lerma (at the western edge of the city), then returns to New Orleans; [OCT. 1: MAO ZEDONG PROCLAIMS THE PEOPLE'S REPUBLIC OF CHINA.] OCT.: 27: **Burroughs** takes **Joan Vollmer**, **Julie**, and **Billy Burroughs** and flees New Orleans for Mexico City; NOV. 18: **Gerald Nicosia** is born in

Berwyn, Illinois; NOV. 21: **William S. Burroughs**, 35, applies for admission to Mexico City College on the GI Bill; DEC.: **Jonas Mekas**, 27, immigrates to the United States; he settles in Williamsburg, Brooklyn, New York and begins to make experimental films; Gallimard (Paris) publishes **Jean Genet's** *Journal du voleur* (*The Thief's Journal*); DEC.: **Joan Vollmer** quits Benzedrine but begins to drink heavily; Osmond Beckwith at Breaking Point (New York) publishes *Love & Death: A Study in Censorship* by **Gershon Legman**; DEC. 4: New Directions publishes *The Sheltering Sky* by **Paul Bowles**; DEC. 31: On hospital furlough for the holidays, **Allen Ginsberg** meets **Helen Parker** at a New Year's Eve party; **Charles Olson**, writing to **Robert Creeley**, coins the term *postmodern*; **Jean Genet** is threatened with a life sentence after ten felony convictions; **Jean Cocteau** and other prominent figures, including **Jean-Paul Sartre**, **François Mauriac**, **Paul Claudel**, **André Breton**, **André Gide**, and **Pablo Picasso** successfully petition the French president **Vincent Auriol** to have the sentence set aside. [MAX RINKEL (1894–1966), A NEUROPSYCHIATRIST AT CUSHING GENERAL VETERANS HOSPITAL IN BEDFORD, MASSACHUSETTS, BRINGS LSD TO THE UNITED STATES FROM SANDOZ PHARMACEUTICALS IN SWITZERLAND AND INITIATES WORK WITH THE DRUG IN BOSTON.]

1950

JAN. 2: **William Burroughs**, 35, is admitted to Mexico City College (MCC) on the GI Bill; JAN. 26: **Carolyn Cassady** gives birth to a second daughter, **Melany Jane Cassady**, nicknamed **Jamie**; FEB.: **Neal Cassady** gets his new girlfriend, **Diana Hansen**, pregnant; [FEB. 9: IN WHEELING, WEST VIRGINIA, SENATOR **JOSEPH R. MCCARTHY** (R-WISCONSIN) ACHIEVES INSTANT NOTORIETY BY MAKING A SPEECH CLAIMING THERE ARE DOZENS OF COMMUNISTS IN THE U.S. STATE DEPARTMENT.] FEB. 27: After eight months of psychiatric treatment, **Allen Ginsberg**, 23, is released from the hospital and moves in with his father and new stepmother at 416 E. Thirty-Fourth Street, Paterson, New Jersey; **Ginsberg** begins dating women, hoping that his hospital stay has "cured" him of his homosexuality; MARCH 2: Harcourt, Brace & World publishes **Jack Kerouac's** first novel, *The Town and the City*; the reviews are good but the sales are moderate (about 5,000 copies sold); **Allen Ginsberg** publishes a poem, "Song: Fie My Fum," in *Neurotica*, no. 6 (Spring 1950); it contains the line "pull my daisy," later used as a Beat film title); SPRING: **William Everson** moves into Maurin House—the first Dorothy Day House of Hospitality on the West Coast—located at Fifth and Washington (near skid row), Oakland, California; he soon becomes its

codirector; APRIL: **Burroughs** becomes readdicted
to horoin in Mexico City; MAY: **Kerouac** takes a book
publicity trip to Denver; he stays with **Ed White**
and has a brief relationship with **Beverly Burford**;
MAY 20: **Lew Welch**, 23, finishes his senior thesis
on **Gertrude Stein**; JUNE: **Lew Welch** graduates
from Reed College; [JUNE 6: DIZZY GILLESPIE AND
CHARLIE PARKER RECORD AN ALBUM TOGETHER
IN NEW YORK CITY ENTITLED *BIRD AND DIZ;* JUNE
22: COUNTERATTACK, A RIGHT-WING NEWSLETTER,
PUBLISHES "RED CHANNELS," A PAMPHLET THAT
BLACKLISTS 151 WRITERS, MUSICIANS, ACTORS, AND
OTHER ARTISTS.] JUNE: **Gary Snyder**, 20, marries
Alison Gass, 18, a fellow student at Reed College;
JUNE 23: **Jack Spicer** is terminated from his teaching
assistant job at Berkeley for refusing to sign an
anticommunist loyalty oath; he leaves to teach at the
University of Minnesota; JUNE 24: **Jack Kerouac**,
Neal Cassady, and **Frank Jeffries** arrive in Mexico
City and take a cheap place next to **Burroughs**
and his family, who are now living in a third-floor
apartment at 37 Cerrada de Medellín; SUMMER:
Brion Gysin and **Paul Bowles** attend a *moussem*
(festival) at Sidi Kacem, 100 miles south of Tangier,
Morocco, and hear Sufi trance music performed by
local musicians; summer: **Gary Snyder** works for the
U.S. National Park Service and helps excavate the

archaeological site of Fort Vancouver (Washington State) [JUNE 25: THE KOREAN WAR BEGINS.] JUNE 26: **Carolyn Cassady**, alone in San Francisco, gives birth to her second daughter, **Jamie Cassady**; JULY 1–4: **Allen Ginsberg** spends the long Fourth of JULY weekend with his new girlfriend, **Helen Parker**, at her cottage in Provincetown, Massachusetts; he meets **Bill Cannastra**; JULY: **Brion Gysin** arrives in Tangier as a guest of **Paul Bowles**; JULY 10: **Neal Cassady** commits bigamy by marrying **Diana Hansen**; SUMMER: **Joan Haverty** meets **Bill Cannastra**, 28, a Harvard Law School graduate (also a bisexual and an alcoholic) in Provincetown, Massachusetts, and follows him when he returns to Manhattan and takes a loft apartment at 125 W. Twenty-First Street in Chelsea; AUG.: **Lucien Carr** and his girlfriend, **Liz Lehrman**, arrive in Mexico City for a one-week visit with **Burroughs** and his family; **Joan Vollmer Burroughs** goes to Cuernavaca to file for divorce; [SEPT. 19: THE BATTLE OF INCHON ENDS IN VICTORY FOR THE UNITED NATIONS.] SEPT. 17: **William Carlos Williams** visits Reed College in Oregon; he meets **Lew Welch**, **Gary Snyder**, and **Philip Whalen** and reads their poetry; OCT. 11: While drinking with **Carl Solomon** and **Bob Steen** at the San Remo (189 Bleecker Street, Greenwich Village), **Ginsberg** spots **Bill Cannastra** with **Tennessee Williams** and is jealous; OCT. 12: **Bill Cannastra** is instantly killed when he leans out—and gets stuck in—the window of a moving New York City subway train at the Bleecker Street station on the IRT Lexington Avenue line; late OCT.: **Allen Ginsberg** ends his four-month affair with **Helen Parker**; NOV.: **Diana Hansen** gives birth to a son, **Curtis** (**Neal Cassady** is the father); NOV. 3: **Jack Kerouac**, 28, meets **Joan Haverty**, 19, at a party at **Bill Cannastra's** former loft on W. Twenty-First Street; mid-NOV.: **Alison Gass** separates from **Gary Snyder** after five months of marriage; NOV. 17: **Kerouac** marries **Joan Haverty** in New York City; he moves into the W. Twenty-First Street loft; DEC. 17: **Neal Cassady** writes the 28,000-word "Joan Anderson" letter to **Kerouac**; DEC.: Released from Clinton State Prison (Dannemora, New York) after serving a three-year sentence for robbery, **Gregory Corso** meets **Ginsberg** and **Kerouac** at the Pony Stable, a lesbian bar at 150 W. Fourth Street in Manhattan's West Village; **Ginsberg** takes a temporary job at the Paterson Post Office; **Burroughs** and his family move to apartment 5 of 201 Orizaba, Mexico City (above the Bounty Bar, a favorite watering hole for American expatriates); **Peter Orlovsky**, 17, drops out of high school his senior year to help support his family; **Anton Rosenberg**, 23, opens a print shop on Christopher Street in Greenwich Village, New York City.

KELLS ELVINS,
1913 - 1961

1951

JAN.: **Allen Ginsberg**, 24, seduces **Gregory Corso**, 20; **Jack Kerouac** and his new wife, **Joan Haverty**, move to 454 West Twentieth Street; **Burroughs's** friend, psychologist **Kells Elvins** and **Elvins's** wife, **Marianne**, visit him in Mexico City; MARCH–APRIL: **Burroughs** temporarily kicks his heroin addiction but starts drinking heavily; APRIL: **Kerouac** writes the Teletype-roll manuscript of *On the Road* in three weeks of frenetic labor; [APRIL 11: PRESIDENT TRUMAN FIRES GENERAL DOUGLAS MACARTHUR FOR ATTEMPTING TO WIDEN THE WAR IN KOREA.] MAY: **Jack Kerouac** and **Joan Haverty** separate; **Gary Snyder** graduates from Reed College with a bachelor of arts in literature and anthropology (his senior thesis at Reed is later published as *He Who Hunted Birds in His Father's Village: The Dimensions of a Haida Myth*); **Ted Joans** graduates from Indiana University with a bachelor

LEWIS MARKER AND WILLIAMS S. BURROUGHS IN
THE BOUNTY BAR, MEXICO CITY, 1951

of fine arts; **Harold Norse** earns a masters degree
from New York University; **Philip Whalen** graduates
from Reed with a bachelor of arts in literature and
languages; he moves to San Francisco, then to Venice
(a Los Angeles seaside suburb), where a friend is
living; both get jobs at the North American Aviation
plant in Downey, California (east L. A.); **Burroughs**
meets **Adelbert Lewis Marker**, 21, a student at MCC,
and begins a relationship; JUNE: **Kerouac** gets **Joan
Haverty** pregnant; **LeRoi Jones**, 18, graduates from
Barringer High School, Newark, New Jersey; summer:
Gary Snyder, 21, works as a timber scaler in Warm
Springs Indian Reservation in North-Central Oregon;
late JUNE–early JULY: **Burroughs** and **Lewis Marker**
travel to Puyo, Ecuador in an unsuccessful search for
yagé (ayahuasca, pronounced *ah-yah-waska*); AUG.:
Kerouac goes to his sister's home in Rocky Mount,

North Carolina; late AUG.: **Ginsberg** travels to Mexico with **Lucien Carr**; SEPT.: **Lew Welch** enrolls at the University of Chicago to study for a masters degree in the history of philosophy; **Leonard Cohen** enrolls at McGill University, Montreal; SEPT. 5: On the return trip from Mexico, **Lucien Carr's** automobile breaks down in Houston, Texas; **Carr** flies back to his job in New York, leaving **Ginsberg** to oversee repairs; SEPT. 6: During a party hosted by **John Healy** at apartment 10, 122 Monterrey Street, Mexico City (also attended by MCC students **Bob Addison**, **Eddie Woods**, **John Herrmann**, and **Lewis Marker**) **William S. Burroughs**, 37, accidentally shoots and kills his wife, **Joan Vollmer Adams Burroughs**, 27, with a Star .380 automatic handgun—supposedly in a drunken game of William Tell, but the circumstances are never fully clarified; SEPT. 8: **Burroughs's** brother, **Mortimer Burroughs Jr.**, 40, arrives in Mexico City to lend his support; SEPT.: **Joan Vollmer's** parents arrive in Mexico City and take charge of Joan's daughter, **Julie**; **Billy Burroughs** is sent to live with his grandparents; SEPT. 19: After serving thirteen days in jail, **Burroughs** is released after posting bond; he must report to authorities every week for the next year; SEPT.: **Carolyn Cassady** gives birth to a third child, **John Allen Cassady**; OCT. 25: Inspired by **Neal Cassady's** "Joan Anderson" letter, **Jack Kerouac** formulates the tenets of "spontaneous prose"; AUTUMN: **Ginsberg** moves into a two-room attic apartment at 346 W. Fifteenth Street, New York City; DEC.: Ace Books gives **Kerouac** $250 advance for *On the Road*; DEC.: **Lew Welch** suffers a nervous breakdown and quits graduate school; DEC. 18: **Jack Kerouac**, unable to ship out as a merchant seaman with his friend, **Henri Cru**, moves in with **Neal Cassady** and **Carolyn Cassady** at 29 Russell Street, San Francisco, and begins to train as a brakeman on the Southern Pacific Railroad; **Gary Snyder** reads D.T. Suzuki's *Essays in Zen Buddhism*; **Ray Bremser**, 17, goes AWOL from the U.S. Air Force and is briefly imprisoned before receiving a dishonorable discharge; **Slim Brundage** opens the second College of Complexes at 1651 N. Wells Street, Chicago.

CHAPTER THREE

THE PEAK WRITING PERIOD 1952– 1960

1952

JAN.: **Ginsberg** sends a sheaf of his poems to **William Carlos Williams** and receives an enthusiastic response; JAN. 4: **Lucien Carr** marries **Francesca "Cessa" von Hartz**, the daughter of the national news editor of *The New York Times*, in New York City; **Ginsberg** attends the wedding and is depressed by **Carr's** newfound commitment to heterosexual marriage; FEB. 8: **Kerouac**, arrested for drunkenness, fails to show up for **Neal Cassady's** twenty-sixth birthday; **Carolyn Cassady**, 28, is temporarily stricken with Bell's palsy (partial facial paralysis), probably triggered by emotional stress; FEB. 16: **Kerouac's** daughter with **Joan Haverty**, **Janet "Jan" Michelle Kerouac**, is born in Albany, New York; MARCH 1: Random House publishes *Let It Come Down*, **Paul Bowles's** second novel; APRIL:

Ginsberg sends **William Carlos Williams** *Empty Mirror*, his poetry manuscript; **Charles Bukowski**, 31, takes a post office job in Los Angeles; MAY: **Alexander Trocchi** becomes editor of *Merlin*, a Paris-based literary journal published by **Alice Jane Lougee**; it lasts until 1955; MAY: **Kerouac** leaves the **Cassady** household after a five-month stay and returns to his mother; SPRING: **Elise Cowen**, 19, is introduced to **Allen Ginsberg**, 26, by **Donald A. "Don" Cook** (1926–1996), then a psychology graduate student at Barnard; **Cowen** and **Ginsberg** discover that they both know **Carl Solomon**; **David Amram**, 21, graduates from George Washington University with a degree in European history; **Carl Solomon** suffers another psychotic episode; **Jack Kerouac** joins **William S. Burroughs** in Mexico City, imposes on his hospitality, and writes *Doctor Sax* (published in 1959) in **Burroughs's** bathroom while high on marijuana; SUMMER: **Lew Welch**, 26, moves to New York City and takes a job in advertising; JULY 1: **Kerouac** leaves Mexico for 1328 Tarboro Street, Rocky Mount, North Carolina to live with his mother and his sister, **Nin**, but **Neal Cassady** soon persuades him to come live in San Jose and work as a brakeman on the Southern Pacific Railroad; SEPT.: **Jack Spicer**, 27, returns to Berkeley, signs a now-modified loyalty oath, and resumes PhD work;

SEPT.: **Kerouac** moves out of the **Cassadys'** house after a quarrel with **Neal Cassady** and takes a room at the Cameo Hotel, 389 Third Street, San Francisco; OCT.: **Kerouac**, deeply depressed, writes "October in the Railroad Earth"; **Allen Ginsberg**, attempting to go straight, takes a job as a market analyst with George Fine Market Research and moves into apartment 16 at 206 E. Sixth Street on the Lower East Side, New York City; [NOV. 1: THE U.S. DETONATES ITS FIRST THERMONUCLEAR DEVICE, THE H-BOMB, AT ENIWETOK ATOLL IN THE MARSHALL ISLANDS; NOV. 5: DWIGHT D. EISENHOWER IS ELECTED THIRTY-FOURTH PRESIDENT IN A LANDSLIDE VICTORY.] mid-NOV.: **Burroughs** leaves Mexico for the U.S.; NOV. 16: Scribner's publishes **John Clellon Holmes's** novel *Go*, the first Beat novel, to mixed reviews; **Holmes** sells the paperback rights to Bantam for $20,000; **Holmes** also publishes an article titled "This Is the Beat Generation" in *The New York Times*, officially launching the term *Beat*; DEC.: **Kerouac**, after six months on the road, returns to New York to live with his mother again; **Ray Bremser**, 18, is remanded to Bordentown Reformatory in New Jersey for armed robbery; **Gary Snyder** and **Alison Gass** divorce; Editions Gallimard publishes *Saint Genet, comédien et martyr*, an adulatory study of **Jean Genet** by **Jean-Paul Sartre**.

1953

JAN.: **Ginsberg** visits his mother, **Naomi Ginsberg**, at Pilgrim State Hospital, Brentwood, New York; **William S. Burroughs**, 39, sets out alone from his parents' home in Palm Beach, Florida, on an eight-month excursion through South America (Panama, Ecuador, Colombia, and Peru) in search of *yagé*, an extremely powerful natural hallucinogen used ritually by Amazonian Indians; in the course of his travels in the Amazon region, Burroughs meets legendary ethnobotanist **Richard Evans Schultes** (1915–2001); JAN.–FEB.: **Jack Kerouac**, in New York City, writes *Maggie Cassidy* (published in 1959), a novel set in Lowell in 1938–39 about his relationship with **Mary Carney**; FEB.: **Kerouac** returns to San Jose; MARCH: **Kerouac**, back in New York, meets editor **Malcolm Cowley**, who expresses genuine interest in his work; SPRING–SUMMER: **Ginsberg** dates **Elise Cowen**; [MARCH 5: JOSEPH STALIN, 74, DIES OF A STROKE.] APRIL 10: **Neal Cassady** is seriously injured in an accident on the job with the Southern Pacific Railroad; APRIL: **Kerouac** begins working for Southern Pacific; [APRIL 13: THE CIA'S SECRET DRUG-FACILITATED MIND-CONTROL PROJECT, MK-ULTRA, BEGINS.] MAY: **Burroughs** publishes his first novel, *Junkie*, under the pseudonym William Lee; Ace Books prints an edition of one hundred thousand

JUNKIE, WILLIAM S. BURROUGHS'S FIRST NOVEL

copies at thirty-five cents each; **Burroughs's** editor, **Aaron A. Wyn** (1898–1967), is **Carl Solomon's** uncle; **Kerouac** quits his railroad job and signs on with the USS *William Carruthers*, a freighter out of San Francisco bound for Panama; [MAY 15: DIZZY GILLESPIE, CHARLIE PARKER, BUD POWELL, CHARLES MINGUS, AND MAX ROACH PERFORM TOGETHER AT MASSEY HALL, TORONTO.] MAY 22–25: **Ginsberg** writes "The Green Automobile"; SUMMER: **Gary Snyder**, 23, works as a fire warden at Sourdough Mountain Lookout in the northern Cascades; JUNE 8: **Lawrence Ferlinghetti** and **Peter D. Martin** open City Lights, the first all-paperback bookstore in the U.S., at 261 Columbus Avenue, San Francisco; [JUNE 19: ATOMIC ESPIONAGE CONVICTS **JULIUS** AND **ETHEL**

ROSENBERG ARE EXECUTED AT SING SING PRISON.]
JUNE 23: **Kerouac** is discharged from the *Carruthers* in New Orleans; [JUNE 27: AFTER THREE YEARS OF FIGHTING, THE KOREAN WAR ARMISTICE IS SIGNED.] JULY: After throwing the *I Ching*, **Allen Ginsberg** and **John Clellon Holmes** both decide to leave New York; **Holmes** moves to Old Saybrook, Connecticut (on Long Island Sound), where he buys a house and renovates it with proceeds from *Go*; **Ginsberg** plans a major trip south; AUG.: **Ginsberg** begins to write "Howl"; AUG.: **Kerouac** returns to New York and has a brief, intense affair with **Alene Lee**, a young black woman employed by **Ginsberg** and **Burroughs** as a typist; AUG. 23: **Kerouac** has a sexual encounter with **Gore Vidal**; **Kerouac** writes *The Subterraneans*—about his affair with **Alene Lee** ("Mardou Fox")—in three nights; SEPT.: **William S. Burroughs** moves from Mexico City to New York and begins a short, intense affair with **Allen Ginsberg** (at 206 E. Seventh Street, on the Lower East Side) while preparing *The Yagé Letters* for publication; NOV. 10: **Peter Orlovsky**, 20, is drafted into the U.S. Army; [NOV.: *THE WILD ONE,* STARRING MARLON BRANDO, PREMIERS IN NEW YORK CITY; NOV. 28: FRANK OLSON, 43, A U.S. ARMY SCIENTIST INVOLVED WITH BIOLOGICAL WEAPONS RESEARCH AT FORT DETRICK, FREDERICK, MARYLAND, DIES UNDER MYSTERIOUS CIRCUMSTANCES AFTER BEING GIVEN

ALENE LEE, C.1953

DEC. 1: After four months in New York, **William S. Burroughs** begins a voyage to Rome on the Greek liner TSS *Nea Hellas*; he arrives in Rome on DEC. 10 and spends the rest of the year in Rome with **Alan Ansen**; [DEC.: **HUGH HEFNER AND ELDON SELLERS** BEGIN PUBLISHING *PLAYBOY* MAGAZINE.] DEC.: **Kerouac** begins an intense study of Buddhism after examining **Dwight Goddard's** *A Buddhist Bible* (1932) at the San Jose Public Library; DEC. 14: A Mexican court finds **William S. Burroughs** guilty of homicide in absentia and sentences him to two years in prison (minus thirteen days served), but the sentenced is suspended; DEC. 15: **James Grauerholz** is born in Coffeyville, Kansas; DEC. 19–31: **Allen**

Ginsberg leaves New York City and hitchhikes south to Washington, D.C.; from Washington he travels to Jacksonville, Florida; then to Palm Beach to visit **William S. Burroughs's** parents; then to Key West via Miami; then he takes a boat to Cuba; DEC. 26: A trial run of **Jane Bowles's** play, *In the Summer House*, in Washington, D.C., stirs controversy; DEC. 29–FEB. 13: *In the Summer House*, directed by **José Quintero** and starring **Judith Anderson**, runs for fifty-five performances at the 865-seat Playhouse Theatre, 137 W. Forty-Eighth Street, New York; **Lew Welch** takes a job in Montgomery Ward's retail advertising department (Chicago), where he prepares ads for the stores in the Ward retail chain; **Alan Watts** begins a regular radio program on KPFA that lasts twenty years (until his death in 1973); **Edward Marshall**, 20, moves from New Hampshire to Boston, Massachusetts; he meets poet **Stephen Jonas**, with whom he shares a room, and also **Joe Dunn** (founder of the White Rabbit Press) and **John Wieners**.

1954

JAN. 1: **Allen Ginsburg**, 27, takes his first plane ride, a 494-mile flight from Havana, Cuba, to Mérida, Mexico, on the Yucatán peninsula; JAN. 2: **Ginsberg** visits the Mayan ruins at Chichén Itzá; [JAN.: GALLUP POLLS SHOW THAT THE RED-BAITING SENATOR JOSEPH first week of JAN.: **William S. Burroughs**, 39, arrives in Tangier, Morocco, after a short stay in Gibraltar and resides in various hotels over the next three weeks; JAN.–MAY: **Ginsberg** explores Mayan ruins in the Yucatán, Mexico and experiments with various psychoactive drugs; JAN. 27: **Kerouac** leaves New York for San Jose, California; early FEB.: **Burroughs** rents a room for fifty cents a day at 1 Calle de los Arcos, a male brothel in Tangier's Socco Chico (Little Market) where he will live for the next ten months; FEB. 7: Harper and Row publishes **Aldous Huxley's** *The Doors of Perception*, his account of a quasi-mystical hallucinogenic drug experience; FEB. 8: **Kerouac** moves back in with the **Cassadys** and takes a job as a parking lot attendant; **Neal** and **Carolyn Cassady** develop a fascination with **Edgar Cayce** (1877–1945), a Californian mystic and channeler known as the "sleeping prophet"; MARCH: **Jack Kerouac** moves out after a bitter quarrel with **Neal Cassady** (who quite rightly accuses **Kerouac** of freeloading); **Kerouac** takes a room for a month in the Cameo Hotel, 389 Third Street, San Francisco; he meets **Al Sublette** and writes *San Francisco Blues*, a book of poetry; MARCH: **Robert Creeley** moves to Asheville, North Carolina, to teach at Black Mountain College and to edit *Black Mountain Review*; [MARCH

16: THE ARMY–MCCARTHY HEARINGS ARE HELD IN WASHINGTON.] APRIL: **Kerouac** returns to New York; **Charles Bukowski**, 34, nearly dies from a bleeding stomach ulcer; *New World Writing* publishes an extract from *On the Road* titled "Jazz of the Beat Generation"; fearing that the piece will be used against him as evidence against of unpaid child support, **Kerouac** uses his first name, Jean-Louis, as a pseudonym; [APRIL 21–22: THE UNITED STATES SENATE SUBCOMMITTEE ON JUVENILE DELINQUENCY HOLDS HEARINGS ON THE ALLEGED ADVERSE EFFECTS OF COMIC BOOKS ON AMERICA'S YOUTH; MAY 8: THE BATTLE OF DIEN BIEN PHU ENDS AND THE FRENCH ARE DEFEATED IN VIETNAM; MAY 17: THE U.S. SUPREME COURT DECIDES *BROWN V. BOARD OF EDUCATION* AND ORDERS THE DESEGREGATION OF PUBLIC SCHOOLS.] mid-MAY: **Ginsberg** is in Mexico City; JUNE: **John Wieners**, 20, graduates from Boston College with an AB degree; **LeRoi Jones**, 19, graduates from Howard University, Washington, D.C. with a BA in English; **Ginsberg** arrives at the **Cassadys'** house (East Santa Clara Street, San Jose, California) for an extended stay; JULY 12: After eight months' service, **Peter Orlovsky** receives a psychiatric discharge from the Army; AUG.: **Neal** and **Carolyn Cassady** buy a house in Los Gatos, California; AUG. 19: **Carolyn Cassady** catches **Allen Ginsberg** performing oral sex on **Neal Cassady**; she ejects **Ginsberg** from her home; he takes up residence at the Marconi Hotel, 554 Broadway (between Kearney and Colombus), San Francisco, where he meets **Sheila Williams, Al Sublette**, and **Peter Du Peru**; AUG. 21: *The Saturday Review* publishes "Invitation to Innovators," an essay by **Malcolm Cowley** that introduces **Kerouac's** work; SUMMER: after **Gary Snyder** is blacklisted, **Philip Whalen** takes his place as a fire warden at Sourdough Mountain Lookout in the northern Cascades, Washington State; **Sterling Lord** becomes **Kerouac's** literary agent; JUNE: Little, Brown rejects *On the Road*; [AUG. 24: EISENHOWER SIGNS INTO LAW THE COMMUNIST CONTROL ACT OF 1954, WHICH OUTLAWS THE COMMUNIST PARTY OF THE UNITED STATES OF AMERICA (CPUSA).] SUMMER and AUTUMN: **Gary Snyder** works for Warm Springs Lumber Company in Oregon; OCT.–DEC.: **LeRoi Jones** enlists in the U.S. Air Force and undergoes eight and a half weeks of basic training at Lackland Air Force Base, San Antonio, Texas; OCT. 5: During Hurricane Hazel, **John Wieners** attends a **Charles Olson** poetry reading at the Charles Street Meeting House, Boston and decides to enroll at Black Mountain College; OCT. 17: **Ginsberg**, high on peyote at the Pine Street apartment he shares with **Sheila Williams**, peers out the window at the Sir Francis Drake Hotel (450

ALLEN GINSBERG
POINTS AT THE
SIR FRANCIS DRAKE
HOTEL, HIS VISION
OF MOLOCH

Powell Street) and has a vision of the building as "the robot skullface of Moloch," which inspires part 2 of "Howl"; OCT.: **Neal Cassady** meets **Natalie Jackson**; OCT.: **Kerouac** goes back to Lowell by bus; he visits his first love, **Mary Carney**, tours his childhood haunts, and goes to the basement chapel of Sainte Jeanne d'Arc Church (129 Fourth Street) where he has an epiphany about the word *beat* (i.e., that it really means *beatific*); he goes to live with his mother in New York and revises *On the Road*; [NOV. 1: THE ALGERIAN WAR BEGINS.] NOV. 9: **Allen Ginsberg's** ten-week relationship with **Sheila Williams** falters; [DEC. 2: SENATE VOTES BY A TWO-THIRDS MARGIN TO CENSURE SENATOR MCCARTHY.] DEC.: After basic training, **LeRoi Jones**, 20, is assigned (until January 1957) to the Seventy-Second Bombardment Wing, Heavy, Strategic Air Command (SAC), as a gunner and aerial climatographer on a huge Convair B-36 "Peacemaker" bomber based at Ramey Air Force Base near Aguadilla, Puerto Rico; **Ginsberg**, 28, meets **Peter Orlovsky**, 21, artist and artist's model, at **Robert LaVigne's** apartment (1403 Gough Street, San Francisco); **Burroughs** moves from Calle de los Arcos to the Villa Muniria, 1 Calle Magallanes, in the Spanish Quarter of Tangier; **Brion Gysin** and **Mohamed Hamri** open 1001 Nights, a restaurant located in Dar Menebhi Palace on the Marshan in Tangier (it will permanently close in January 1958); **Jack Kerouac** is arrested for nonsupport of his daughter, **Jan Kerouac**; DEC. 19: **Kerouac** writes in his journal, "At the lowest beatest ebb of my life"; DEC. 27: Knopf rejects **Kerouac's** *On the Road*; Olympia Press (Paris) publishes **Alexander Trocchi's** first novel, *Young Adam*; **LeRoi Jones** drops out of Howard University and joins the U.S. Air Force; **Kenneth Patchen** introduces him to **Lawrence Ferlinghetti**; **Dick McBride**, 26, starts a fifteen-year stint working as store manager at City Lights.

1955

JAN.: **Carolyn Cassady** learns of **Neal Cassady's** affair with **Natalie Jackson**; **Neal Cassady** moves out; he stays with **Allen Ginsberg** and **Peter Orlovsky** at their apartment in San Francisco and begins to gamble on horse races with $2,500 illegally expropriated from **Carolyn's** savings account; JAN. 18: **Joan Haverty** forces **Jack Kerouac** to appear before a domestic relations court for nonpayment of child support for his daughter, **Jan Kerouac**; the judge suspends the case for one year because **Kerouac** is unable to work due to his phlebitis condition; FEB.: **Kerouac** goes to Rocky Mount, North Carolina to live with his sister's family; SPRING: **John Wieners**, 21, enrolls at Black Mountain College; [MARCH 12: CHARLIE PARKER, 34, DIES OF A HEART ATTACK AT THE STANHOPE HOTEL, 995 FIFTH AVENUE, NEW YORK CITY.] APRIL: **Robert Frank** is awarded a Guggenheim Fellowship and uses the money to buy a car and travel all over the U.S. in 1955–56; he takes more than 27,000 black-and-white photographs (760 rolls of film) that will be distilled into a book entitled *The Americans*; JUNE: **Richard Fariña** graduates from Brooklyn Technical High School; SUMMER: **Seymour Krim**, 33, becomes manic and is briefly hospitalized in a mental institution; **Philip Whalen**, 31, spends his second summer as a fire warden at Sourdough Mountain Lookout in the northern Cascades; **Gary Snyder**, 25, works on a trail crew at Yosemite National Park, East-Central California; [JUNE 29–30: R. GORDON WASSON AND ALLEN RICHARDSON SAMPLE HALLUCINOGENIC MUSHROOMS IN THE REMOTE

AL SUBLETTE AT ALLEN GINSBERG'S APARTMENT AT 1010 MONTGOMERY ST., SAN FRANCISCO, SPRING 1955

MAZATEC VILLAGE OF HUAUTLA DE JIMÉNEZ IN THE STATE OF OAXACA, SOUTHERN MEXICO.] JULY: **Gary Snyder** becomes a Buddhist; Viking Press accepts *On the Road*; JULY 18: San Francisco artist-poet-musician-composer **Weldon Kees**, 41, disappears and is presumed to have committed suicide; AUG.: **Kerouac** starts hitchhiking from Rocky Mount to San Francisco to visit Ginsberg but ends up in Mexico City; he lives on the roof of Orizaba 210, Roma Norte, Cuauhtémoc (above **Bill Garver's** apartment, which formerly belonged to **William S. Burroughs**); he smokes pot, injects heroin, has an affair with his dealer, a Mexican prostitute named **Esperanza Villanueva**, and writes *Mexico City Blues*; AUG. 10: City Lights publishes its first book, **Ferlinghetti's** poetry collection *Pictures of the Gone World*; AUG. 25: **Ginsberg** begins to write the first section of "Howl"; [AUG. 28: AFTER ALLEGEDLY WHISTLING AT A WHITE WOMAN IN MONEY, MISSISSIPPI, **EMMETT TILL**, 14, IS

KIDNAPPED, BRUTALLY BEATEN, SHOT, AND DUMPED IN THE TALLAHATCHIE RIVER, HIS MUTILATED CORPSE BARELY IDENTIFIABLE.] SEPT.: **Richard Fariña** starts college at Cornell University, Ithaca, New York; **Allen Ginsberg** moves to a cottage at 1624 Milvia Street, Berkeley, California, near the university; SEPT. 9: **Kerouac** takes a bus to El Paso, Texas, and then hitchhikes to California to visit **Ginsberg** in Berkeley, as originally planned; SEPT.: Kerouac meets **Gary Snyder**; [SEPT. 30: JAMES DEAN, 24, IS KILLED IN A CAR ACCIDENT NEAR CHOLAME, CALIFORNIA.]

OCT.: **Alexander Trocchi** becomes involved with the Letterist International (LI), a Paris-based collective of radical artists and theorists active between 1952 and 1957; the collective provides the link between **Isidore Isou's** letterist group and the Situationist International; OCT. 7: For an audience of about one hundred fifty people, **Ginsberg** reads "Howl" (part 1) at the historic "Six Poets at the Six Gallery" reading (the Six Gallery is a small art gallery converted from an auto repair garage at 3119 Fillmore Street, San Francisco); the other poets reading are **Philip Whalen, Gary Snyder, Michael McClure, Philip Lamantia, and Kenneth Rexroth; Jack Kerouac, Neal Cassady, Natalie Jackson, and Ann Charters**, 19 (a student at Berkeley), are among those in the audience; OCT.: **Gary Snyder, John Montgomery,**

NATALIE JACKSON,
1931 - 1955

and **Jack Kerouac** climb Matterhorn Peak (12,264 feet) in the Sierra Nevada chain, at the northern boundary of Yosemite National Park, California (**Kerouac** later writes about the experience in *The Dharma Bums*); OCT. 26: **Ed Fancher**, **Dan Wolf**, and **Norman Mailer** launch *The Village Voice*; [OCT. 27: JAMES DEAN'S LAST FILM, *REBEL WITHOUT A CAUSE*, IS RELEASED FIVE WEEKS AFTER HIS DEATH; A DEAN CULT EMERGES.] NOV. 5: Random House publishes *The Spider's House* by **Paul Bowles**; NOV. 7: **Robert Frank** is arrested while driving on U.S. Route 65 near McGehee, Arkansas, and is briefly jailed as a "suspicious person"; NOV. 9: **Kerouac**, **Ginsberg**, and **Phil Whalen** take a walk in San Francisco's dock area; noticing a bedraggled sunflower, **Kerouac** pronounces it a victim of civilization, thus inspiring **Ginsberg** to write "Sunflower Sutra"; NOV. 30: **Neal Cassady's** mistress, **Natalie Jackson**, 24, suffering from acute, amphetamine-induced paranoia, commits suicide by jumping off the roof of her apartment building at 1041 Franklin Street, San Francisco—despite **Jack Kerouac's** earlier efforts to keep her calm; [DEC. 1: ROSA PARKS IS ARRESTED FOR REFUSING TO MOVE TO THE BACK OF A CITY BUS IN BIRMINGHAM, ALABAMA, AN EVENT THAT SIGNALS THE START OF THE MOST ACTIVIST PHASE OF THE CIVIL RIGHTS MOVEMENT.] DEC. 14: **Richard Brautigan**, 20, is arrested for throwing a rock through a police station window; he is sent to Oregon State Hospital, where he is administered electroshock treatments; DEC. 22: **Kerouac** returns to his sister's house in Rocky Mount, North Carolina; Richard Brukenfeld publishes *The Vestal Lady on Brattle, and Other Poems* by **Gregory Corso**.

1956

JAN. 1–16: **Jack Kerouac** writes *Visions of Gerard*, a novel about the death of his older brother, **Gerard Kerouac**, in 1926; the novel is published in 1963; JAN. 17: **Ginsberg** completes "America" in Berkeley; [JAN. 27: RCA RELEASES ELVIS PRESLEY'S "HEARTBREAK HOTEL" AS A 45 RPM SINGLE AND ELVIS BECOMES AN INSTANT POP SENSATION.] FEB.: **Elise Cowen**, 22, graduates from Barnard College,

New York City; she and her lesbian lover, **Sheila**, move in with **Allen Ginsberg** and **Peter Orlovsky**; FEB.: **William S. Burroughs** travels to London to take the apomorphine (i.e., nonaddictive morphine) cure devised by **John Yerbury Dent** (1888–1962); MARCH 15: **Kerouac** completes *Some of the Dharma* (published in 1997); MARCH 17: **Jack Kerouac**, 34, borrows fifty dollars from his mother and begins hitchhiking cross-country, from Rocky Mount, North Carolina, to California, to report for his fire watch job; MARCH 18: **Ginsberg** reads "Howl" at a poetry reading at the Town Hall Theater in Berkeley; the participating poets are the same as the Six Gallery bill; APRIL: **Kerouac** arrives in California and settles into *Marin-an* (Japanese for "Horse Grove Hermitage"), a small cabin owned by **Gary Snyder** at 370 Montford Avenue, Mill Valley, California (just east of Mount Tamalpais State Park), on land belonging to **Locke McCorkle**, a carpenter and a Buddhist; MAY: **Kerouac** meets **Locke McCorkle** and poets **Robert "Bob" Creeley** and **Bob Donlin**; MAY 5: On a scholarship from the First Zen Institute of America, **Gary Snyder** sails by freighter for Japan to study Rinzai Zen under **Miura Isshu Roshi** at Daitokuji Temple, Kyoto; After bidding farewell to **Snyder** from the dockside, **Kerouac** and **Robert Creeley** are thrown out of the Cellar (a tavern at 576 Green Street, San Francisco); **Kerouac** asks **Creeley** if he would like to spend the night at **Snyder's** Mill Valley cabin and **Creeley** agrees, bringing with him **Kenneth Rexroth's** wife, **Marthe Rexroth**; **Rexroth**—a jealous philanderer—comes to mistakenly believe that **Kerouac** is also sexually involved with his wife, inciting **Rexroth's** lifelong antipathy for **Kerouac**; MAY 7: **Wilhelm Reich** is convicted of contempt of court and sentenced to two years in prison; MAY 28: **Kerouac** begins *Old Angel Midnight*, a long narrative poem (published in 1993); JUNE 9: **Ginsberg's** mother, **Naomi Ginsberg**, 62, dies of a stroke at Greystone State Mental Hospital, Morristown, New Jersey; JUNE: **William S. Burroughs**, finally cured of his thirteen-year heroin addiction, returns to Tangier via Algeria; JUNE 18: **Jack Kerouac** begins hitchhiking north to report for his sixty-three-day summer stint in a remote fire-watch tower on Desolation Peak, Mount Hozomeen in the Cascade Mountains (Washington State); [AUG. 11: NEAR EAST HAMPTON, LONG ISLAND, **JACKSON POLLOCK**, 44, IS KILLED IN A SINGLE-CAR ACCIDENT WHILE DRIVING UNDER THE INFLUENCE; A PASSENGER, **EDITH METZGER**, 25, IS ALSO KILLED; ANOTHER PASSENGER—POLLOCK'S MISTRESS—**RUTH KLIGMAN**, 26, SURVIVES; AUG. 23: THE FDA BURNS SEVERAL TONS OF **WILHELM**

DESOLATION PEAK LOOKOUT WITH MT. HOZOMEEN IN THE BACKGROUND, NORTH CASCADES MOUNTAINS, WASHINGTON STATE, ELEVATION: 6,102 FT.

REICH'S CONFISCATED WRITINGS IN A NEW YORK CITY GARBAGE INCINERATOR; AUTUMN: BLACK MOUNTAIN COLLEGE CLOSES AFTER TWENTY-FOUR YEARS IN OPERATION.] SEPT. 13: **Kerouac**, down from Mount Hozomeen, takes the bus to San Francisco from Seattle; **Kerouac** agrees to change names and some locations so that *On the Road* can be published; SEPT.: **Kerouac** returns to Mexico City, where he writes the first part of *Desolation Angels*; The September 19, 1956 issue of *Downbeat* features "Art Pepper Tells the Tragic Role Narcotics Played in Blighting His Career and Life" by **John Tynan**; OCT. 30: **Ginsberg**, responding to a heckler, takes off his clothes at a poetry reading in Los Angeles; NOV.: **Ginsberg**, **Corso**, **Peter Orlovsky**, and his brother, **Lafcadio Orlovsky**, join **Kerouac** in Mexico City; appalled by the dire poverty he encounters in Mexico, **Corso** flies back to Washington, D.C.; **Kerouac**, **Ginsberg**, **Peter Orlovsky**, and **Lafcadio Orlovsky** drive a rented car back to New York City; **Ginsberg**, **Peter Orlovsky**, and **Kerouac** meet **Salvador Dalí** (1904–1989) at the Russian Tea Room, 150 W. Fifty-Seventh Street, New York City; Nov 1: City Lights publishes *Howl, and Other Poems*; Jonathan Williams in Big Sur, California, publishes **Michael McClure's** first book of poetry, *Passage*; McGill Poetry Series publishes *Let Us Compare Mythologies*, **Leonard Cohen's** first book.

1957

JAN. 1: Through **Ginsberg's** auspices, **Jack Kerouac**, 34, meets **Joyce Glassman**, 21, a graduate student at Barnard; they begin a two-year on-again, off-again relationship; JAN. 11: **Kerouac** signs his contract with Viking Press for *On the Road*; **Kerouac** lives with **Joyce Glassman** (at 554 W. 113th Street, New York City) after **Helen Weaver** kicks him out of her apartment; JAN.: **LeRoi Jones** is discharged from the U.S. Air Force; FEB. 15: With $200 borrowed from **Ferlinghetti**, **Jack Kerouac** sails for Africa on the Yugoslavian freighter SS *Slovenija* to visit **Burroughs** who is still living at the Villa Muniria in Tangier; FEB. 24: **Gregory Corso** departs New York for Europe on the SS *America*; MARCH: **Hettie Roberta Cohen**

LORD BUCKLEY LP
COVER DESIGN BY
JIM FLORA, 1955

meets **LeRoi Jones** when he applies for a job at
the *Record Changer* in New York City; MARCH 8:
Ginsberg and **Orlovsky** ship out of Hoboken, New
Jersey, on SS *Extavia*, a 6,535-ton freighter bound
for Casablanca and Tangier, Morocco, via Lisbon;
Kerouac, in Morocco, receives a forwarded letter
from editor **Malcolm Cowley** (dated February
24) rejecting *Desolation Angels*; MARCH 25: U.S.
Customs seizes all 520 copies of the second printing
of *Howl, and Other Poems*, which the printer in
England had shipped to City Lights; MARCH 19:
After eleven days at sea, **Ginsberg** and **Orlovsky**
join **Kerouac** and **Burroughs** in Tangier, Morocco;
Ginsberg feels snubbed by **Jane Bowles**; [MARCH
22: WILHELM REICH IS SENT TO LEWISBURG FEDERAL
PENITENTIARY.] APRIL 4: **Jane Bowles**, 40, suffers
a mild stroke; APRIL 5: After six weeks in Tangier
helping to collate and type **Burroughs's** *Naked
Lunch* manuscript, **Kerouac** leaves for Marseille,

France; **Ginsberg** and **Orlovsky** take over **Kerouac's** vacated room; APRIL 20: After two weeks in France, **Kerouac** begins his return trip to New York on board the Dutch ocean liner SS *Neiuw Amsterdam*; **Norman Mailer** publishes "The White Negro" in the spring issue of *Dissent* magazine; [MAY 2: SENATOR JOSEPH R. MCCARTHY, 48, DIES OF CIRRHOSIS OF THE LIVER.] early MAY: **Kerouac** and his mother arrive in Berkeley by bus from Orlando, Florida; they settle into an apartment at 1943 Berkeley Way (near the University of California, Berkeley); **Kerouac** works on "Old Angel Midnight" and *Book of Dreams*; MAY 21: Two plainclothes police officers enter City Lights, buy copies of *Howl, and Other Poems*, and leave; they return to arrest the clerk, **Shigeyoshi "Shig" Murao**; **Lawrence Ferlinghetti** is not present but is later served a warrant stating he sought to "willfully and lewdly print, publish and sell obscene and indecent writings, papers, and books, to wit: *Howl and Other Poems*"; an August trial is set; JUNE 10: *Life* magazine publishes **R. Gordon Wasson's** illustrated article "Seeking the Magic Mushroom"; JUNE 11: **Ginsberg** and **Orlovsky** take the ferry across the Strait of Gibraltar from Tangier to Algeciras, Spain; they spend two nights in Seville before moving on to Córdoba; the next day (JUNE 14) they take the night train to Madrid; they stay in Madrid for a few days, then travel

LAWRENCE FERLINGHETTI AND SHIG MURAO, SEATED FRONT AND CENTER, ON TRIAL FOR PUBLISHING "HOWL," AUGUST 1957

to Marseille, France; JULY 1: **Ginsberg** and **Orlovsky** arrive in Venice; JULY 15: After ten weeks in Berkeley, **Kerouac** and his mother move back to Florida; JULY 20: **Kerouac** travels to Mexico City but finds out that **Herbert Huncke's** friend, **Bill Garver**, has committed suicide during heroin withdrawal the month before; AUG.: **Gary Snyder** boards USS *Sappa Creek* (a World War II–era T-2 oil tanker) in Yokohama, Japan; he works as a wiper in the engine room and subsequently sails to the Persian Gulf (five times), Italy, Turkey, Okinawa, Wake Island, Guam, Ceylon, and Pago Pago, Samoa; **Ginsberg** and **Orlovsky** begin a tour of Italy; AUG. 16–SEPT. 3: The obscenity trial against **Lawrence Ferlinghetti** is held in San Francisco Municipal Court; **Ferlinghetti** is prosecuted by **Ralph McIntosh** and defended by **Jacob W. "Jake" Ehrlich** (1900–1971) and the ACLU; nine literary experts testify about *Howl*, including **Mark Schorer, Luther Nichols, Walter Van Tilburg Clark, Herbert Blau, Arthur Foff, Kenneth Rexroth,** and **Vincent McHugh**; AUG. 17: **Kerouac** returns to Orlando, Florida, from Mexico, after almost a month away; AUG. 22: **Ginsberg** flies to Rome; SEPT. 4: **Kerouac** arrives in New York City, after a thirty-hour trip on a Greyhound bus from Florida, and stays with **Joyce Glassman**; SEPT. 5: Six years after he wrote it, **Kerouac's** *On the Road* is finally published by Viking Press; **Gilbert Millstein's** famous, adulatory review appears in *The New York Times* and makes **Kerouac** an instant celebrity; SEPT. 8: **David Dempsey's** more skeptical review of *On the Road* appears in *The New York Times*; Sept 10: **Kerouac** appears on the TV show *Night Beat* with **Joseph "Sepy" Dobronyi**; SEPT. 16: **Ginsberg** and **Orlovsky** arrive in Paris from Italy; OCT. 3: Judge **Clayton W. Horn** acquits **Ferlinghetti** of obscenity charges; AUTUMN: **Edward Marshall's** "Leave the Word Alone," a poem about his mother's madness, appears in *Black Mountain Review*, no. 7; **Ginsberg** later cites it as a key inspiration for "Kaddish"; OCT.: First collaborative poetry-jazz performance— featuring **Howard Hart, Philip Lamantia, Jack Kerouac,** and **David Amram**—is staged at the Brata Gallery, 89 E. Tenth Street, New York City; OCT.: **Lew Welch** and his wife, **Mary Welch**, move from Chicago to

San Francisco after **Welch** is granted a transfer to the Montgomery Ward office in Oakland; [OCT. 4: SOVIETS SHOCK THE WORLD BY LAUNCHING *SPUTNIK 1*, THE FIRST ARTIFICIAL SATELLITE.] OCT. 14: **Kerouac** returns to Florida and lives with his mother at 1418 1/2 Clouser Street, Orlando; OCT. 15: **Ginsberg** and **Orlovsky** join **Burroughs** and **Corso** at a cheap, dirty, forty-two-room flophouse that becomes famous as the "Beat Hotel" (No. 9 rue Git le Coeur, Latin Quarter, Paris); **Ginsberg** brings **Burroughs's** *Naked Lunch* manuscript to **Maurice Girodias**, but **Girodias** initially rejects it as not commercial enough; [NOV. 3: WILHELM REICH, 60, DIES OF HEART FAILURE WHILE INCARCERATED AT THE FEDERAL PENITENTIARY IN LEWISBURG, PENNSYLVANIA.] NOV. 13: **Ginsberg** (at the Café Select in Paris) begins writing "Kaddish," an elegy for his mother, **Naomi Ginsberg**; NOV. 24: **Peter Orlovsky** writes his first poem; DEC. 9: **Kerouac** finishes *The Dharma Bums*; DEC.: **Ginsberg** writes "Death to van Gogh's Ear" in Paris; DEC. 19–25: **Kerouac** visits New York to do a series of readings of his work at the Village Vanguard (178 Seventh Avenue South); the first show is a disaster but subsequent readings, accompanied by **Steve Allen** on piano, are highly successful; Troubadour Press (New York City) publishes **Jack Micheline's** first book of poetry, *River of Red Wine, and Other Poems* (with an introduction by **Jack Kerouac**); **John Mitchell**

(Village nightclub entrepreneur) and **Alene Lee** have a daughter, **Christina Mitchell**; **Barney Rosset** (Grove Press) founds *Evergreen Review* (which runs until 1973); **Barbara Moraff**, 18, meets **Jack Kerouac**, 35; he calls her "the baby of the Beat Generation"; **Jane Bowles**, 40, suffers another stroke, which leaves her partially incapacitated for the remaining seventeen years of her life.

1958

JAN.: A hostile **Mike Wallace** interviews **Jack Kerouac** for the *New York Post*; JAN. 16: **William S. Burroughs** arrives in Paris on a flight from Tangier, Morocco; he moves in with **Allen Ginsberg** at the Beat Hotel and meets **Maurice Girodias** of Olympia Press; JAN.: **Lew Welch** begins studying for a masters degree in English from San Francisco State College; he is subsequently fired from Montgomery Ward; FEB. 2: **Allen Ginsberg** arrives in England for a two-week stay; FEB.: City Lights publishes *Gasoline* by **Gregory Corso** and *Memoirs of a Shy Pornographer* by **Kenneth Patchen**; FEB.: *Esquire* publishes "The Philosophy of the Beat Generation" by **John Clellon Holmes**; Grove Press publishes **Kerouac's** *The Subterraneans*; **David Dempsey**, book critic for *The New York Times*, gives it a negative review, but MGM buys the movie rights from **Kerouac** for

HUBERT "HUBE THE CUBE" LESLIE (1921-1986), A SAN FRANCISCO NEWSPAPER STAND PROPRIETER (AND DRUG ADDICT), HIRED IN 1958 BY HENRY LENOIR OF VESUVIO CAFE (255 COLUMBUS AVE., SF) TO SIT IN THE WINDOW, ADD BEAT AMBIENCE, AND ATTRACT CUSTOMERS

$15,000—the first substantial sum of money he has ever had in his life; MARCH: **Kerouac** returns to New York to look for a home; with the money from MGM, **Kerouac** buys a house at 34 Gilbert Street in the village of Northport, on the north shore of Long Island; the Spring 1958 issue of *Chicago Review* devotes most of its pages to writers "From San Francisco," including **Lawrence Ferlinghetti**, **Robert Duncan**, **Allen Ginsberg**, **John Wieners**, **Michael McClure**, **Kirby Doyle**, **Philip Lamantia**, and **Philip Whalen**; MARCH: **Kerouac** cuts a spoken-word LP for Dot Records, accompanied by **Steve Allen** on piano, but the album is never officially released because it offends Dot Records president **Randy Wood**; MARCH: **LeRoi** and **Hettie Jones** begin publishing *Yūgen*, a Beat literary magazine (eight issues are published over the next five years); APRIL 2: San Francisco newspaper columnist **Herb Caen** signals the start of a backlash against the Beats when he coins the derisive term *beatnik*, an amalgam of *Beat* and *Sputnik* that associates the Beats with the threat of Soviet communism; APRIL 3: **Eugene Burdick's** "The Innocent Nihilists Adrift in Squaresville," published in *The Reporter*, offers a more sympathetic view of the Beats; SPRING: **Brion Gysin** leaves Morocco and moves into the Beat Hotel in Paris; early APRIL: While leaving the Kettle of Fish (114 MacDougal Street, New York City) with **Gregory Corso**, **Jack Kerouac** is severely beaten by two men; he sustains a broken nose, a broken arm, and a concussion; he is bleeding so profusely when he returns to **Joyce Glassman's** Morningside Heights apartment that she takes him to the hospital where he tells doctors to "cauterize" his wounds; APRIL: **Gary Snyder** returns to the U.S.; MAY: **Kerouac** moves into his new home in Northport with his mother; MAY 4: After a poetry reading at the Corcoran Gallery in Washington, D.C., **Kenneth Rexroth** dismisses the Beat Generation as a "gimmick"; MAY 6: **Ginsberg** and **Corso** read their poetry at Oxford; a melee ensues when the audience misinterprets **Corso's** satiric poem "Bomb" as being in favor of nuclear armaments; MAY 15: Robert Delpire (Paris) publishes **Robert Frank's** *Les Américains*, a French edition of **Frank's** photography book *The Americans*, which includes writings by **Simone de Beauvoir**,

Erskine Caldwell, William Faulkner, Henry Miller, and John Steinbeck; late MAY: Ginsberg and Corso return to Paris; JUNE: Gary Snyder, 28, meets Joanne Kyger, 24; JUNE 1: Citadel Press publishes *The Beat Generation and the Angry Young Men*, edited by Gene Feldman and Max Gartenberg; JUNE: Ginsberg, in Paris, writes "To Aunt Rose"; JUNE 15 and 22: *San Francisco Chronicle* runs "Life and Loves among the Beatniks," a two-part article by Allen Brown; JUNE 17: Danna Connie Sublette (a.k.a., Danna Lewis and Connie Swanson), 20, the common-law wife of Al Sublette (a friend of Kerouac from his Cameo Hotel days), is strangled to death by an African American sailor named Frank Harris, 32, in an alley between 432 and 436 Lyon Street, San Francisco, during a sexual encounter gone wrong; Harris is subsequently arrested, tried, and convicted of murder; JULY 4: Neal Cassady, 32, begins serving a two- to five-year sentence in San Quentin Prison for trading two marijuana cigarettes to undercover narcotics cops in exchange for a ride to work; JULY 8: Ginsberg and Burroughs visit Louis-Ferdinand Céline (1894–1961) at his home in Bas Meudon, a Paris suburb; JULY 17: Ginsberg sails for New York (having been abroad for sixteen months); he arrives in New York on JULY 23; Alan Watts's "Beat Zen, Square Zen, and Zen" appears in the summer issue of *Chicago Review*; AUG.: **Paul Krassner**, 26, begins publishing *The Realist*, a magazine of "free thought, criticism and satire" from 225 Lafayette Street, New York City; **Ginsberg** and **Orlovsky** take an apartment (for sixty dollars a month) at 170 E. Second Street, East Village, New York City; **Gary Snyder** hikes one hundred twenty miles and climbs Mount Tyndall (14,025 feet) and adjacent to Mount Whitney (14,505 feet) in Sequoia National Park, East-Central California; AUG. 10: Random House publishes **John Clellon Holmes's** jazz novel *The Horn*, which is loosely based on the lives of **Lester Young** and **Charlie Parker**; SEPT.: **Ken Kesey** and **Ken Babbs** meet while both are taking a graduate creative writing course at Stanford University; **Robert Brustein's** article "The Cult of Unthink" (*Horizon* 1, no. 1) attacks the Beats for "inarticulateness, obscurity, and self-isolation"; **Norman Podhoretz** attacks the Beats for anti-intellectualism in "The Know-Nothing Bohemians," *Partisan Review*; SEPT. 29: **Ginsberg**, **Kerouac**, and **Franz Kline** go on an all-night binge in New York City; OCT.–DEC.: **Jane Bowles** is hospitalized at Cornell Medical Center, White Plains, New York; OCT. 2: Viking Press publishes **Kerouac's** *The Dharma Bums*, which is favorably reviewed by **Nancy Wilson Ross** in *The New York Times*; OCT.: **Kerouac** meets artist **Dody Müller** at **Robert Frank's** loft in the Bowery at Ninth Street and begins an affair that lasts until mid-February 1959; **Ferlinghetti** publishes *A Coney Island of the Mind* (City Lights); **Gregory Corso's** *Gasoline / The Vestal Lady on Brattle* is published by City Lights; OCT. 8: **Allen Ginsberg** stages a passionate two-hour poetry reading to an enthusiastic audience of two hundred people at Muhlenberg College, Allentown, Pennsylvania; OCT. 13: **Hettie Cohen** and **LeRoi Jones** marry; OCT. 15: **Kerouac's** *The Dharma Bums* is published; **Kerouac**, **Allen Ginsberg**, and **Peter Orlovsky** meet Zen expert **Daisetz Teitaro Suzuki** in New York City; NOV. 6: **Jack Kerouac** (drunk) joins **Kingsley Amis**, **Ashley Montagu**, **James Wechsler** (*New York Post* editorial writer), and **Joseph Kauffman** (acting as moderator) before an SRO audience at Hunter College to debate the question "Is There a Beat Generation?"; though each speaker is allotted ten minutes, **Kerouac** speaks for almost an hour, generally mugs and clowns, then repeatedly goes offstage to refill his brandy glass when the others speak; the evening is a fiasco; NOV. 7–11: **Kerouac** edits galleys of *The Subterraneans*; NOV. 22–27: **Kerouac** indulges in a "five-day bender"; NOV.: **Ray Bremser** is released from Bordentown Reformatory; DEC. 28: **Brion Gysin** has a quasi-mystical experience while dosing on a bus traveling from Paris to Marseilles, an experience that leads to the development of the "dream machine"; Auerhahn Press (San Francisco) publishes *Hotel Wentley Poems* by **John Wieners**, illustrated by **Robert LaVigne**; Birth Press publishes the first issue of *Birth*, a Beat journal edited by **Tuli Kupferberg**.

1959

[JAN. 1: **FIDEL CASTRO'S** TWENTY-SIXTH OF JULY MOVEMENT OVERTHROWS CUBAN DICTATOR **FULGENCIO BATISTA**.] JAN.: City Lights publishes *Selected Poems* by **Robert Duncan**; Grove Press publishes the first U.S. edition of **Robert Frank's** photography book *The Americans* (containing an introduction by **Jack Kerouac** but omitting the prose selections from the French edition, which are deemed anti-American); JAN. 18: Appearing with **Dorothy Parker** and **Norman Mailer** on **David Susskind's** TV program, *Open End* (Channel 13, New York City), **Truman Capote** snidely characterizes **Kerouac's** work as "typing, not writing"; JAN. 28: **Ginsberg**, **Orlovsky**, and **Corso** fly back to the U.S. via Chicago; their arrival is front-page news in the *Chicago Sun-Times*; JAN.: **Burroughs** finishes *Naked Lunch*; FEB. 5: **Allen Ginsberg**, **Gregory Corso**, and **Peter Orlovsky** read their poetry to a standing-room-only crowd of fourteen hundred students at Columbia University's McMillin

Theater; **Ginsberg's** father, **Louis Ginsberg**, is in the audience when an emotion-choked **Ginsberg** reads a draft version of "Kaddish" in public for the first time; FEB. 15: **Ginsberg**, **Corso**, and **Ray Bremser** read their poetry at the Gaslight, 116 MacDougal Street, New York City; MARCH 2: At a poetry reading at the Living Theatre, 530 Sixth Avenue at Fourteenth Street, New York City, a drunken **Jack Kerouac** heckles poet **Frank O'Hara**: "You're ruining American poetry, O'Hara!" **O'Hara** retorts, "That's more than you could ever do!" MAY: **Ginsberg**, at the behest of anthropologist **Gregory Bateson**, participates in clinical testing of LSD-25 at Stanford's Mental Research Institute in Palo Alto, California; MAY 1: Grove Press publishes **Kerouac's** *Doctor Sax*; the novel is very harshly reviewed by **David Dempsey** in *The New York Times*; MAY: Julian Messner publishes *The Holy Barbarians*, a sympathetic assessment of the Beats by **Lawrence Lipton**; MAY 9: **Bob Kaufman**, **Allen Ginsberg**, **John Kelley**, and **William Margolis** begin publishing *Beatitude* magazine in San Francisco; MAY 23: A benefit poetry reading for **John Wieners's** literary magazine, *Measure*, takes place at Garibaldi Hall, San Francisco; **Ginsberg**, **Wieners**, **Meltzer**, **Whalen**, **McClure**, **Duncan**, **Spicer**, and **James Broughton** participate; JUNE: The June issue of *Playboy* magazine contains a transcript of **Kerouac's** November 6, 1958, Hunter College talk titled "The Origins of the Beat Generation"; JUNE 2: **Ginsberg** writes the poem, "Lysergic Acid" after taking LSD; JULY 3: *The Beat Generation*, an exploitation movie written by **Richard Matheson** and **Lewis Meltzer**, directed by **Charles F. Hass**, and starring **Steve Cochran** and **Mamie Van Doren**, is released by MGM; University of Chicago student **Paul Carroll** brings out *Big Table*, a new literary journal, to publish "Ten Episodes from *Naked Lunch*" by **William S. Burroughs**; JUNE: Origin Press publishes **Gary Snyder's** first book of poems, *Riprap*; **Snyder** returns to Japan, where he will live for the next six years; **Janine Pommy**, 17, takes a job at Café Bizarre, 106 W. Third Street, New York; JULY: Avon Books publishes **Kerouac's** *Maggie Cassidy*, which is favorably reviewed by **David Dempsey** in the *New York Times*; a brief report on a scientific study of the Beats by **Francis Rigney**, staff psychiatrist at a Veterans Administration hospital in San Francisco, appears in *Science Digest* under the headline: "Beatniks Just Sick, Sick, Sick"; [JULY 17: BILLIE HOLIDAY, 44, DIES OF CIRRHOSIS OF THE LIVER WHILE UNDER POLICE GUARD IN METROPOLITAN HOSPITAL, NEW YORK CITY.] AUTUMN: **Lew Welch**, 33, begins working at the Bemis Bag Company, San Francisco subsidiary, as a rubber cutter; SEPT.: **Robert Zimmerman (Bob**

THE BEAT GENERA-TION MOVIE POSTER

Dylan) begins college at the University of Minnesota in Minneapolis; **Lou Reed** begins college at Syracuse University; **William S. Burroughs** and **Brion Gysin** make their first "cut-ups" (word collages) using newspapers and magazines; SEPT. 25: **Burroughs** appears before a French magistrate on a drugs charge; he is found guilty but given a suspended sentence and fined the equivalent of eighty dollars; SEPT. 26–OCT. 1: **Burroughs** is in England getting another apomorphine treatment from **John Yerbuy Dent** and visiting **Ian Sommerville**; SEPT. 29: *The Many Loves of Dobie Gillis*, a sitcom featuring **Maynard G. Krebs** (played by **Bob Denver**), a "beatnik," premiers on CBS; OCT.: **Brion Gysin** introduces **Burroughs** to the pseudoreligion of

BOB DENVER AS
NON-THREATENING
TV BEATNIK
MAYNARD G. KREBS

Scientology; **Kerouac** takes mescaline; **Kerouac** begins
a brief affair with another Northport resident, **Lois
Sorrells**, 24; Oct 31: **Kenneth Patchen's** jazz play *Don't
Look Now* opens at the Outside at the Inside Theater,
High Street, Palo Alto, California; produced by the
Troupe Theatre group under the direction of **Phillip
Angeloff**, it runs for six weeks; NOV. 11: **Alfred Leslie**
and **Robert Frank** release *Pull My Daisy*, a twenty-six-
minute black-and-white film about the Beats written
and narrated by **Kerouac** and featuring **Allen Ginsberg**,
Peter Orlovsky, **Gregory Corso**, artists **Larry Rivers**
and **Alice Neel**, musician **David Amram**, actors **Richard
Bellamy**, **Delphine Seyrig**, **Sally Gross**, and **Pablo
Frank** (**Robert Frank's** young son); NOV. 16: **Kerouac**
appears on *The Steve Allen Plymouth Show* (taped
in Hollywood) and reads passages from *On the Road*
to **Steve Allen's** jazz piano accompaniment; NOV. 17:

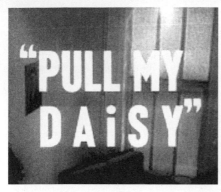

PULL MY DAISY
TITLE CARD

Kerouac travels to San Francisco to attend a screening of *Pull My Daisy* at the San Francisco Film Festival, where he meets **Lew Welch** and **Albert Saijo**; NOV. 21: **Kerouac** fails to make a promised visit to **Neal Cassady** at San Quentin; **Cassady** perceives this as a snub and takes it hard; NOV. 28: Grove Press publishes **Kerouac's** *Mexico City Blues*; NOV. 29: **Kenneth Rexroth** savages the book in a *New York Times* review; NOV.: Olympia Press, Paris, publishes **Burroughs's** *Naked Lunch* in an edition of ten thousand copies; after appearing on a talk show in Philadelphia to advocate the legalization of marijuana, **Ray Bremser** is arrested for violating the terms of his parole and is remanded to Trenton State, where he serves a six-month sentence; *Pull My Daisy* is screened at the San Francisco Film Festival and met with hostility; NOV. 30: **Paul O'Neil's** damning article "Beats: Sad but Noisy Rebels" appears in *Life* magazine; late NOV.–early DEC.: **Lew Welch**, **Albert Saijo**, and **Jack Kerouac** travel cross-country from San Francisco back to Northport in **Welch's** Willys Jeepster (nicknamed "Willy"); **Ken Kesey** participates in a study of psychoactive drugs at the Menlo Park (California) Veterans Administration Hospital; City Lights publishes **Bob Kaufman's** *Second April*; Hanover Records releases *Poetry for the Beat Generation* (Hanover LP 5000), a spoken-word recording by **Jack Kerouac**, accompanied by **Steve Allen** on piano; the recording includes "October in the Railroad Earth," "Deadbelly," "Charlie Parker," "The Sounds of the Universe Coming in My Window," "One Mother," "Goofing at the Table," "Bowery Blues," "Abraham," "Dave Brubeck," "I Had a Slouch Hat Too One Time," "The Wheel of the Quivering Meat Conception," "McDougal Street Blues," "The Moon Her Majesty," "I'd Rather Be Thin than Famous," and "Readings from *On the Road* and *Visions of Cody*"; at the invitation of **Keith S. Ditman** of the Neuropsychiatric Clinic at UCLA Medical School, **Alan Watts** takes LSD-25; **Ian Sommerville**, 20, meets **William S. Burroughs**, 45, and **Brion Gysin**, 43, in Paris; **Sommerville** subsequently moves into the Beat Hotel in Paris; Tibor de Nagy Gallery Editions publishes three hundred copies of *The Old Religion*, **Alan Ansen's** first book of poetry; Signet publishes *Beat Beat Beat: A Hip Collection of Cool Cartoons about Life and Love among the Beatniks* by **William F. Brown**.

1960

JAN.: **Brion Gysin** and **Ian Sommerville** both read **W. Grey Walter's** *The Living Brain* (first published in 1953); inspired, they begin to design a "Dreamachine," a flickering stroboscopic light device—consisting of a 100-watt light bulb, a motor, and a rotating cylinder with cutouts—that causes light to oscillate at the alpha wave rate (i.e., eight to thirteen times per second); meant to be experienced with the eyes closed, the Dreamachine can trigger dream states; **Ginsberg** and **Ferlinghetti** fly to South America to take part in a literary conference at the University of Concepción, Santiago, Chile; after the conference, **Ferlinghetti** visits La Paz, Bolivia, on his way home; **Ginsberg** remains in Chile until late April; *The Flower Thief*, **Ron Rice's** no-budget underground film about San Francisco's North Beach scene (starring future **Andy Warhol** "superstar" **Taylor Mead** as a gay flower thief and featuring North Beach habitués **Bob Kaufman**, **Eric Nord**, **Barry Clark** and others) is released on sixteen-millimeter black-and-white film from surplus USAAF World War II film stock used in aerial gunnery; JAN. 30: **Gary Snyder** and **Joanne Kyger** depart from San Francisco for Japan aboard Yamashita-Shinnihon Line's MV *Nachiharu Maru*; FEB.: **Snyder**, 29, marries **Kyger**, 25, in Japan; FEB. 6: **John Ciardi** publishes "Epitaph for the Dead Beats" in the *Saturday Review*, no. 43 which predictably accuses the Beats of anti-intellectualism; FEB.: **LeRoi** and **Hettie (Cohen) Jones** move into an apartment at 324 E. Fourteenth Street, New York City; FEB.: **Janine Pommy**, 18, graduates as valedictorian of her high school class; **William S. Burroughs** discovers the work of **Harold S. Schroeppel**, an analytical chemist and self-development teacher; FEB. 27: **George Blair's** *The Hypnotic Eye*, a low-budget camp horror-Beat exploitation film, featuring **Jacques Bergerac**, **Lawrence Lipton** as "King of the Beatniks," **Eric "Big Daddy" Nord** as a bongo drummer, and **Fred Demara** (a.k.a., "The Great Imposter"), is released by "poverty row" studio Allied Artists; MARCH: *Holiday* magazine publishes "The Vanishing American Hobo," by **Kerouac** and **Corso**; MARCH 25: **Ianthe Brautigan**, daughter of **Richard Brautigan** and **Virginia Alder**, is born in San Francisco; APRIL 5: Gold Medal Books publishes **Seymour Krim's** *The Beats*—the first Beat literature anthology—in a cheap paperback edition; APRIL 25: Grove Press publishes **Alexander Trocchi's** *Cain's Book*; [MAY 1: A U-2 SPY PLANE IS SHOT DOWN OVER THE SOVIET UNION AND ITS PILOT, CAPTAIN FRANCIS GARY POWERS, IS CAPTURED, CAUSING AN INTERNATIONAL INCIDENT.] late APRIL: **Ginsberg** visits Machu Picchu, the lost city of the Incas, in Peru; MAY: **Bob Dylan** drops out of college at the end

THE HYPNOTIC EYE
MOVIE POSTER

of his freshman year; City Lights publishes *Rimbaud* by **Jack Kerouac**; MAY 23: **Ginsberg** takes *yagé* for the first time in his room at the Hotel Comercio, Lima, Peru; MAY 31: **Ginsberg** sets out for Pucallpa, Peru, where **Burroughs** found *yagé* in 1953; he takes the drug in marathon sessions with locals; JUNE: **Ginsberg** returns home to New York City after six months in South America; SUMMER: **Lenore Kandel**, 28, moves from New York City to San Francisco and settles in the Haight-Ashbury district; The summer issue of *Provincetown Review* features "Tralala," a short story by **Hubert Selby Jr.** (later incorporated into *Last Exit to Brooklyn*); City Lights publishes **Ginsberg's** *Kaddish, and Other Poems: 1968–1960*; JUNE 3: **Neal Cassady** is paroled from San Quentin after serving almost two years; he takes a job at Los Gatos Tire Company, 575 University Avenue, Los Gatos, recapping tires on the night shift; JUNE 19: Avon publishes *Tristessa*, **Kerouac's** novel about his 1956 affair with **Esperanza Villanueva**; **Daniel Talbot** gives it a positive review in *The New York Times*; JUNE 23: MGM releases its film version of *The Subterraneans*, starring **George Peppard** (as the **Kerouac** figure) and **Leslie Carron** (a white woman, playing the **Alene Lee** figure); reviews are dismissive; JULY: City Lights publishes *Hiparama of the Classics* by **Lord (Richard) Buckley**; JULY 17: In New York, **Kerouac** boards a train bound for California at **Lawrence Ferlinghetti's** invitation; JULY 23: **LeRoi Jones** arrives in Cuba to attend a mass anniversary rally for the Twenty-Sixth of July Movement; AUG.: **Timothy Leary** travels to Cuernavaca, Mexico and tries psilocybin mushrooms for the first time, an experience that changes the course of his life; AUG. 26: Grove Press publishes *The New American Poetry, 1945–1960*, edited by **Donald M. Allen**; poet **Harvey Shapiro** gives it a negative review in *The New York Times*; SEPT. 3: **Kerouac** suffers an alcohol-induced nervous breakdown at **Lawrence Ferlinghetti's** isolated cabin in Bixby Canyon, near Big Sur, California; SEPT. 13: **Kerouac** takes a TWA "Ambassador flight" back to New York; SEPT.

15: **Ginsberg** completes "Kaddish" (typed by **Elise Cowen**); SEPT. 23: **Ginsberg**, **Orlovsky**, **LeRoi Jones**, and others meet **Fidel Castro** while he is in New York to deliver a speech before the United Nations; OCT. 7: **Jack Kerouac** and **Allen Ginsberg** take *yagé* together; **Ginsberg** records **Kerouac's** reactions in his journal; OCT. 7: *Route 66*, a CBS TV series inspired by *On the Road*, starring **Martin Milner** and **George Maharis**, premiers (it runs for four seasons); Birth Press (New York City) publishes *Birth 3, Book 1* (Autumn 1960; a special issue "on Alcohol, Marihuana, Hashish, Peyote, Mescaline, LSD, etc.") edited by **Tuli Kupferberg**; NOV.: McGraw-Hill publishes **Kerouac's** *Lonesome Traveler*; the book is favorably reviewed by **Daniel Talbot** in *The New York Times*; [NOV. 8: MASSACHUSETTS SENATOR JOHN F. KENNEDY, 43, IS ELECTED THIRTY-FIFTH U.S. PRESIDENT BY A VERY NARROW MARGIN OVER RICHARD NIXON.] NOV. 12: **Lord Buckley**, 54, dies suddenly at Columbus Hospital, 229 E. Nineteenth Street, New York City; NOV. 14: At a grand jury hearing into police corruption, **Lord Buckley's** attorney, **Maxwell T. Cohen**, accuses the NYPD of contributing to **Buckley's** death by lifting his cabaret card several weeks earlier; Police Commissioner **Stephen Kennedy** takes umbrage and a fistfight nearly ensues; NOV. 21: At 5:00 AM, after a party at their apartment at 250 W. Ninety-Fourth

LEROI JONES AND DIANE DI PRIMA AT THE CEDAR
STREET TAVERN, NYC, APRIL 5, 1960

Street, New York City, **Norman Mailer** stabs his
second wife, **Adele (Morales) Mailer**, with a penknife
and nearly kills her; he is subsequently committed
to Bellevue for observation; NOV. 26: **Ginsberg** takes
psilocybin at **Timothy Leary's** house in Newton
Center, Massachusetts; DEC. 17: Pantheon Books
publishes **Alan Watts's** *This is It, and Other Essays on
Zen and Spiritual Experience*; NOV.–DEC.: *Evergreen
Review* publishes "Cuba Libre," **LeRoi Jones's** account
of his visit to Cuba; New Directions publishes **Gregory
Corso's** *The Happy Birthday of Death*; Auerhahn
Press (San Francisco) publishes **Burroughs** and
Gysin's *Exterminator!*; Hanover Records releases
Blues and Haikus (Hanover LP 5006), a spoken-
word recording of poetry readings by **Jack Kerouac**,
accompanied by **Al Cohn** and **John Haley "Zoot" Sims**;
the recording includes "American Haikus," "Hard

Hearted Old Farmer," "The Last Hotel & Some of the Dharma," "Poems from the Unpublished *Book of Blues*," and "Old Western Movies"; **Wilder Bentley** at the Bread and Wine Press (San Francisco) publishes **Dick McBride's** first collection of poetry, *Oranges*, illustrated with woodcuts by the artist and actor **Victor Wong**; Two Cities (Paris) and Beach Books (San Francisco) publish *Minutes to Go* by **William S. Burroughs, Sinclair Beiles, Gregory Corso**, and **Brion Gysin**.

CHAPTER FOUR

THE LATE PERIOD 1961–1969

1961

JAN. 1: New Directions publishes **Kenneth Patchen's** antiwar novel *The Journal of Albion Moonlight*; JAN. 13: At **Timothy Leary's** house in Newton Center, Massachusetts, **Ginsberg** and **Kerouac** take psilocybin provided by **Leary**; JAN. 20: **Kerouac** sends **Leary** his "Dear Coach" letter describing his reactions to the psychedelic drug experience; JAN: City Lights publishes **Kerouac's** *Book of Dreams*; [JAN. 17: IN HIS FAREWELL ADDRESS TO THE NATION, PRESIDENT DWIGHT D. EISENHOWER WARNS OF THE DANGERS TO DEMOCRACY OF A "MILITARY-INDUSTRIAL COMPLEX."] JAN.: **Robert Zimmerman (Bob Dylan)**, 19, moves to New York City to pursue a career as a folk singer-songwriter; FEB. 2: **Lenny Bruce** appears at Carnegie Hall in the midst of a blizzard; the performance—recorded and later released in 1961 as *The Carnegie Hall Concert*—is widely regarded as one of his best; FEB.: **Ginsberg** writes "Television Was a Baby Crawling Toward That Death Chamber"; FEB.: **Neal Cassady** meets **Anne Murphy** in San Francisco; the two begin a five-year relationship; MARCH: **Joan Haverty's** lawyer serves **Kerouac** with a summons for $17,500 in back payment for child support; a shaken **Kerouac** hires lawyer **Eugene Brooks** (**Allen Ginsberg's** brother) to fight the suit; MARCH 23: **Ginsberg** and **Orlovsky** sail from New York to Le Havre, France, on the liner SS *America*; early APRIL: **Ginsberg** and **Orlovsky** arrive in Paris in search of **Burroughs** but discover he left days before, for Tangier; they spend the rest of the month with **Gregory Corso**; [APRIL 17–19: ANTI-CASTRO CUBAN EXILES, SUPPORTED BY THE CIA, LAUNCH AN UNSUCCESSFUL INVASION OF CUBA AT THE BAY OF PIGS.] APRIL: Olympia Press (Paris) publishes *The American Express*, **Gregory Corso's** first and only novel; **Janine Pommy** meets **Bill Heine**; **Pommy** begins an amphetamine habit; she rents a newly renovated apartment on Sixth Street and Avenue C, East Village, New York City, with **Herbert Huncke** and **Lafcadio Orlovsky** (**Alexander Trocchi** and his wife, **Lyn**, move in briefly); APRIL 29: City Lights publishes **Ginsberg's** *Kaddish, and Other Poems*; APRIL: **Alexander Trocchi** is charged with supplying

NEAL CASSADY AND
HIS GIRLFRIEND,
ANNE MURPHY,
SAN FRANCISCO,
SUMMER OF 1963

drugs to a minor; he flees the U.S. for Britain to
avoid prosecution; APRIL–MAY: **Jack Kerouac** sells
the house in Northport and he and his mother move
to a ranch house at 1309 Alfred Drive in Orlando,
Florida; MAY 3–7: **Ginsberg**, **Orlovsky**, **Corso**, and
jazz saxophonist **Allen Eager** (1927–2003) attend the
Twenty-Second Annual Cannes Film Festival; JUNE:
Kerouac travels to Mexico for literary inspiration; he
takes a room on Cerrida Medellion, Mexico City, and
writes the second part of *Desolation Angels*; JUNE
1: **Ginsberg**, **Corso**, and **Orlovsky** arrive in Tangier
aboard the SS *Azemour* to visit **Burroughs**; JUNE:
Citadel Press publishes *Dinners and Nightmares*
by **Diane di Prima**; JULY: **Kerouac** returns home to
Orlando; **Timothy Leary** arrives in Tangier to visit

Burroughs (on **Ginsberg's** recommendation); **Leary** also meets **Paul Bowles**; **Peter Orlovsky**, shunned by **Burroughs**, leaves Tangier for Israel; AUG.: *Confidential* magazine publishes a ghostwritten story "by" **Joan Haverty** titled "My Ex-husband, **Jack Kerouac**, Is an Ingrate"; **Neal Cassady** travels to Denver to visit his father; AUG. 24: **Ginsberg** leaves Tangier for Athens; he stays in Greece until January 1962; SEPT.: After a shopping errand, **Janine Pommy** comes home to find the East Village apartment empty; **Herbert Huncke** and **Bill Heine** had been arrested (**Lafcadio Orlovsky** had already left for home in Long Island two weeks earlier); **Pommy** gathers her few possessions and goes back to her parents' house; SEPT. 18: **Kerouac** begins writing *Big Sur*; SEPT. 29: **Lenny Bruce** is arrested for possession of narcotics in Philadelphia (the charges are later dropped); OCT.: Legendary record producer **John Henry Hammond II** (1910–1987) signs **Bob Dylan** to a recording contract with Columbia Records; OCT. 4: **Lenny Bruce** is arrested for obscenity at the Jazz Workshop in San Francisco; NOV.: **Kerouac** ventures to coastal Maine, Vermont, and Cape Cod in search of land on which to build a cabin; DEC.: **Barbara Moraff**, 22, moves to Vermont with her lover; they build a small one-room cabin on land belonging to a former Black Mountain College student with whom they exchange work for rent; DEC.: **Lenny Bruce** is arrested for obscenity at the Gate of Horn nightclub in Chicago; he is released on bail and returns to work at the club; Wesleyan University Press publishes *Disorderly Houses* by **Alan Ansen**; Corinth Books publishes Ginsberg's *Empty Mirror*; E.P. Dutton publishes **Seymour Krim's** *Views of a Nearsighted Cannoneer*; Olympia Press (Paris) publishes **Burroughs's** *The Soft Machine*; Birth Press (New York City) publishes *1001 Ways to Live without Working* by **Tuli Kupferberg**; **Kells Elvins**, 48, dies in New York City; Wesleyan Press publishes *Disorderly Houses: A Book of Poems* by **Alan Ansen**.

1962

JAN.: **Kerouac's** literary agent, **Sterling Lord**, sells two of **Kerouac's** novels—*Big Sur* and *Visions of Gerard*—for a $10,000 advance; **Kerouac** subjects himself to a "30 day drunk" during a visit to New York; JAN. 21: **Ginsberg** meets **Peter Orlovsky** in Tel Aviv, Israel; In Jerusalem, **Ginsberg** meets theologian **Martin Buber** (1878–1965) and kabbalah scholar and friend of the late **Walter Benjamin, Gershom Scholem** (1897–1982); **Ginsberg** and **Orlovsky** depart for Nairobi, Kenya; JAN. 28: Athenaeum publishes *Come and Join the Dance*, **Joyce Glassman's** first novel; JAN.–FEB.: **Kerouac** types up *Big Sur* in Orlando, Florida; FEB. 1: **Elise Nada Cowen**, 29, commits suicide by jumping through the locked window of her parents' seventh floor apartment on Bennett Avenue, Washington Heights, New York City; FEB. 5–15: **Ginsberg** and **Orlovsky** sail from Mombasa, Kenya, to Bombay, India, on the SS *Amra*; FEB. 16: **Ginsberg** and **Orlovsky** travel from Bombay to Calcutta by train; FEB. 20: At a Brooklyn diner, **Kerouac**, 39, meets his daughter, **Jan**, 10, for the first time; MARCH: **Gary Snyder** and **Joanne Kyger** join **Ginsberg** and **Orlovsky** in Delhi; they travel to Dharamsala (in northern India) to visit **Tenzin Gyatso**, 26, the fourteenth **Dalai Lama**; Grove Press publishes an American edition of **Burroughs's** *Naked Lunch*; MARCH: **Lenny Bruce** is tried for obscenity in San Francisco and acquitted; APRIL 20: **Walter Pahnke** (a graduate student of theology at Harvard Divinity School), under the supervision of **Timothy Leary** and the Harvard Psilocybin Project, conducts the Marsh Chapel Experiment (a.k.a. the Good Friday Experiment) at Boston University; a group of graduate divinity student volunteers are given psilocybin and another group of volunteers are given a placebo; the ones given the drug tend to have quasi-mystical religious experiences; [JUNE 15: TOM HAYDEN, FIELD SECRETARY OF STUDENTS FOR A DEMOCRATIC SOCIETY (SDS), COMPLETES THE *PORT HURON STATEMENT* AT AN SDS CONVENTION

IN LAKEPORT, MICHIGAN; JULY: HOUGHTON MIFFLIN PUBLISHES **RACHEL CARSON'S** CONTROVERSIAL EXPOSÉ OF THE PESTICIDE INDUSTRY, *SILENT SPRING*—A KEY MOMENT IN THE DEVELOPMENT OF THE ENVIRONMENTAL MOVEMENT.] JULY: **Janine Pommy** meets Peruvian painter **Fernando Vega**; JULY 9–AUG. 4: **Andy Warhol** has his first one-man show at **Irving Blum's** Ferus Gallery, 723 N. La Cienega Boulevard, West Hollywood, California; SUMMER: The San Francisco Poetry Festival is held at the Museum of Art; the festival is comprised of eight programs over four days; **Rexroth**, **Ferlinghetti**, and **Whalen** do poetry readings, but **Robert Duncan**, **Jack Spicer**, and **Michael McClure** boycott the festival; **Neal Cassady** meets **Ken Kesey** at his home on Perry Lane in Palo Alto, California; [AUG. 5: **MARILYN MONROE**, 36, IS FOUND DEAD OF A DRUG OVERDOSE IN HER HOME IN BRENTWOOD, CALIFORNIA; SUICIDE IS SUSPECTED.] AUG. 20–24: The International Writers Conference is held in Edinburgh, Scotland as part of the Edinburgh International Festival; participants include **Norman Mailer**, **Colin MacInnes**, **Henry Miller**, **Alexander Trocchi**, **Mary McCarthy**, **William S. Burroughs**, **Aldous Huxley**, and many others; AUG.: **Robert Zimmerman** legally changes his name to **Bob Dylan** and hires **Albert Grossman** as his manager; AUTUMN: Stanford graduates **Michael**

Murphy and **Dick Price** found the Esalen Institute in
Big Sur, California; SEPT.: **Lenny Bruce** is officially
banned from Australia; after finding evidence of his
cheating on her again, **Carolyn Cassady** asks **Neal
Cassady** for a divorce; SEPT. 11: **Kerouac's** *Big Sur*
is published by Farrar, Straus & Giroux and garners
excellent reviews; OCT. 6: **Lenny Bruce** is arrested
for drug possession and is later acquitted; OCT. 12:
Lenny Bruce is arrested again on obscenity charges;
[OCT. 14–28: THE CUBAN MISSILE CRISIS BRINGS THE
UNITED STATES AND THE SOVIET UNION TO THE BRINK
OF NUCLEAR WAR.] OCT. 19: **Sheldon N. Grebstein**, a
professor of English at the University of South Florida,
is suspended for teaching **Norman Podhoretz's** "The
Know-Nothing Bohemians" (which includes direct
quotations from Beat writings); NOV. 18: **Grebstein** is
reinstated on appeal; DEC. 10: **Ginsberg** and **Orlovsky**
travel to Benares by train; **Ginsberg** and **Orlovsky**
spend Christmas at the Taj Mahal in Agra, India; DEC.:
Janine Pommy and **Fernando Vega** leave New York for
Israel; they marry shortly thereafter; **Ginsberg**, while
in Calcutta, writes to the *Harvard Crimson* regarding
a reference to LSD and other "mind distorting drugs";
he suggests it would be more accurate to write
"mind expanding or consciousness-widening" drugs,
a correction based on "about thirty experiences
(with LSD-25, psilocybin, mescaline, peyote and

KEN KESEY,
1935-2001

banisteriopsis caapi [*yagé*]) spaced out over the last decade"; Viking Press publishes **Ken Kesey's** *One Flew Over the Cuckoo's Nest*; Olympia Press (Paris) publishes **William S. Burroughs's** *The Ticket That Exploded*; **Ed Sanders** begins publishing *Fuck You: A Magazine of the Arts*; **Jim Carroll**, 13, becomes addicted to heroin in New York City; **Billy Burroughs** accidentally shoots his best friend in the neck with a rifle, causing an almost fatal wound; the incident precipitates a nervous breakdown; Totem Press/Corinth Books publishes *Four Young Lady Poets: Carol Bergé, Barbara Moraff, Rochelle Owens, Diane Wakoski;* the jacket illustration is by **Jesse Sorrentino** and the introductory "Note on the Authors" is by **LeRoi Jones**.

1963

JAN.: **Lenny Bruce** is arrested for possession of narcotics in Los Angeles but is later acquitted; [FEB.

11: AMERICAN POET **SYLVIA PLATH**, 30, COMMITS SUICIDE AT HER HOME IN LONDON.] MARCH 15: **Lenny Bruce** is sentenced to a year and a day on obscenity charges in Chicago; MARCH 20: **William Carlos Williams**, 79, dies in Rutherford, New Jersey; on the same day, **Ginsberg**, in Benares, writes an elegy to **Williams** titled "Death News"; APRIL: **Lenny Bruce** is barred from entering the U.K.; [APRIL: W.W. NORTON PUBLISHES BETTY FRIEDAN'S *THE FEMININE MYSTIQUE*.] MAY: **Alan Ansen** privately prints *Field Report*, a seventy-seven-page poetry book; MAY 6: Harvard University fires **Timothy Leary** and his colleague **Richard Alpert** (later known as **Baba Ram Dass**) for unauthorized LSD experimentation; MAY 19: **Hunter S. Thompson**, 26, and **Sandra Dawn Tarlo** marry; MAY 26: **Ginsberg** flies to Bangkok, Thailand, from Calcutta; he visits the Angkor Wat temple complex in Cambodia; JUNE 4–7: **Ginsberg** stops over in Saigon, South Vietnam, on his way back to North America, to investigate the political situation; JUNE 11: **Ginsberg** arrives in Tokyo; travels to Kyoto to visit **Gary Snyder** and **Joanne Kyger**; JUNE: **Allen Ginsberg** meets **Bob Dylan** in New York City; JUNE: **Gregory Corso**, 33, marries **Sally November**, 25, the daughter of a Cleveland florist; [JUNE 12: CIVIL RIGHTS LEADER **MEDGAR EVERS** IS ASSASSINATED IN JACKSON, MISSISSIPPI, BY A WHITE

RUINS OF ANGKOR WAT TEMPLE COMPLEX,
CAMBODIA

SUPREMACIST NAMED **BYRON DE LA BECKWITH**, WHO
IS ULTIMATELY CONVICTED OF THE MURDER IN 1994
AFTER TWO MISTRIALS IN 1964.] JULY 17: **Ginsberg**
arrives in Vancouver, British Columbia, to attend a
poetry conference; JULY 18: **Ginsberg** writes "The
Change: Kyoto-Tokyo Express"; JULY 24–AUG. 8:
Ginsberg participates in the 1963 Vancouver (British
Columbia) Poetry Conference, which spans three
weeks and involves about sixty people who register
for a program of discussions, workshops, lectures,
and readings; the conference was created by **Warren
Tallman** and **Robert Creeley** as a summer course at
the University of British Columbia; JULY 25: **Neal
Cassady** visits **Jack Kerouac** in Northport; AUG.:
Ginsberg arrives in San Francisco and stays with
the **Ferlinghettis**; **Neal Cassady** briefly shares an
apartment with **Allen Ginsberg** and **Charles Plymell**

at 1403 Gough Street, San Francisco; **Lucien Carr** pays a surprise visit; [AUG. 28: REVEREND MARTIN LUTHER KING JR. DELIVERS HIS "I HAVE A DREAM" SPEECH BEFORE AN IMMENSE CROWD AT THE LINCOLN MEMORIAL IN WASHINGTON, D.C.] AUG. 28: Farrar, Straus & Giroux publishes **Jack Kerouac's** *Visions of Gerard*; City Lights publishes *Reality Sandwiches* by **Ginsberg** and *The Yagé Letters* by **Ginsberg** and **Burroughs**; [SEPT. 15: A BOMB PLANTED BY WHITE SUPREMACISTS KILLS FOUR YOUNG AFRICAN AMERICAN GIRLS ATTENDING SUNDAY SCHOOL AT THE SIXTEENTH STREET BAPTIST CHURCH IN BIRMINGHAM, ALABAMA.] SEPT. 25: William Morrow publishes *Blues People: Negro Music in White America* by **LeRoi Jones**; it garners excellent reviews; OCT. 30: **Allen Ginsberg** participates in his first street demonstration, against **Trân Lê Xuân** (a.k.a. "**Madame Nhu**" and "the Dragon Lady"), the imperious sister-in-law of South Vietnam's president, **Ngô Đình Diêm**, when she arrives in San Francisco on a "lecture tour"; [NOV. 1: NGÔ ĐÌNH DIÊM AND HIS BROTHER, NGÔ ĐÌNH NHU, ARE ASSASSINATED AFTER A CIA-ASSISTED MILITARY COUP OVERTHROWS THEIR REGIME.] NOV.: While giving a speech at Ohio University in Athens, Ohio, social critic, erotic folklorist, and former publisher of *Neurotica*, **Gershon Legman** coins the phrase, "Make love, not war"; [NOV. 22: JFK IS

ASSASSINATED IN DALLAS BY AN EX-MARINE NAMED LEE HARVEY OSWALD––PROMPTING **BOB KAUFMAN** TO BEGIN A DECADE-LONG PERIOD OF SILENCE.] NOV. 22: **Aldous Huxley**, 69, dies of cancer while under the influence of LSD, administered at his request by his wife, **Laura Archera Huxley**; [NOV. 24: DALLAS NIGHTCLUB OWNER **JACK RUBY** SHOOTS AND KILLS LEE HARVEY OSWALD IN THE BASEMENT OF DALLAS POLICE HEADQUARTERS––A MURDER COMMITTED ON LIVE TELEVISION AND WITNESSED BY TENS OF MILLIONS OF VIEWERS.] **Robert Frank** becomes a U.S. citizen; **Billy Burroughs**, 16, lives with his father in Tangier, Morocco, for six months (and later maintains that his father's friends sexually molested him); **Anthony Balch's** eleven-minute thirty-five-millimeter black-and-white film, *Towers Open Fire*, written and narrated by **William S. Burroughs**, is released; Alan Swallow (Denver) publishes *Lonely the Autumn Bird: Two Novels* by **Richard "Dick" McBride**.

1964

JAN. 22: Grove Press publishes **Richard Brautigan's** novel *A Confederate General from Big Sur*; JAN. 28: **Andy Warhol** opens his first "factory" (studio) at 231 E. Forty-Seventh Street, New York City; [MARCH 13: CATHERINE SUSAN "KITTY" GENOVESE, 28, IS STABBED TO DEATH ON A STREET IN QUEENS, NEW YORK, WHILE

MARCH 13: **Sally Corso** gives birth to a daughter, **Miranda Corso**; MARCH 23: **Sandy Thompson** (**Hunter Thompson's** wife) gives birth to a son, **Juan Fitzgerald Thompson**; MARCH 24: **Kerouac** gives a reading of his work to students at Lowell House, Harvard University; MARCH 25: *Dutchman*, the controversial one-act play by **LeRoi Jones**, opens at the Cherry Lane Theater, 38 Commerce Street, New York City (*Play* by **Samuel Beckett** and *The Two Executioners* by **Fernando Arrabal** are also on the bill); APRIL: **Lenny Bruce** is arrested for obscenity twice in one week at the Café Au Go Go in Greenwich Village, New York City, and is later convicted; MAY 3: E.P. Dutton publishes **John Clellon Holmes's** third novel, *Get Home Free;* [JUNE 10: CONGRESS PASSES THE CIVIL RIGHTS BILL.] MAY: **Ed White** visits **Kerouac** in Northport; MAY 25: *Dutchman* by **LeRoi Jones** wins an Obie for the best off-Broadway play of the 1963–64 season; MAY: **Lou Reed** graduates from Syracuse University; JUNE: The divorce of **Neal Cassady** and **Carolyn Cassady** is finalized; **Neal Cassady** goes on a road trip to Denver with **Anne Murphy** and **Bradley Hodgman**; **Cassady's** father, **Neal Marshall Cassady**, 73, dies penniless in Denver; JUNE 9: **Bob Dylan** first records "Mr. Tambourine Man"; **Emmett Grogan** and **Ramblin' Jack Elliott** sing backup; JUNE 12: **Gary**

Snyder, **Lew Welch**, and **Philip Whalen** give a "Free Way Reading" of their poetry at Longshoreman's Hall, San Francisco; JUNE: On appeal, the Illinois State Supreme Court unanimously upholds **Lenny Bruce's** guilty verdict on obscenity charges; JUNE 20: **Ginsberg**, in New York City, writes the poem, "I Am a Victim of Telephone"; [JUNE 21: CIVIL RIGHTS WORKERS JAMES CHANEY, 21, ANDREW GOODMAN, 20, AND MICHAEL SCHWERNER, 24, ARE KIDNAPPED AND MURDERED BY THE KU KLUX KLAN IN MERIDIAN, MISSISSIPPI; JUNE 22: THE U.S. SUPREME COURT DECIDES TWO OBSCENITY CASES (*JACOBELLIS V. OHIO* AND *GROVE PRESS INC. V. GERSTEIN*) THAT ALLOW FOR MORE CULTURAL FREEDOM.] JUNE 30: **William S. Burroughs's** *The Ticket That Exploded* appears in *The Insect Gazette* (Summer 1964); JULY 14: **Ken Kesey**, **Neal Cassady**, and other LSD cohorts self-dubbed the "Merry Pranksters" begin an eleven-day cross-country journey in a converted 1939 IHC school bus that they purchased for $1,500, refitted, painted psychedelic colors, and named "Furthur" [*sic*]; JULY 16: **Ken Kesey** and his Merry Pranksters visit **Larry McMurtry** in Houston, Texas; JULY 21: The Merry Pranksters arrive in New Orleans; JULY 25: The Merry Pranksters arrive in New York City; **Neal Cassady** drives **Kerouac** to New York City to meet **Ken Kesey** and the Merry Pranksters at a party in a Park Avenue apartment; the

A PENSIVE KEN BABBS RIDES SHOTGUN WITH
NEAL CASSADY ON FURTHER, THE MERRY
PRANKSTERS' BUS, IN THE SUMMER OF 1964

meeting is not a success; JULY: Viking Press publishes
Ken Kesey's second novel, *Sometimes a Great Notion*;
JULY 27: **Orville Prescott** savages **Kesey's** novel in
a *New York Times* review; JULY: **Andy Warhol** shoots
Couch, a silent, forty-eight-minute, sixteen-millimeter
pornographic film that features **Corso**, **Ginsberg**,
Kerouac, **Orlovsky**, and **Warhol** associates **Billy Linich**
(Billy Name), **Taylor Mead**, **Baby Jane Holzer**, **Gerard**
Malanga, **Ivy Nicholson**, **Rufus Collins**, **Kate Heliczer**,
and **Ondine** cavorting on Warhol's red couch at his
Forty-Seventh Street factory; [AUG. 7: U.S. CONGRESS
PASSES THE GULF OF TONKIN RESOLUTION (PUBLIC
LAW 88-408), AUTHORIZING LYNDON B. JOHNSON TO
USE MILITARY FORCE IN SOUTHEAST ASIA WITHOUT
DECLARING WAR.] AUG. 26: **Kerouac** has a farewell
party at his Northport house; after the party he takes
a brief vacation on Fire Island; AUG. 28: **Bob Dylan**

meets the **Beatles** at the Delmonico Hotel, 502 Park Avenue at Fifty-Ninth Street, New York City, and introduces them to marijuana; SEPT: Folklorists **Gershon Legman**, **Alan Dundes**, and **Vance Randolph** are writers-in-residence for the 1964–65 academic year at the University of California, La Jolla; SEPT. 19: **Kerouac's** sister, **Nin**, dies of a coronary occlusion at the age of 45; [OCT. 1: THE FREE SPEECH MOVEMENT BEGINS AT THE UNIVERSITY OF CALIFORNIA, BERKELEY.] NOV.: Grove Press publishes **William S. Burroughs's** *Nova Express* and **Hubert Selby Jr.'s** *Last Exit to Brooklyn*; NOV.: **Ginsberg**, **Corso**, and **Orlovsky** give readings at Harvard and Brandeis; DEC. 16: *The Slave* and *The Toilet*—two short plays by **LeRoi Jones**—open at Saint Marks Playhouse, Second Avenue and Eighth Street, New York City, to good reviews; **Ed Sanders** rents a former kosher butcher shop at 147 Avenue A at E. Tenth Street, New York City, and transforms it into the Peace Eye Bookstore, which opens in February 1965 and soon becomes an underground cultural center; **Kerouac** meets **Kurt Vonnegut Jr.** in Barnstable, Massachusetts; Renegade Press (Cleveland) publishes *Marrahwanna Quarterly*, no. 3 (Winter 1964–65); contributors include **Tuli Kupferberg**, **Marguerite Harris**, **Doug Blazek**, **Steven Richmond**, **szabo**, and **Kent Taylor**; **Dick McBride** moves to the United Kingdom for six months to help "bohemianize" **Tony Godwin** (1930–1976), founder and owner of the store Better Books (94 Charing Cross Road, London).

1965

JAN. 15: **Allen Ginsberg** attends a literary conference in Cuba sponsored by the Writer's Union, but he soon gets into trouble with Cuban authorities for protesting against Cuban persecution of homosexuals and for saying that **Fidel Castro's** brother **Raúl Castro** is gay and that Castro is "cute"; JAN.: News of **Ginsberg's** antics alienates **Kerouac**, who breaks off contact for a while; Grove Press publishes *The Dead Lecturer*, a book of poetry by **LeRoi Jones**; JAN. 31: **Richard Elman** gives *The Dead Lecturer* a negative review in *The New York Times*; FEB. 18: Cuban officials put **Ginsberg** on a flight to Prague; [FEB. 21: MALCOLM X IS ASSASSINATED WHILE GIVING A SPEECH AT THE AUDUBON BALLROOM, 165TH STREET, HARLEM, NEW YORK CITY.] MARCH 18: **Ginsberg** visits Moscow and meets Russian poets **Yevgeny Yevtushenko** and **Andrei Voznesenski**; MARCH 28: Guggenheim grants are awarded to **Allen Ginsberg** and **LeRoi Jones**, among many others; APRIL: Police raid **Ken Kesey's** home in La Honda and arrest him on marijuana charges; APRIL 22: **William S. Burroughs** and **Mack Thomas** read their fiction to an audience of one hundred thirty people at the home of painter **Wynn Chamberlain**, 222 Bowery, Manhattan; **Brion Gysin**, **Andy Warhol**, **Kenward Elmslie**, **Frank O'Hara**, **Ted Berrigan**, **Ron Padgett**, **Diane Arbus**, **Richard Avedon**, **Barnett Newman**, and **Karl Heinz Stockhausen** are also in attendance; MAY 1: **Allen Ginsberg** is elected *Kral Majales* (May King) at the May Day Festival in Prague, Czechoslovakia; MAY 3: Coward-McCann publishes **Kerouac's** *Desolation Angels* (with an introduction by **Seymour Krim**); MAY 7: Czech authorities seize his notebook and deport **Ginsberg**, who flies to London; he writes "Kral Majales" en route; **Bob Dylan**, on tour in the U.K., invites **Ginsberg** to attend his Royal Albert Hall concerts, which are scheduled for MAY 9 and MAY 10; MAY: **Donn Alan Pennebaker** shoots an early forerunner of the music video, a film clip promoting **Bob Dylan's** song "Subterranean Homesick Blues," featuring **Dylan** (with **Allen Ginsberg** visible in the background, near London's Savoy Hotel); the clip is incorporated into **Pennebaker's** documentary film on **Dylan**, *Don't Look Back* (released in 1967); SUMMER: With photographer **Leroy Lucas**, **Ed Dorn** visits Indian reservations for *The Shoshoneans*, a book commissioned by William Morrow & Co. Press; JUNE: Grove Press publishes **LeRoi Jones's** first novel, *The System of Dante's Hell*; JUNE 1: **Kerouac** flies to Paris on Air France to do genealogical research on the **Kerouac** family; he also travels to the family's ancestral home in Brittany; JUNE 8: **Ginsberg**, in London, writes the poem "Who Be Kind To"; JUNE 8: **Kerouac** flies back to Florida; JUNE 11: **Ginsberg** organizes the "Wholly Communion: International Poetry Incarnation" event at London's Royal Albert Hall; participants (seventeen white male poets) include **Ginsberg**, **Gregory Corso**, **Lawrence Ferlinghetti**, **Andrei Voznesenski**, **Michael Horovitz**, **Harry Fainlight** (whom the audience heckles), **Adrian Mitchell**, **Christopher Logue**, **Ernst Jandl**, **Alexander Trocchi**, and **Simon Vinkenoog**; seven thousand people attend, and filmmaker **Peter Lorrimer Whitehead** creates a thirty-three-minute film record entitled *Wholly Communion*, which is shown at the 1966 New York Film Festival; JUNE: **Ginsberg** gives a series of readings in England and studies William Blake's manuscripts at the Fitzwilliam Museum, Cambridge; **Ginsberg** meets American poet **Tom Clark** and submits to a four-hour tape-recorded interview at **Clark's** flat (24 Newmarket Road, Cambridge); the interview is published in *The Paris Review*, no. 37 (Spring 1966); it is perhaps **Ginsberg's** most revealing; JUNE 29: **Ginsberg** is strip-searched at customs when he reenters the United States; JULY: **Anne Waldman** travels across the country

ALLEN GINSBERG'S APOTHEOSIS: READING HIS POETRY AT LONDON'S ROYAL ALBERT HALL, JUNE 11, 1965

with her younger brother, Carl, and a school friend; **Ginsberg** returns to California for the Berkeley Poetry Conference, which is slated for JULY 12–23; other poets participating in readings, seminars, or lectures include **Gary Snyder, Charles Olson, Ed Dorn, Robert Duncan, Jack Spicer, John Wieners, Robin Blaser, George Stanley, Ron Loewinsohn, Joanne Kyger, Lew Welch, Richard Durerden**, and many others; JULY 16: At **Robert Duncan's** reading, **Anne Waldman**, 20, meets **Lewis Warsh**, 20; according to **Waldman**, "We become fast friends, romantic comrades hitchhiking to Mexico at the end of the poetry conference, hitching back to New York City, founding *Angel Hair* magazine and books, living together (even marrying in 1967 at Saint Mark's Church [New York City] in a gala wedding studded with poet friends)"; the marriage lasts until 1970; JULY: **Ginsberg** and **Neal Cassady** are filmed in conversation at City Lights

Bookstore; **Kerouac** writes *Satori in Paris* in seven nights; JULY 25: **Bob Dylan** angers folk music purists by "going electric" at the Newport Folk Festival; [AUG. 11–16: THE WATTS RACE RIOT RAGES IN LOS ANGELES; 34 PEOPLE ARE KILLED, 1,032 ARE INJURED, AND 3,952 ARE ARRESTED; PROPERTY DAMAGE IS IN THE MILLIONS.] AUG. 7: The Merry Pranksters invite the local Hell's Angels chapter to a party at **Ken Kesey's** home in La Honda, Colorado; **Neal Cassady's** girlfriend, **Anne Murphy**, allows herself to be "gang-banged" by the bikers as **Cassady** looks on; AUG. 12: Vintage publishes *The Joyous Cosmology: Adventures in the Chemistry of Consciousness* by **Alan W. Watts** (with a foreword by **Timothy Leary** and **Richard Alpert**); AUG. 16: New Directions publishes *Solitudes Crowded with Loneliness* by **Bob Kaufman**; AUG. 17: **Jack Spicer**, 40, dies of alcoholism in San Francisco; AUTUMN: British poet and scholar **Donald Davie** invites **Ed Dorn** to join the literature department he is creating at the new University of Essex (U.K.); SEPT. 5: **Michael Fallon**, writing for the *San Francisco Examiner*, coins the word *hippie*; OCT.: **Lenny Bruce** is declared legally bankrupt in San Francisco; he requests a federal court in San Francisco to keep him out of jail in New York; NOV.: **Kerouac** drives north with Florida friends **Cliff Anderson** and **Paddy Mitchell** through Chapel Hill, North Carolina (where he briefly meets **Russell Banks**) to Connecticut to see **John Clellon Holmes** and to Lowell to see **Tony** and **Stella Sampas** and other Lowell friends; **Fernando Vega** dies of a heroin overdose on the Spanish island of Ibiza while **Janine Pommy Vega** is stranded, penniless, in Paris; DEC.: **Ginsberg** writes the poem "First Party at **Ken Kesey's** with Hell's Angels" (see the August 7 entry); DEC.: **Drew Wagnon** and **Terry Wagnon** edit and publish *Wild Dog*, nos. 19–20, a mimeographed poetry magazine with contributions by **Allen Ginsberg**, **Robert Duncan**, **Clark Coolidge**, **Tuli Kupferberg**, **Robert Kelly**, **Joanne Kyger**, **Diane Wakoski**, **Thomas Clark**, **Paul Blackburn**, and others; DEC. 18: **Michael McClure's** play, *The Beard*, opens at Actor's Workshop Theater in San Francisco but is quickly closed down by police; DEC. 20: **Timothy Leary** is arrested at the U.S.–Mexico border for possession of marijuana; Coward-McCann publishes **Kerouac's** *Desolation Angels*; Paperback Gallery publishes **Ray Bremser's** *Poems of Madness*, his first book of poetry; radicalized by his Cuba trip (1960), the murder of Malcolm X (1965), and the rise of black militancy, **LeRoi Jones** divorces **Hettie Cohen** then moves to Harlem to form the Black Arts Repertory Theatre; **Allen Ginsberg** is classified as an "internal security" risk and comes under surveillance by the FBI and the CIA; The

Poets Press (New York) publishes *Huncke's Journal* by Herbert Huncke.

1966

JAN. 1: NYPD officers raid the Peace Eye Bookstore a few hours after a midnight New Year's Eve concert of the Fugs at the Bridge Theater (4 Saint Mark's Place); they seize copies of *Fuck You* magazine, letters, books, and files and arrest **Ed Sanders** for obscenity; the ACLU soon takes the case, which ultimately goes to trial in the summer of 1967 (Sanders wins acquittal); JAN. 16: **Ken Kesey** is arrested a second time for marijuana possession; he jumps bail and flees to Mexico after faking suicide; JAN. 21–23: Producers **Stuart Brand** and **Ramon Sender** present the Trips Festival at Longshoremen's Hall, 400 North Point Street, San Francisco (8:00 PM–midnight); FEB. 14: **Ginsberg** finishes the antiwar poem "Wichita Vortex Sutra"; Grove Press publishes **Burroughs's** *The Soft Machine* and **Kerouac's** *Satori in Paris*; MARCH: **Kerouac** sells his Saint Petersburg home and buys a house on Cape Cod at 20 Bristol Avenue, Hyannis, Massachusetts; APRIL 28: Random House publishes *Been Down So Long It Looks Like Up to Me* by **Richard Fariña**; APRIL 30: **Richard Fariña**, 29, is killed in a motorcycle accident near Carmel, California, after leaving a book signing event;

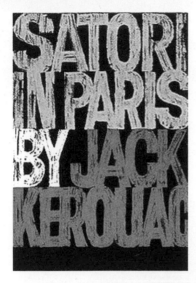

SATORI IN PARIS
BOOK COVER

JUNE: **Anne Waldman**, 21, graduates from Bennington College in Vermont; JUNE 14: **Allen Ginsberg** testifies before the U.S. Senate Judiciary Subcommittee on Juvenile Delinquency and argues against making LSD possession illegal; [JULY 14: RICHARD SPECK, A PSYCHOPATHIC DRIFTER, RAPES AND MURDERS EIGHT STUDENT NURSES IN CHICAGO.] JULY 21: **Stella Sampas** accepts **Kerouac's** marriage proposal; JULY 24–25: With the **Mothers of Invention** at the Fillmore (San Francisco), **Lenny Bruce** gives his last performances; JULY 25: **Frank O'Hara**, 40, poet and art curator, is run over by a dune buggy on the beach at Fire Island and dies of his injuries; JULY 29: **LeRoi Jones** and three friends assault and rob **Shepard Sherbell**, 21, editor of the *West Side Review*, after **Jones** claimed that **Sherbell** owed him one hundred dollars for a play published in the magazine; an assault charge is filed in court but is dismissed on January 20, 1967; [AUG. 1: CHARLES WHITMAN, 25, KILLS TWELVE AND WOUNDS THIRTY-TWO WITH A HUNTING RIFLE FROM THE 307-FEET-TALL CLOCK TOWER AT THE UNIVERSITY OF AUSTIN, TEXAS, BEFORE BEING SHOT TO DEATH BY POLICE.] AUG. 4: **Lenny Bruce**, 40, dies of a heroin overdose at his home in Los Angeles; the police allow the media to photograph his naked corpse on the floor of his bathroom; AUG. 16–17: **Ann Charters** visits **Jack Kerouac** in Hyannis, Massachusetts (on Cape Cod), and works with him on a **Kerouac** bibliography; SEPT.: **Emmett Grogan**, **Peter Berg**, and **Peter Cohon** (**Peter Coyote**) organize members of the San Francisco Mime Troupe into the Diggers, a political theater–anarchist –collective named after a communist religious sect in seventeenth-century England; **Conrad Rooks's** drug film, *Chappaqua*, premieres at the Venice Film Festival with cinematography by **Robert Frank** and musical score by **Philip Glass** and **Ravi Shankar** (**Burroughs**, **Ginsberg**, **Ed Sanders**, the **Fugs**,

TIMOTHY LEARY AT THE HEIGHT OF HIS
NOTORIETY IN THE 1960S

Moondog, **Ornette Coleman**, and **Peter Orlovsky**
appear in it); SEPT. 9: **Kerouac's** mother, **Gabrielle**,
suffers a massive stroke that leaves her partially
incapacitated; SEPT. 19: **Timothy Leary** founds the
League for Spiritual Discovery (LSD); SEPT. 27:
Kerouac flies to Italy to promote the Italian edition
of *Big Sur*; **Kerouac**, very drunk, is interviewed by
Beats translator **Fernanda Pivano** on Italian TV;
[OCT.: HUEY P. NEWTON AND BOBBY SEALE FOUND THE
BLACK PANTHER PARTY FOR SELF-DEFENSE (BPP) IN
OAKLAND, CALIFORNIA; OCT. 6: LSD IS MADE ILLEGAL
IN THE UNITED STATES.] **Gary Snyder** returns to the
U.S. after a six-year stay in Kyoto, Japan; OCT. 21: *The
Berkeley Barb* prints the first mention of the Diggers;
OCT. 27: Sir **Cyril Black** (1902–1991), a conservative
member of Parliament from Wimbledon, brings an
obscenity lawsuit against the British publishers of

Hubert Selby's *Last Exit to Brooklyn*; NOV. 17: San Francisco Police raid City Lights Bookstore and the Haight-Ashbury District's Psychedelic Shop, confiscate copies of **Lenore Kandel's** *The Love Book* on the grounds that it "excites lewd thoughts," and make three arrests; NOV. 18: **Kerouac** marries **Stella Sampas** (Sammy's older sister) in Hyannis, Massachusetts; NOV. 30: Farrar, Straus & Giroux publishes *The Collected Works of Jane Bowles* with an introduction by **Truman Capote**; O. Layton Press publishes *1001 Ways to Beat the Draft* by **Tuli Kupferberg**; **Barbara Moraff's** first child, **Alesia**, is born; shortly afterward **Moraff**, 27, buys a remote hilltop farm in Strafford, Vermont, where she teaches herself organic farming practices, keeps a cow and two goats, and raises the family's food; Alan Swallow (Denver) publishes *Memoirs of a Natural-Born Expatriate* by Richard McBride.

1967

JAN: **Kerouac** moves to 271 Sanders Avenue, Lowell, Massachusetts, with his mother and wife, **Stella**; **Charles Bukowski** starts writing "Notes of a Dirty Old Man," a column for *Open City*, an underground newspaper in Los Angeles; JAN. 12: San Francisco Beat poets **Gary Snyder, Lenore Kandel, George Stanley, Ron Loewinsohn, Lew Welch, Richard**

Brautigan, David Meltzer, and William Fritchey hold a benefit for the Diggers at Gino and Carlo's Tavern, 548 Green Street (between Bannam Place and Jasper Place), San Francisco; Jan 14: The "Gathering of the Tribes: The Human Be-In" event is held in San Francisco's Golden Gate Park; more than twenty thousand people attend; **Ginsberg**, **Gary Snyder**, **Timothy Leary**, and **Lenore Kandel** are prominently featured; FEB. 28: **Gene Persson's** fifty-five-minute film version of **LeRoi Jones's** *Dutchman* opens at the Little Carnegie Theater, Fifty-Seventh Street, New York City; MARCH 7: While in Montreal for Expo '67, **Jack Kerouac** is interviewed by **Fernand Séguin** (1922–1988) on *Le Sel de la Semaine* (*The Week's Salt*) (CBC-TV) in joual (i.e., French-Canadian patois); MARCH: **Gary Snyder** returns to Japan and lives in "Banyan Ashram" on Suwanose-jima in the northern Ryukyu Islands; MAY 28: After a five-week trial, a San Francisco jury finds **Lenore Kandel's** *The Love Book* obscene and without redeeming social value; MAY 29: **Jean Genet**, 56, depressed and exhausted, attempts suicide in a hotel room in Domodossola, Italy; JULY 5: **Ginsberg** travels to the Spoleto Festival in Italy; JULY 9: **Ginsberg** is arrested and subsequently prosecuted for using supposedly obscene language in the poem "Who Be Kind To"; JULY 12: **Ginsberg** gives a reading at Queen

Elizabeth Hall, London; [JULY 12–17: NEWARK RACE RIOTS—26 PEOPLE DIE IN THE RIOTING, 1,500 PEOPLE ARE INJURED, 1,400 PEOPLE ARE ARRESTED, AND 300 FIRES ARE SET.] JULY 20: **Ginsberg** attends the Dialectics of Liberation International Congress in London; other attendees during the JULY 15–JULY 30 event include **Paul Sweezy**, **Paul Goodman**, **Herbert Marcuse**, and **Stokely Carmichael**; JULY 29: **Ginsberg**, on LSD at his publisher's house in Wales, begins the poem "Wales Visitation"; he finishes the poem in London on August 3; [JULY 23–30: DETROIT RACE RIOTS—40 PEOPLE ARE KILLED, 2,000 ARE INJURED, AND 5,000 ARE LEFT HOMELESS; DAMAGE IS ESTIMATED AT $2 BILLION.] AUG. 6: **Gary Snyder**, 37, marries **Masa Uehara** on the rim of an active volcano on the Japanese island of Suwanose-jima; SEPT. 23: Accompanied by his Italian translator, **Fernanda Pivano**, **Ginsberg** meets **Ezra Pound** (1885–1972) in Portofino, Italy; **Ginsberg** does almost all the talking; [OCT. 7: ERNESTO "CHE" GUEVARA, 39, IS CAPTURED AND SHOT BY COUNTERINSURGENCY FORCES IN LA HIGUERA, BOLIVIA.] OCT. 12: Delacorte Press publishes **Richard Brautigan's** *Trout Fishing in America*; OCT. 21: **Ginsberg** joins thousands of other antiwar activists in a ritual "attempt" to levitate the Pentagon; NOV. 1: **Ken Kesey** is paroled after serving a five-month sentence at the San Mateo County Jail and Sheriff's Honor Camp; NOV. 23: A British jury finds **Hubert Selby's** *Last Exit to Brooklyn* obscene; **Neal Cassady** travels to Puerto Vallarta, Mexico, with Merry Prankster **George "Barely Visible" Walker** and **Anne Murphy**; Grove Press publishes **Burroughs's** *The Ticket That Exploded*; Phoenix Bookshop publishes **Ann Charters's** *A Bibliography of Works by Jack Kerouac (Jean Louis Lebris De Kerouac) 1939–1975*; City Lights publishes **Bob Kaufman's** *Golden Sardine*; DEC. 5: **Ginsberg** is arrested at an antiwar rally in New York City (along with 265 other protestors, including **Benjamin Spock**).

1968

JAN. 18: **Allen Ginsberg** and his father, **Louis Ginsberg**, give a joint poetry reading at Brooklyn Academy; [JAN. 31: THE TET OFFENSIVE BEGINS IN VIETNAM; THE NORTH VIETNAM ARMY AND VIET CONG FORCES ATTACK ALL MAJOR CITIES IN SOUTH VIETNAM.] FEB. 4: **Neal Cassady**, 41, dies of alcohol-Seconal intoxication and exposure on railroad tracks near San Miguel de Allende, Guanajuato (central Mexico); FEB. 5: **Carolyn Cassady** calls **Kerouac** with news of **Neal Cassady's** death; **Kerouac** refuses to believe it at first; FEB. 6: Coward-McCann publishes **Kerouac's** *Vanity of Duluoz: An Adventurous Education, 1935–46*; MARCH: **Ginsberg** moves to

A WAN NEAL CASSADY NEAR THE END OF HIS LIFE

a communal farm outside Cherry Valley, New York; **Kerouac** takes a brief trip to Europe with **Tony** and **Nick Sampas** and squanders $2,000 on booze and prostitutes in ten days; Kulchur Press publishes *Bean Spasms* by **Ted Berrigan** and **Ron Padgett**; Mother Press publishes *Poems* by **John Giorno**; City Lights publishes *Selected Poems, 1943–1966* by **Philip Lamantia**; Tompkins Square Press publishes *Angel* by **Ray Bremser**; [MARCH 22–JUNE 5: CHARLES DE GAULLE'S GOVERNMENT IS ALMOST TOPPLED BY MASS STUDENT-LABOR STRIKES AND PROTESTS; MARCH 31: LBJ ANNOUNCES ON NATIONAL TELEVISION THAT HE WILL NOT SEEK REELECTION.] APRIL: **Kai Snyder**, the first son of **Gary Snyder** and **Masa Uehara**, is born in Kyoto, Japan; APRIL: City Lights publishes *Poems to Fernando* by **Janine Pommy Vega**; [APRIL 4: JAMES

JOHN GIORNO

EARL RAY, A WHITE SUPREMACIST, ASSASSINATES MARTIN LUTHER KING JR. IN MEMPHIS, TENNESSEE; RIOTS BREAK OUT ALL OVER THE U.S.] JUNE 3: At Warhol's factory, **Valerie Solanas**, 32, radical feminist author of *S.C.U.M.* [Society for Cutting Up Men] *Manifesto*, shoots **Andy Warhol** and severely wounds him; **Mario Amaya**, art curator and critic, is also slightly wounded; [JUNE 5: SIRHAN SIRHAN, A DISAFFECTED PALESTINIAN, ASSASSINATES SENATOR ROBERT F. KENNEDY AT THE AMBASSADOR HOTEL IN LOS ANGELES, RIGHT AFTER KENNEDY WINS THE CALIFORNIA DEMOCRATIC PRIMARY.] JULY: **Allen Ginsberg** buys a farm in Cherry Valley, New York (thirty miles southeast of Utica); JULY 29: **Mohamed Hamri** and **Brion Gysin** take **Brian Jones** (founder of the **Rolling Stones**) to Jajouka—a village in the Ahl-Srif mountains in the southern Rif, Morocco—to hear Sufi trance music; Jones records the performances, released in 1971 as the LP *Brian Jones Presents the Pipes of Pan at Joujouka* (Coc/ATCO no. 49100); AUG. 1: A British court of appeals finds **Hubert Selby's** *Last Exit to Brooklyn* not obscene; [AUG. 21: SOVIET UNION AND WARSAW PACT ALLIES INVADE CZECHOSLOVAKIA, BRINGING AN END TO A BRIEF PERIOD OF LIBERALIZATION KNOWN AS THE PRAGUE SPRING.] AUG. 24–30: On assignment for *Esquire* magazine, **Allen Ginsberg**, **William S. Burroughs**, **Jean Genet**, and **Terry Southern** attend the Democratic National Convention in Chicago; SEPT. 3: **Jack Kerouac** (drunk) and **Ed Sanders** appear on **William F. Buckley's** TV program, *Firing Line*, to discuss "hippies" (**Ginsberg** is in the studio audience); AUTUMN: In Florida at **Cliff Anderson's** cabin in the woods, **Kerouac** takes a large dose of LSD; SEPT.: Drained by the events at the Democratic National Convention in Chicago, **Allen Ginsberg** repairs to his property in Cherry Valley, New York, for the winter, hires young photographer-filmmaker **Gordon Ball** to manage the farm with **Peter Orlovsky**, and begins setting some of William Blake's work to music for release on the **Beatles'** Apple Records label; NOV.: City Lights publishes **Ginsberg's** *Planet News*; **Jack**, **Stella**, and **Gabrielle Kerouac** move into

A FRAME FROM ROBERT FRANK'S *ME AND MY BROTHER;* ALLEN GINSBERG IS ON THE LEFT; PETER ORLOVSKY IS IN THE MIDDLE; JULIUS ORLOVSKY IS ON THE RIGHT

a house at 5169 Tenth Avenue, Saint Petersburg, Florida; DEC.: **Gary Snyder** and his family leave Japan to live in the U.S.; Coward-McCann publishes **Kerouac's** *The Vanity of Duluoz;* Black Sparrow Press publishes *The Gunslinger* by **Ed Dorn**.

1969

JAN.: World publishes **Timothy Leary's** *High Priest* and G.P. Putnam's publishes **Leary's** *The Politics of Ecstasy;* FEB. 2: *Me and My Brother*—**Robert Frank's** quasi-fictional documentary film about the relationship between **Peter Orlovsky** and his catatonic schizophrenic brother, **Julius Orlovsky**—is released in New York City (**Ginsberg** and **Christopher Walken** also appear in the film); APRIL: **Gen Snyder**, **Gary Snyder's** second son with **Masa Uehara**, is born in California; MAY: New Directions publishes **Gary Snyder's** *Earth House Hold*; City Lights publishes **Ginsberg's** *Indian Journals*; JUNE–JULY: **Allen Ginsberg**, at Apostolic Studios (W. Tenth Street near Broadway, New York City), records some of William Blake's *Songs of Innocence* and *Songs of Experience*, set to music accompanied by musicians **Don Cherry**, **Elvin Jones**, and **Jon Sholle** (released by MGM in 1970); JUNE: **Janine Pommy Vega**, 27, leaves California for Woodstock, New York, where she rents a house, goes on methadone maintenance, and takes a job as a waitress; [JUNE 28: SOME TWO THOUSAND GAYS RIOT AGAINST POLICE HARASSMENT OUTSIDE THE STONEWALL INN, 53 CHRISTOPHER STREET, GREENWICH VILLAGE, NEW YORK CITY; THE EVENT IS CONSIDERED THE BEGINNING OF THE GAY LIBERATION MOVEMENT; JULY 14: COLUMBIA PICTURES RELEASES THE COUNTERCULTURE ROAD MOVIE *EASY RIDER*; JULY 29: U.S. ASTRONAUT **NEIL ARMSTRONG** OF APOLLO 11 BECOMES THE FIRST HUMAN BEING TO SET FOOT ON THE MOON; AUG. 9–10: **CHARLES MANSON** "FAMILY" MEMBERS COMMIT MASS MURDER IN LOS ANGELES; AUG. 15–18: THE WOODSTOCK MUSIC AND ARTS FESTIVAL IS HELD IN BETHEL, NEW YORK; ATTENDANCE IS ESTIMATED AT HALF A MILLION PEOPLE.] JULY 28: **John Sinclair**, radical poet, is sentenced to nine-and-a-half to ten years in prison on a marijuana charge in Michigan; he serves two-and-a-half years before his conviction is overturned; AUG.: Harcourt, Brace & World publishes **Philip Whalen's** *On Bear's Head*; SEPT. 3: **Kerouac** is beaten up—sustaining cracked ribs and possible internal injuries—at the Cactus Bar in Saint Petersburg and is jailed for drunkenness; OCT. 1: Farrar, Straus & Giroux publishes **Tom Wolfe's** *The Electric Kool-Aid Acid Test*; New Directions publishes **Kenneth Patchen's** *Collected Poems*; [OCT. 8–10: WEATHERMEN (SDS FACTION) STAGE "DAYS OF RAGE" RIOTS IN CHICAGO.] OCT. 20: **Kerouac** sends a letter to his nephew, **Paul Blake Jr.**, stating his intention to leave his estate to his mother, and if she predeceases him, to his nephew, and to not "leave a dingblasted fucking goddamn thing to my wife's one hundred Greek relatives"; OCT. 21: **Jack Kerouac**, 47, dies at Saint Anthony's Hospital, 5169 Tenth Avenue, Saint Petersburg, Florida, of a massive abdominal hemorrhage brought on by more than twenty years of alcoholism; OCT. 24: **Kerouac's** funeral is held at Saint Jean Baptiste Roman Catholic Church in Lowell and is attended by over two hundred mourners (including **Allen Ginsberg**, **Gregory Corso**, **Jimmy Breslin**, and **John Cleland**); Grove Press publishes **William S. Burroughs's** *The Wild Boys*; Random House publishes **Jane Kramer's** *Allen Ginsberg in America*; Twayne publishes **Thomas**

F. Merrill's *Allen Ginsberg*; [NOV. 12: SEYMOUR HERSH BREAKS THE STORY OF THE MY LAI MASSACRE (I.E., AMERICAL DIVISION SOLDIERS ON A RAMPAGE KILL THREE HUNDRED TO FOUR HUNDRED UNARMED VIETNAMESE CIVILIANS—INCLUDING OLD MEN, WOMEN, CHILDREN, AND INFANTS—ON MARCH 16, 1968); DEC. 4: CHICAGO POLICE KILL BLACK PANTHER LEADER FRED HAMPTON IN A PREDAWN SHOOT-OUT; DEC. 6: THREE HUNDRED THOUSAND PEOPLE ATTEND THE ALTAMONT FREE CONCERT NEAR SAN FRANCISCO; THREE ACCIDENTAL DEATHS AND A HOMICIDE OCCUR.] Doubleday publishes **Brion Gysin's** novel *The Process*; Dec: **Ginsberg** testifies at the "Chicago Seven" conspiracy trial; Croton Press publishes *Troia: Mexican Memoirs* by **Bonnie Bremser** (**Ray Bremser's** wife, now known as **Brenda Frazer**).

CHAPTER FIVE

AFTERMATH AND REASSESSMENT
1970–
THE PRESENT

1970

JAN. 1: **Charles Olson**, 59, dies of liver cancer (partly the result of alcoholism) in New York; JAN. 9: **Charles Bukowski**, 49, quits his post office job to write full time; JAN. 21: **Timothy Leary** receives a ten-year prison sentence for his 1968 marijuana offense, with a further ten added later (while in custody) for a previous arrest in 1965—a total of twenty years to be served consecutively for less than a half ounce of marijuana; MARCH 2: **Jimmy Breslin** files a million-dollar libel suit against **Seymour Krim** and *The New York Times* after **Krim** reviews **Breslin's** *The Gang That Couldn't Shoot Straight* and reports an alleged anti-Semitic remark made by **Breslin**; MARCH: Black Panther Party International Coordinator **Connie Matthews** travels to Paris to enlist the help of **Jean Genet** after the arrest of BPP cofounder **Bobby**

Seale; MARCH–MAY: **Jean Genet** accompanies Black Panther Party officials on a cross-country speaking tour of the U.S.; [MARCH 6: WEATHER UNDERGROUND MEMBERS DIANA OUGHTON, TED GOLD, AND TERRY ROBBINS DIE WHEN THE BOMB THEY ARE MAKING EXPLODES PREMATURELY IN THEIR SAFE HOUSE AT 18 W. ELEVENTH STREET, GREENWICH VILLAGE, NEW YORK CITY; MAY 4: OHIO NATIONAL GUARDSMEN SHOOT AND KILL FOUR COLLEGE STUDENT ANTIWAR PROTESTORS AND WOUND MANY OTHERS AT KENT STATE UNIVERSITY; MAY 14–15: POLICE OPEN FIRE ON A DORM AT JACKSON STATE COLLEGE IN MISSISSIPPI; TWO STUDENTS ARE KILLED AND TWELVE ARE WOUNDED.] JUNE: **Janine Pommy Vega** travels to Peru; AUG.: **Allen Ginsberg** has a chance meeting with **Chögyam Trungpa Rinpoche** while hailing a cab in New York City; the two men begin a seventeen-year association; SEPT.: **Ed Dorn** begins a one-year teaching appointment at Northeastern Illinois University in Chicago; Sept 12: **Timothy Leary**, with the help of members of the Weather Underground, escapes from the California Men's Colony, a low security prison in San Luis Obispo; he subsequently seeks asylum with **Eldridge Cleaver** in Algeria; [SEPT. 18: JIMI HENDRIX, 27, DIES IN LONDON OF BARBITURATE-ALCOHOL INTOXICATION; OCT. 4: JANIS JOPLIN, 27, DIES OF A HEROIN OVERDOSE IN LOS

ANGELES.] New Directions publishes **Gregory Corso's** *Elegiac Feelings American*; Olympia Press (New York City) publishes **Billy Burroughs's** first novel, *Speed*; Cape Goliard Press (London) publishes **William S. Burroughs's** *The Last Words of Dutch Schultz*; **Gary Snyder** and his family move to San Juan Ridge, north of the South Yuba river, in the foothills of the Sierra Nevada; **Gary Snyder**, with the help of friends and students, builds a house called *Kitkitdizze* (the Wintu Indian word for *Chamaebatia foliolosa*, an indigenous aromatic shrub) on a hundred-acre parcel of land; **Snyder** also builds a small cabin for **Allen Ginsberg** to stay in when he visits; History Compass publishes *The Beat Generation*, edited by **Juliet Mofford.**

1971

MAY: City Lights publishes **Jack Kerouac's** *Scattered Poems*; MAY 23: **Lew Welch**, 44, suffering from depression and alcoholism, presumably commits suicide in the Sierra Nevada foothills near **Gary Snyder's** new home (**Welch's** body is never found); JUNE: **Dusan Makavejev's** film about **Wilhelm Reich**, *W.R.—Misterije organizma* (*W.R.—Mysteries of the Organism*), opens at the Twenty-First Berlin International Film Festival; JUNE: New Directions publishes **Gary Snyder's** *The Back Country*; City Lights publishes **Allen Ginsberg's** *Planet News:*

ALLEN GINSBERG AND LEW WELCH OUTSIDE
CITY LIGHTS BOOKSTORE, SAN FRANCISCO,
OCTOBER 30, 1963

1961–1967; [JULY 3: JIM MORRISON, 27, DIES IN
PARIS, PERHAPS OF HEART FAILURE.] AUG.: Scribner's
publishes **Bruce Cook's** *The Beat Generation*, the
first critical assessment of the Beats; SEPT.: *Esquire*
magazine publishes an exposé of **William S. Burroughs**
by his son, **Billy Burroughs**; [AUG. 21: BLACK PANTHER
GEORGE JACKSON, 29, DIES IN A SHOOT-OUT WHILE
TRYING TO ESCAPE FROM SAN QUENTIN PRISON.]
SEPT.: **Ginsberg** visits India and West Bengal, which
are hard hit by drought and famine; [SEPT. 9–13:
ATTICA PRISON (NEW YORK) UPRISING—STATE
POLICE MASSACRE TWENTY-NINE INMATES AND TEN
HOSTAGES.] OCT.: *Rolling Stone* magazine serializes
Hunter S. Thompson's *Fear and Loathing in Las
Vegas: A Savage Journey to the Heart of the American
Dream*; NOV. 9: **Bob Dylan** attends a poetry reading
by **Allen Ginsberg** at New York University's Loeb

Auditorium; afterward, the two repair to **Ginsberg's** apartment for an impromptu jam session; **Dylan** then invites **Ginsberg** to join him in the recording studio on November 17; NOV. 14–16: **Ginsberg** writes "September on Jessore Road" about his recent trip to India; NOV. 17: **Bob Dylan**, **Allen Ginsberg**, **Happy Traum**, **Arthur Russell**, **Steven Taylor**, **David Amram**, and others convene in a New York recording studio to collaborate (the resulting work is released as *First Blues* in 1983); DEC. 10: A "Free John [Sinclair] Now" rally is held at Ann Arbor's Crisler Arena; the event attracts fifteen thousand people and brings together a who's who of left-wing luminaries, including **John Lennon** (who recorded the song "John Sinclair" on his 1972 *Some Time in New York City* album), **Yoko Ono**, **David Peel**, **Stevie Wonder**, **Phil Ochs**, and **Bob Seger**, jazz artists **Archie Shepp** and **Roswell Rudd**, and speakers **Allen Ginsberg**, **Abbie Hoffman**, **Rennie Davis**, **David Dellinger**, **Jerry Rubin**, and **Bobby Seale**; DEC. 13: **John Sinclair** is released from prison; City Lights publishes **Neal Cassady's** unfinished autobiographical novel *The First Third*; Coward-McCann publishes **Jack Kerouac's** *Vanity of Duluoz*; Grove Press publishes **Kerouac's** *Pic*; Dell publishes **Seymour Krim's** *Shake It for the World, Smartass*; Grove Press publishes **Burroughs's** *The Wild Boys: A Book of the Dead*; City Lights publishes *Revolutionary*

Letters by **Diane di Prima** and **Charles Plymell's** *The Last of the Moccasins*.

1972

FEB. 10: **Robert Kalfin** directs a theatrical version of **Ginsberg's** "Kaddish," which is staged at the Chelsea Theater Center (Brooklyn Academy of Music) as a theater-video work and garners a positive review from *New York Times* theater critic **Clive Barnes**; APRIL: G.P. Putnam's Sons publishes *Without Stopping: An Autobiography* by **Paul Bowles**; MAY: Little, Brown publishes **Emmett Grogan's** quasi-autobiographical *Ringolevio: A Life Played for Keeps*, a book that takes a refreshingly skeptical view of the sixties' counterculture; JUNE 8: **Kenneth Patchen**, 61, dies in Palo Alto, California; JULY: Random House publishes **Hunter S. Thompson's** *Fear and Loathing in Las Vegas: A Savage Journey to the Heart of the American Dream* in book form; AUG.: **Walter Becker** and **Donald Fagen** form the jazz-rock fusion group Steely Dan, the name derived from the name of a dildo in **William S. Burroughs's** *Naked Lunch*; [SEPT. 5–6: BLACK SEPTEMBER, A PALESTINIAN TERRORIST GROUP, KIDNAPS AND MURDERS THE ELEVEN MEMBERS OF THE ISRAELI OLYMPIC TEAM IN MUNICH, GERMANY.] NOV. 8: The first film screened on HBO, a new cable TV network, is *Sometimes a*

Great Notion, based on **Ken Kesey's** novel; NOV.:
Pantheon Books publishes **Alan Watts's** *In My Own
Way: An Autobiography, 1915–1965*; DEC.: McGraw-
Hill publishes **Kerouac's** *Visions of Cody* (with an
introduction by **Allen Ginsberg**); **Ginsberg's** *Fall of
America* wins the National Book Award for Poetry.

1973

JAN.: Covent Gardens Press publishes **William S.
Burroughs's** novel *Port of Saints*; **Burroughs** moves
from London to New York City to teach a creative
writing course at City College of New York; FEB.:
Ginsberg is elected a member of the National
Institute of Arts and Letters; MARCH: **Ginsberg**
breaks his leg after slipping on icy flagstone outside
his farmhouse in Cherry Valley, New York; APRIL:
City Lights publishes **Ginsberg's** *The Fall of America*;
Viking Press publishes **Burroughs's** *Exterminator!*;
MAY 4: **Jane Bowles**, 56, dies at the Clínica de los
Angeles in Málaga, Spain of alcohol-related illnesses;
JUNE: Something Else Press publishes *Brion Gysin
Let the Mice In*, by **Brion Gysin**, **William Burroughs**,
and **Ian Sommerville**; [SEPT. 11: CHILE'S PRESIDENT
SALVADOR ALLENDE, 65, A POPULARLY ELECTED
MARXIST, IS OVERTHROWN IN A MILITARY COUP LED
BY GENERAL AUGUSTO PINOCHET; ALLENDE COMMITS
SUICIDE.] OCT.: **Jack Kerouac's** mother, **Gabrielle**

ALAN WILSON WATTS,
1915-1973

Kerouac, 78, dies in Saint Petersburg, Florida;
NOV. 16: **Alan Watts**, 58, dies in his sleep from the
effects of long-term alcoholism at his home in Mill
Valley, California; DEC. 17: Black Sparrow Press
publishes *South of No North: Stories of the Buried
Life* by **Charles Bukowski**; E.P. Dutton publishes **Billy
Burroughs's** second novel, *Kentucky Ham*; Straight
Arrow Books publishes **Ann Charters's** *Kerouac: A
Biography*; **Bob Kaufman**, 47, starts to speak and
write again after a decade of silence.

1974

FEB.: **William S. Burroughs**, 60, meets **James
Grauerholz**, 21, who soon becomes his bibliographer
and secretary (until **Burroughs's** death twenty-
three years later in 1997); FEB. 28: *Rolling Stone*
publishes a dialogue between **William S. Burroughs**

and **David Bowie**; MARCH: **Billy Burroughs**, 26, visits his father at **William S. Burroughs's** sublet apartment at 452 Broadway, New York City, and meets **James Grauerholz**; MARCH 18–25: **Allen Ginsberg**, **Lawrence Ferlinghetti**, **Gregory Corso**, **Michael McClure**, **Shig Murao**, **Peter Orlovsky**, **Miriam Patchen**, **Kenneth Rexroth**, and **Gary Snyder** attend the Fifth Annual North Dakota Writers Conference, sponsored by the English Department of the University of North Dakota (Grand Forks); [AUG. 8: RICHARD NIXON RESIGNS IN DISGRACE OVER THE WATERGATE COVER-UP; GERALD FORD ASSUMES THE PRESIDENCY.] SUMMER: **Allen Ginsberg** and **Anne Waldman** found The **Jack Kerouac** Society for Disembodied Poetics at the Naropa Institute (which was also founded in 1974 but was renamed Naropa University in 1999) at 2130 Arapahoe Avenue, Boulder, Colorado; **Burroughs** teaches there; DEC.: **Ginsberg** introduces **Barbara Moraff** to **Chögyam Trungpa**; New Directions publishes **Gary Snyder's** *Turtle Island*; City Lights publishes *Iron Horse* by **Allen Ginsberg**; Ithaca Press publishes *Visions of Kerouac: The Life of Jack Kerouac* by **Charles E. Jarvis**.

1975

[APRIL 30: THE FALL OF SAIGON MARKS THE END OF THE VIETNAM WAR.] APRIL 11: **Gary Snyder** wins the

Pulitzer Prize for Poetry for *Turtle Island;* APRIL 17: **Allen Ginsberg**, **Peter Orlovsky**, **Gregory Corso**, and **William S. Burroughs** read their work at Columbia University in New York City; SEPT. 24–28: **William S. Burroughs** and **Brion Gysin** attend "Le Colloque de Tanger," a conference about their work; **Gérard-Georges Lemaire** and **François Lagarde** organize the event in Geneva, Switzerland; OCT. 17: **Ginsberg** writes "Gospel Noble Truths" on a New York City subway train; OCT. 31: During a wild Halloween party at his Snowmass, Colorado seminary, a drunken **Chögyam Trungpa** has subordinates forcibly detain and strip poet **W.S. Merwin** and his girlfriend, **Dana Naone**—an incident that causes a major scandal in poetry circles; **Ginsberg**, called upon to repudiate **Chögyam Trungpa**, refuses; OCT. 27: **Ginsberg** joins **Bob Dylan's** Rolling Thunder Revue as it tours the Northeast; NOV. 2: **Bob Dylan** and **Allen Ginsberg** visit **Kerouac's** grave at Edson Cemetery in Lowell, Massachusetts (as recorded in Dylan's 1978 film *Renaldo and Clara*); Coach House (Toronto) publishes **Victor-Lévy Beaulieu's** *Jack Kerouac: A Chicken Essay*; NOV. 19: **Milos Forman's** film adaptation of **Ken Kesey's** *One Flew Over the Cuckoo's Nest* (starring **Jack Nicholson**) is released to critical and popular acclaim; DEC. 18: Black Sparrow Press publishes *Factotum* by **Charles Bukowski**.

THE CITY LIGHTS IN NORTH DAKOTA CONFERENCE, IN GRAND FORKS, NORTH DAKOTA, MARCH 18, 1974. CLOCKWISE FROM TOP LEFT: GREGORY CORSO, MIRIAM PATCHEN, KENNETH REXROTH, ALLEN GINSBERG, LAWRENCE FERLINGHETTI, PETER ORLOVSKY (CUT IN HALF), GARY SNYDER, JANIE McCLURE, SHIG MURAO, CURATOR (NAME UNKNOWN), JOANNE McCLURE.

1976

FEB. 5: **Ian M. Sommerville**, 36, **William S. Burroughs's** longtime artistic collaborator (and sometimes lover), is killed in a single-car accident in Bath, England; APRIL 21: California governor **Jerry Brown** orders the release of **Timothy Leary** from prison; MAY: McGraw-Hill publishes **John Tytell's** *The Naked Angels: The Lives and Literature of the Beat Generation*; JULY 7: **Allen Ginsberg's** father, **Louis Ginsberg**, 80, dies from natural causes; JULY 8: **Ginsberg** writes "Father Death Blues" en route to his father's funeral; JULY: Creative Arts publishes **Carolyn Cassady's** *Heartbeat: My Life* *with Jack and Neal;* AUG. 7: **Allen Ginsberg**, **Anne Waldman**, **Chögyam Trungpa Rinpoche**, and **William S. Burroughs** give a poetry reading at the Naropa Institute, Boulder, Colorado; AUG.: **Billy Burroughs** receives a liver transplant; the operation is performed by **Thomas Starzl** (considered the father of modern transplantation) at the University of Colorado, Denver; **William S. Burroughs** moves to Boulder to be close to his ailing son; OCT.: Holt, Rinehart & Winston publish **Emmett Grogan's** crime novel, *Final Score*; OCT.: The Four Seasons Foundation publishes *The Collected Poems of Edward Dorn, 1956–1974*; OCT.: North Atlantic Books publishes *Selected Poems, 1956–1975* by **Diane di Prima**; OCT.: Full Court Press publishes *Collected Poems* by **Edwin Denby**; [NOV. 2: JIMMY CARTER IS ELECTED THIRTY-NINTH U.S. PRESIDENT.] NOV. 25: **Lawrence Ferlinghetti** reads "Last Prayer" on stage during the Band's farewell concert at Winterland in San Francisco (as seen in **Martin Scorsese's** 1978 film *The Last Waltz*); DEC.: *Visions of Kerouac*, a play by **Martin Duberman**, opens at the Lion Theater, 410 W. Forty-Second Street, New York City; McGraw-Hill publishes **Kerouac's** *Visions of Cody*; **Burroughs** moves into the so-called Bunker, a basement apartment in a former YMCA at 222 Bowery Street, New York City; **Seymour Krim** wins a Guggenheim Fellowship.

1977

FEB. 23: **Allen Ginsberg** and **Robert Lowell** do their only poetry reading together at Saint Mark's Place, New York City; MAY: *Oui* magazine publishes "The Band's Perfect Goodbye: A Behind the Scenes Report" by **Emmett Grogan**; AUG.: Grey Fox Press publishes *On Bread and Poetry: A Panel Discussion between Gary Snyder, Lew Welch and Philip Whalen*; SEPT.: City Lights publishes three hundred copies of the hardcover edition of **Ginsberg's** *Mind Breaths: Poems, 1972–1977*; OCT.: Grove Press publishes *Journals: Early Fifties, Early Sixties* by **Allen Ginsberg**, edited by **Gordon Ball**; NOV. 25: Creative Arts publishes *As Ever: The Collected Correspondence of Allen Ginsberg and Neal Cassady*, edited by **Barry Gifford**; DEC. 1: **Richard Brautigan** and **Akiko Nishizawa Yoshimura** marry in Richmond, California; DEC. 13: Grey Fox Press publishes *I, Leo: An Unfinished Novel* by **Lew Welch**, edited by **Donald Allen**; Cherry Valley Editions publishes **Dan Propper's** *The Tale of the Amazing Tramp*; *The Beat Diary*, edited by **Arthur Winfield Knight** and **Kit Knight**, appears as volume 5 of *the unspeakable visions of the individual*.

1978

JAN. 1: City Lights publishes **Ginsberg's** *Mind Breaths: Poems, 1972–1977* in paperback; JAN. 10:

EMMETT GROGAN,
1943–1978 (IN 1978)

Ecco Press publishes *My Sister's Hand in Mine: An
Expanded Edition of the Collected Works of Jane
Bowles*, with an introduction by **Truman Capote**;
JAN. 25: **Bob Dylan's** 232-minute surrealist film,
Renaldo and Clara (featuring **Allen Ginsberg**),
is released at selected venues and is savaged by
film critics; APRIL 6: **Emmett Grogan**, 35, dies of a
heart attack—probably related to long-term heroin
use—on an *F* train subway car in Coney Island, New
York City; JUNE: Bookpeople publishes **Jim Carroll's**
The Basketball Diaries; JUNE 17: At Lindisfarne-
in-Manhattan, Sixth Avenue and Twentieth Street,
New York City, **Gary Snyder** reads poems from *Turtle
Island* with musical accompaniment by the **Paul
Winter** Consort (an audio recording is later released);
JULY 14: **Ginsberg** completes "Plutonian Ode"; JULY
31: St. Martin's Press publishes *Jack's Book*, an oral
history of **Kerouac** and the Beats compiled by **Barry
Gifford** and **Lawrence Lee**; SEPT. 4: Playboy Press

publishes *Requiem for a Dream* by **Hubert Selby Jr.**;
Sep. 11–16: The P78, One World Poetry Conference is
held at De Kosmos, Amsterdam, Holland; participants
include **Tom Raworth**, **Ted Berrigan**, **Harold Norse**,
Jim Koller, **Joanne Kyger**, **Franco Beltrametti**,
Bill Berkson, **Anne Waldman**, **Lewis MacAdams**,
Stephen Rodefer, **Diane di Prima**, and **Michael
Brownstein**; [NOV. 18: NINE HUNDRED NINE MEMBERS
OF PEOPLES TEMPLE DIE IN JONESTOWN, GUYANA,
IN A MASS SUICIDE ORDERED BY THEIR PSYCHOTIC
LEADER, JIM JONES.] NOV. 30–DEC. 2: Organized
by Columbia professor **Sylvère Lotringer**, **John
Giorno**, and **James Grauerholz**, the Nova Convention
(a tribute to **William S. Burroughs**) is held in the
Entermedia Theater (formerly the Phoenix Theater)
at 189 Second Avenue (at Twelfth Street) and at
other locations around New York City; among those
on stage or in the audience are **Burroughs**, **Giorno**,
Debbie Harry, **Philip Glass**, **Frank Zappa**, **Patti Smith**,
Laurie Anderson, **Ed Sanders**, **Terry Southern**,
Victor Bockris, and **Brion Gysin**; **Keith Richards**, also
scheduled to appear, is persuaded by his lawyers to
cancel; with a Toronto drug possession case pending,
associating with **Burroughs** is deemed an unwise
career move; WINTER: **Joy Walsh** publishes the first
of twenty-eight issues of *Moody Street Irregulars: A
Jack Kerouac Newsletter* from Clarence Center, New

York (near Buffalo); the last issue appears in 1992; **Burroughs** becomes readdicted to heroin during the Lower East Side whitcout of the late 1970s (the "Bunker" is one block from the junk-dealer streets of Stanton and Rivington); **Bob Kaufman** resumes his vow of silence; *The Beat Journey*, edited by **Arthur Winfield Knight** and **Kit Knight**, appears as volume 8 of *the unspeakable visions of the individual*.

1979

APRIL 12: William Morrow publishes **Aram Saroyan's** *Genesis Angels: The Saga of Lew Welch and the Beat Generation*; Random House publishes **Dennis McNally's** *Desolate Angel: Jack Kerouac, the Beats, and America*; JUNE 18: Giorno Poetry Systems (GPS) releases *The Nova Convention*, a double-LP recorded at Entermedia Theater during the previous December's events; SEPT.: Black Sparrow Press publishes *Collected Stories of Paul Bowles, 1939–1976*, with an introduction by **Gore Vidal**; OCT.: **Janine Pommy Vega** inherits $5,000 from her mother and buys a six-room house in Willow, New York, near Woodstock; **Costanzo Allione's** *Fried Shoes, Cooked Diamonds*, a fifty-five-minute documentary about the Jack Kerouac School of Disembodied Poetics (Naropa Institute, Boulder, Colorado) premiers at the Chicago International Film Festival; the film features **Allen Ginsberg**, **Peter**

Orlovsky, Gregory Corso, William S. Burroughs, Anne Waldman, Timothy Leary, and Amiri Baraka; OCT. 14: P79, One World Poetry, a multimedia event dedicated to **Jack Kerouac**, is held in Amsterdam; [NOV. 4: ANGERED BY JIMMY CARTER'S ADMITTING THE DEPOSED SHAH OF IRAN INTO THE U.S. FOR CANCER TREATMENT—A MOVE URGED BY HENRY KISSINGER—IRANIAN STUDENT RADICALS STORM THE U.S. EMBASSY IN TEHRAN AND SEIZE FIFTY-THREE AMERICAN HOSTAGES, IGNITING A CRISIS THAT LASTS 444 DAYS (UNTIL JANUARY 28, 1980) AND ULTIMATELY DESTROYS THE CARTER PRESIDENCY.] NOV. 28: **Allen Ginsberg** gives a poetry reading at De Kosmos, Amsterdam; DEC. 4: **Richard Brautigan** and **Akiko Nishizawa Yoshimura** separate after two years of marriage; they are officially divorced on November 7, 1980; Salem State College publishes the Kerouac issue of *Soundings—East* (vol. 2, no. 2); Schirmer Books (New York) publishes *Straight Life: The Story of Art Pepper* by **Art** and **Laurie Pepper**; Grey Fox Press (Bolinas, CA) publishes *He Who Hunted Birds in His Father's Village: The Dimensions of a Haida Myth*, **Gary Snyder's** 1951 Reed College senior thesis; Calder (London) and Riverrun (New York) publish *Ah Pook Is Here, and Other Texts* by **William S. Burroughs**; Limberlost Press (Pocatello, Idaho) publishes *Death Drag: Selected Poems, 1948–1979* by **John Clellon Holmes**.

1980

JAN. 1: Grey Fox Press publishes *I Remain: The Letters of Lew Welch and the Correspondence of His Friends; Volume 1, 1949–1960* and *I Remain: The Letters of Lew Welch and the Correspondence of His Friends; Volume 2, 1960–1971*; MARCH 4: Film director **Francis Ford Coppola** buys the film rights to *On the Road* for $95,000; APRIL 6: **Antony Balch**, 43, dies of stomach cancer in London; APRIL 25: **John Byrum's** docudrama *Heart Beat*—based on **Carolyn Cassady's** memoir and starring **Nick Nolte** as **Neal Cassady**, **Sissy Spacek** as **Carolyn Cassady**, and **John Heard** as **Jack Kerouac**—opens in New York City to mixed reviews; MAY 26: The Cinema Guild premiers **Philomene Long's** *The Beats: An Existential Comedy*, a forty-six-minute "film poem" (featuring **Shirley Clark**, **Lawrence Ferlinghetti**, **Allen Ginsberg,** and **Viva** and **Andy Warhol**) in Venice, California; JUNE 7: **Henry Miller**, 88, dies at his home in Pacific Palisades, California; SUMMER: **William S. Burroughs** goes on methadone maintenance; SEPT.: **John Clellon Holmes**, 54, takes a teaching job at the University of Arkansas (Fayetteville, Arkansas); SEPT.: Black Sparrow Press publishes *Charles Olson and Robert Creeley: The Complete Correspondence*, edited by **George F. Butterick** and **Richard Belvins**; OCT. 14: **Allen Ginsberg** writes "Birdbrain!" at the

Hotel Subrovka in Dubrovnik, Yugoslavia; [NOV. 4: FORMER B-MOVIE ACTOR AND GENERAL ELECTRIC PITCHMAN RONALD REAGAN, 69, IS ELECTED FORTIETH U.S. PRESIDENT IN A LANDSLIDE VICTORY OVER INCUMBENT JIMMY CARTER.] NOV. 20: Grey Fox Press publishes *Enough Said: Fluctuat Nec Mergitur; Poems, 1974–1979* by **Philip Whalen** in a limited edition of fifty-six copies; the subtitle is Latin for "It is tossed by the waves but does not sink," the motto of the city of Paris; [DEC. 8: JOHN LENNON, 40, IS MURDERED OUTSIDE HIS NEW YORK CITY APARTMENT BUILDING BY MARK DAVID CHAPMAN, 25, A PSYCHOTIC "FAN."] DEC. 15: **Ginsberg** writes "Capitol Air" while flying from Frankfurt, West Germany, to New York City.

1981

JAN. 1: Holt, Rinehart & Winston publishes **Burroughs's** *Cities of the Red Night*; MARCH 3: **William S. "Billy" Burroughs Jr.**, 33, dies of liver failure after a life of heavy drinking and drug abuse; [MARCH 30: JOHN WAYNE HINCKLEY JR. WOUNDS PRESIDENT REAGAN IN AN UNSUCCESSFUL ASSASSINATION ATTEMPT OUTSIDE THE WASHINGTON HILTON HOTEL.] MAY 7: **Jerry Garcia** and **Ken Kesey** appear on **Tom Snyder's** *Tomorrow* show at NBC studios, New York City; MAY 29: New Directions publishes **Bob Kaufman's** *The Ancient Rain: Poems,*

1956–1978; JUNE: Grey Fox Press and City Lights copublish **Jack Kerouac's** *Heaven, and Other Poems*; JUNE 10: **Allen Ginsberg** performs his poem-song "Capitol Air" on stage with the **Clash** at Bond's International Casino, 1530 Broadway (Times Square, between Forty-Fourth and Forty-Fifth Streets), New York City; JUNE 25: **Jay Landesman** publishes the nine issues (1948–1951) of the Beat journal, *Neurotica*, in a single-volume edition with an introduction by **John Clellon Holmes**; AUG. 15: City Lights publishes *The Campaign against the Underground Press: Pen American Center Report*, edited by **Anne Janowitz** and **Nancy J. Peters**, with a foreword by **Allen Ginsberg** and reports by **Aryeh Neier**, **Todd Gitlin**, and **Angus Mackenzie**; OCT. 1: Thunder's Mouth Press publishes *The Holy Goof: A Biography of Neal Cassady* by **William Plummer**; OCT.: **Ginsberg** moves to Boulder, Colorado to be near the Naropa Institute; he settles into a house at 2141 Bluff Street, Boulder; OCT. 21: St. Martin's Press publishes **Jan Kerouac's** *Baby Driver: A Story about Myself*; NOV. 7: **William S. Burroughs** gives a reading of his work on *Saturday Night Live*; NOV. 14: **Allen Ginsberg** gives a twenty-fifth anniversary reading of "Howl" at Columbia University's McMillin Theatre; DEC.: **Burroughs** moves to Lawrence, Kansas; Tombouctou publishes **Joanne Kyger's** *The*

Japan and India Journals, 1960–1964; McFarland publishes *The Beats: Essays in Criticism*, edited by **Lee Bartlett**; Cadmus (Santa Barbara, CA) publishes *Early Routines* by **William S. Burroughs**.

1982

JAN.: V/Search Publications (San Francisco) publishes a "special book issue: of Re/Search #4–5 on **William S. Burroughs**, **Brion Gysin**, and **Throbbing Gristle**; JAN. 23: **Ginsberg** writes "The Little Fish Devours the Big Fish" at the Intercontinental Hotel's bar, Managua, Nicaragua; [APRIL 2–JUNE 14: THE U.K. AND ARGENTINA FIGHT THE FALKLANDS WAR.] JUNE 6: **Kenneth Rexroth**, 76, dies of a massive heart attack in Santa Barbara, California; late JULY: The Naropa Institute holds "*On the Road*: The **Jack Kerouac** Conference" on the twenty-fifth anniversary of the publication of *On the Road* (with opening remarks by **Allen Ginsberg** and **Chögyam Trungpa Rinpoche**, the founder and titular head of Naropa); other participants include **Gregory Corso**, **Peter Orlovsky**, **Robert Creeley**, **Lawrence Ferlinghetti**, **Michael McClure**, **Diane di Prima**, **Ken Kesey**, **Ted Berrigan**, **Carl Solomon**, **Ray Bremser**, **Jack Micheline**, **Robert Frank**, **Herbert Huncke**, **David Amram**, **Anne Waldman**, **Abbie Hoffman**, **Timothy Leary**, and **Jan Kerouac**; SEPT.: **William S. Burroughs** moves to a

1927 LEARNARD STREET, LAWRENCE, KANSAS: WILLIAM S. BURROUGHS'S RESIDENCE FROM SEPTEMBER, 1982 UNTIL HIS DEATH IN AUGUST, 1997

house at 1927 Learnard Street, Lawrence, Kansas; OCT. 7: **William S. Burroughs, John Giorno, Marc Almond, and Heathcote Williams** give a reading at Heaven nightclub in London; City Lights publishes **Allen Ginsberg's** *Plutonian Ode: Poems 1977–1980*; DEC. 21: Houghton Mifflin publishes **Joyce Johnson's** *Minor Characters*.

1983

MARCH 17: **Allen Ginsberg** does a reading at Skidmore College and is interviewed by **Jennie Skerl** on his relationship with **William S. Burroughs**; the interview is published in *Modern Language Studies* 16, no. 3 (Summer 1986); MAY 1: Southern Illinois University Press publishes **Larry Smith's** *Lawrence Ferlinghetti: Poet-at-Large*; E.P. Dutton publishes *Going On: Selected Poems, 1958–1980* by **Joanne**

ALLEN GINSBERG ON *THE DAVID LETTERMAN SHOW*

Kyger; MAY: **William S. Burroughs** is inducted into the American Academy and Institute of Arts and Letters; MAY 13: Gale Group publishes *The Beats: Literary Bohemians in Postwar America* in two volumes edited by **Ann Charters**; JUNE: **Allen Ginsberg** appears on *The David Letterman Show*; JUNE 23: Four Seasons Foundation publishes *Heavy Breathing: Poems, 1967–1980* by **Philip Whalen**; JULY 16: Grove Press publishes *Memory Babe: A Critical Biography of Jack Kerouac* by **Gerald Nicosia**; OCT.: **Howard Brookner's** eighty-six-minute documentary film, *Burroughs*, is shown at the New York Film Festival. [OCT. 25–DEC.: U.S. INVADES THE CARIBBEAN ISLAND NATION OF GRENADA.]

1984

FEB. 10: *Burroughs*, the film, opens at the Bleecker Street Cinema, Greenwich Village, New York City; APRIL: The **Jack Kerouac** Club is founded in Quebec to study **Kerouac** as a French-Canadian writer; JUNE 1: City Lights publishes *The Burroughs File* by **William S. Burroughs**; SEPT. 12: Sierra Club Books publishes *What Shall We Do without Us: The Voice and Vision of Kenneth Patchen*; SEPT. 14: **Richard Brautigan**, 49, commits suicide by shooting himself at his home in Bolinas, Marin County, California; his badly decomposed body is not discovered until several weeks later; OCT.: **Allen Ginsberg**, **Gary Snyder**, **Toni Morrison**, **William Gass**, **Francine du Plessix Gray**, and **Harrison Salisbury** travel to Beijing, China as part of an American Academy of Arts and Letters delegation to the Second Sino-U.S. Writer's Conference, which is held October 20–27; **Ginsberg** travels throughout China during the next two months; [NOV. 6: RONALD REAGAN IS REELECTED IN ANOTHER LANDSLIDE VICTORY.] Harper and Row publishes **Ginsberg's** *Collected Poems, 1947–1980*; the two novels by **William S. "Billy" Burroughs Jr.**—*Speed* and *Kentucky Ham*—are published in one volume by the Overlook Press; Harcourt Brace Jovanovich publishes **Tom Clark's** biography *Jack Kerouac*; Gris Banal (Montpellier, France) publishes *The Beat Hotel* by **Harold Chapman**, translated by **Brice Matthieussent**, with "nostalgia" by **William S. Burroughs** and **Brion Gysin** and captions by Claire Parry.

LINDA LEE BIEGHLE AND CHARLES BUKOWSKI DANCE ON THEIR WEDDING DAY, AUG. 18, 1985

1985

JAN. 1: Thunder's Mouth Press publishes *Kerouac and Friends: A Beat Generation Album*, edited by **Fred W. McDarrah** and **Timothy S. McDarrah**; The University of Michigan Press publishes *On the Poetry of Allen Ginsberg*, edited by **Lewis Hyde**; JAN.: Viking Press publishes **William S. Burroughs's** *Queer* (written 1951–53); APRIL 15: **Alexander Trocchi**, 58, dies of pneumonia in London; AUG. 18: **Charles Bukowski**, 65, marries **Linda Lee Beighle**, 42, at the Church of the People in the Los Feliz neighborhood of Los Angeles; SEPT.: **Gary Snyder** begins to teach writing at the University of California, Davis; SEPT. 6: **John Antonelli's** documentary *Kerouac, the Movie* is released; NOV.: **Burroughs** travels to Paris to visit a terminally ill **Brion Gysin**; NOV. 15: Zephyr Press publishes *Two Novels* (*You Didn't Even Try* and *Imaginary Speeches for a Brazen Head*) by **Philip Whalen**, with an introduction by **Paul Christensen**;

Michael B. Emerton, 19, meets **Burroughs** and **James Grauerholz**; **Emerton** will live with them for the next seven years.

1986

JAN. 12: **Bob Kaufman**, 60, dies in San Francisco of emphysema; FEB.: **Martin Duberman's** play, *Visions of Kerouac*, opens its second run, this time at the American Theater, W. Fifty-Fourth Street, New York City; MARCH: Twayne publishes *William S. Burroughs* by **Jennie Skerl**; APRIL 15: **Jean Genet**, 75, dies in Paris of throat cancer; APRIL 16: **Richard Lerner** and **Lewis Adams's** documentary *What Happened to Kerouac?* premiers at the New Directors/New Films Festival in New York; APRIL 25: Black Sparrow Press publishes *Selected Poems, 1958–1984* by **John Wieners**, edited by **Raymond Foye** with a foreword by **Allen Ginsberg**; JUNE 6–7: Beat Generation Weekend is held at Plymouth Arts Centre in England; JULY 13: **Brion Gysin**, 70, dies (alone in his Paris apartment at 135 Rue Saint Martin, across the street from the Centre Pompidou) of lung cancer; JULY: Harper and Row publishes **Ginsberg's** *White Shroud: Poems 1980–1985*; JULY: Doubleday publishes **Ann Charters's** *Beats and Company*, an oversize book of photographs of Beat writers; Twayne publishes *Kerouac: Novelist of the Beat Generation* by **Warren**

French; JULY 25: The University of California Press publishes a new edition of *The Maximus Poems* by **Charles Olson**, edited by **George E. Butterick**; AUG.: **Ginsberg** visits **Burroughs** at his home in Lawrence, Kansas, and stays a week; SUMMER: **Allen Ginsberg**, 59, accepts a position as distinguished professor of English at Brooklyn College (a job he will hold until his death eleven years later); OCT. 1: Water Row Books publishes a reprint edition of **Ray Bremser's** *Poems of Madness & Angel*; DEC. 30: Lowell City Council votes 8–1 to enter into an agreement with the Lowell Historic Preservation Society to budget $100,000 for the establishment of the **Kerouac** Commemorative (completed in 1988).

1987

FEB.: Artist **Philip Taaffe** visits Burroughs at his home in Lawrence, Kansas to commence a series of artistic collaborations; FEB. 22: **Andy Warhol**, 58, dies of a heart attack following routine gall bladder surgery in New York City; APRIL 4: **Chögyam Trungpa**, 48, dies in Halifax, Nova Scotia, from the effects of long-term alcoholism; MAY 20: **Gary Snyder** is inducted into the American Academy and Institute of Arts and Letters; MAY: **Janet Forman's** documentary, *The Beat Generation: An American Dream*, is released by Renaissance Motion Pictures; Southern Illinois

CHÖGYAM TRUNGPA,
1939-1987

University Press publishes **Regina Weinreich's** *The Spontaneous Poetics of Jack Kerouac: A Study of the Fiction*; JUNE: At a get-together in Boulder, Colorado, **Peter Orlovsky** assaults and injures **R.D. Laing**; **Allen Ginsberg**, also injured, is forced to call the police to stop the fracas; JULY 7: Penguin publishes **Jim Carroll's** *Forced Entries: The Downtown Diaries, 1971–1973*; JULY 27: Alt-rock group 10,000 Maniacs releases *In My Tribe*, an LP that includes the song "Hey **Jack Kerouac**"; AUG. 1: The University of Illinois Press publishes *Word Cultures: Radical Theory and Practice in William S. Burroughs' Fiction* by **Robin Lydenberg**; SEPT. 7–13: *River City Reunion*, a weeklong series of Beat film screenings, poetry readings, concerts, and other events, is held in Lawrence, Kansas; participants include **William S. Burroughs**, **Allen Ginsberg**, **Robert Creeley**, **Jim**

Carroll, Andrei Codrescu, Diane di Prima, Ed Dorn, Timothy Leary, Marianne Faithfull, John Giorno, Ed Sanders, Michael McClure, and Anne Waldman; OCT. 1–4: The Rencontre Internationale **Jack Kerouac** (International **Jack Kerouac** Gathering) is held in Quebec City, Canada; participants include **Gerald Nicosia, Allen Ginsberg, Carolyn Cassady, Lawrence Ferlinghetti, Ann Charters, Lise Bissonnette, Denis Vanier, Roger Brunell**, and others; it also features a photo exhibit by **Robert Frank** at Musée du Québec: "Canuck et clochard céleste: l'universe de **Jack Kerouac**" ("Canuck and Spiritual Vagabond: **Jack Kerouac's** Universe"); OCT. 16: **Barbet Schroeder's** *Barfly*—a film based on **Charles Bukowski's** *Barfly: The Continuing Saga of Henry Chinaski* and starring **Mickey Rourke** and **Faye Dunaway**—premiers to good reviews; **Allen Ginsberg** and **Peter Orlovsky** end their thirty-three-year open relationship but remain close friends until **Ginsberg's** death ten years later; Water Row Press (Sudbury, Massachusetts) publishes *The Vigilantes*, a fragment from an unfinished novel by **Alan Ansen**.

1988

FEB. 1: Henry Holt publishes **Jan Kerouac's** *Train Song*; FEB. 3: **Robert Duncan**, 69, dies of kidney failure in San Francisco; MARCH 2: **John**

Clellon Holmes, 61, dies of cancer in Old Saybrook, Connecticut; JUNE: Paragon House publishes *The Beat Vision: A Primary Sourcebook*, edited by **Arthur Winfield Knight** and **Kit Knight**; JUNE 22–26: The First Annual Lowell Celebrates **Kerouac**! Festival is held; JUNE 25: The city of Lowell officially dedicates the **Jack Kerouac** Memorial Park; OCT.: Henry Holt publishes **Ted Morgan's** *Literary Outlaw: The Life and Times of William S. Burroughs*; **Kevin Ring** starts publishing *Beat Scene* magazine ("The Voice of the Beat Generation") in Coventry, England; [NOV. 8: FORMER CIA DIRECTOR GEORGE H.W. BUSH IS ELECTED FORTY-FIRST U.S. PRESIDENT.] DEC. 7: Penguin publishes *The Western Lands* by **William S. Burroughs**; DEC.: Amok Press publishes a new paperback edition of **Jack Black's** *You Can't Win* (first published in 1926), with an introduction by **William S. Burroughs**; The University of Arkansas Press publishes *Representative Men: The Biographical Essays* by **John Clellon Holmes**.

1989

APRIL: E.P. Dutton publishes *In the Night Café*, **Joyce Johnson's** third novel; MAY 2: **Eric "Big Daddy" Nord** (**Harry Helmuth Pastor**), 69, dies of heart and kidney disease in San Jose, California; JUNE: Dalkey Archive Press publishes *Contact Highs:*

Selected Poems, 1957–1987 by **Alan Ansen**; AUG. 30: **Seymour Krim**, 67, suffering from congestive heart failure and other serious ailments, commits suicide by overdosing on barbiturates at his East Village apartment (120 E. Tenth Street, New York City); AUG.: Simon and Schuster publishes **Barry Miles's** *Ginsberg: A Biography*; SEPT. 22: Skouras Pictures releases **Obie Benz's** *Heavy Petting*, a documentary on fifties sexual mores, featuring interviews with **Allen Ginsberg, William S. Burroughs, Spalding Gray, Abbie Hoffman**, and others; OCT. 6: Avenue Pictures Productions releases **Gus Van Sant's** film *Drugstore Cowboy* (featuring **William S. Burroughs** in a small role as Father Tom Murphy, a junkie priest); OCT. 1: Hearing Eye / Water Row publishes *Exiled Angel: A Study of the Work of Gregory Corso* by **Gregory Stephenson**; **Gary Snyder**, 59, and **Masa Uehara** divorce after twenty-two years of marriage; [NOV. 9: THE BERLIN WALL FALLS, AFTER TWENTY-NINE YEARS.] NOV.: William Morrow publishes *Memoirs of a Bastard Angel* by **Harold Norse**; DEC.: Zeitgeist Press publishes *Imaginary Conversation with Jack Kerouac* by **Jack Micheline**; [DEC. 20, 1989–JAN. 21, 1990: "OPERATION JUST CAUSE"—WITH 27,000 TROOPS, THE U.S. INVADES PANAMA AND CAPTURES PANAMANIAN MILITARY DICTATOR (AND FORMER CIA INFORMANT) MANUEL NORIEGA.] Dalkey Archive Press publishes *Contact Highs: Selected Poems, 1957–1987* by **Alan Ansen**; Sea Cliff Press (New York) publishes *The Table Talk of W.H. Auden* by **Alan Ansen**, edited by **Nicholas Jenkins** with an introduction by **Richard Howard**; Paragon Press publishes *Emergency Messages: An Autobiographical Miscellany* by **Carl Solomon**, edited by **John Tytell**.

1990

FEB. 10: **Jack Kerouac's** third wife, **Stella Sampas (Stavroula Sampatacacus)** dies at the age of 71; **Kerouac's** literary estate—valued in the millions—goes to **Stella's** surviving brother, **John Sampas**; MARCH 11: E.P. Dutton publishes **Hettie Jones's** memoir, *How I Became Hettie Jones*; MARCH 31: **William S. Burroughs's** "musical fable" *The Black Rider: The Casting of the Magic Bullets* (directed by **Robert Wilson** with songs by **Tom Waits**) premiers at the Thalia Theater, 67 Raboisen 20095 Altstadt, Hamburg, Germany; MAY 26: *Hydrogen Jukebox*, a "chamber opera" (music by **Philip Glass**, lyrics by **Allen Ginsberg**) premieres at the Spoleto Music Festival in Charleston, South Carolina; JUNE: Paragon House publishes **Herbert Huncke's** *Guilty of Everything: The Autobiography of Herbert Huncke*; JUNE 12: Rhino Records releases *The Jack Kerouac Collection*, a three-CD, thirty-two-track set of spoken-word recordings and music; **Joan Haverty, Kerouac's** second wife, dies of breast cancer at the age of 69; [AUG. 2: THE FIRST GULF WAR BEGINS AS IRAQI TROOPS INVADE KUWAIT.] SEPT. 18: Fontana Island releases *Dead City Radio*, a seventeen-track collection of spoken-word recordings by **William S. Burroughs**; OCT. 8: **Slim Brundage** dies at the age of 82; NOV.: Citadel Press publishes *Tales of Beatnik Glory* by **Ed Sanders**; DEC.: Viking publishes **Ken Kesey's** *The Further Inquiry*; Thunder's Mouth Press publishes **Paul Perry's** *On the Bus: The Complete Guide to the Legendary Trip of Ken Kesey and the Merry Pranksters and the Birth of the Counterculture*; The Harry Ransom Humanities Research Center, University of Texas at Austin, purchases **Peter Orlovsky's** papers; Carleton University Press (Canada) publishes *Un Homme Grand: Jack Kerouac at the Crossroads of Many Cultures/Jack Kérouac à la confluence des cultures*, edited by **Pierre Anctil**, **Louis Dupont**, **Rémi Ferland**, and **Eric Waddell**; Scarecrow Press publishes *The Bohemian Register: An Annotated Bibliography of the Beat Literary Movement* by **Morgen Hickey**.

1991

FEB.: Random House publishes **Neeli Cherkovski's** *Hank: The Life of Charles Bukowski*; [FEB. 24–28:

"OPERATION DESERT STORM"—COALITION FORCES WREST KUWAIT FROM IRAQI OCCUPATION BUT STOP SHORT OF DEPOSING SADDAM HUSSEIN.] FEB. 28: Southern Illinois University Press publishes *William S. Burroughs at the Front: Critical Reception, 1959–1989*, edited by **Jennie Skerl** and **Robin Lydenberg**; APRIL: **Gary Snyder**, 61, marries **Carole Lynn Koda**, 43, a Japanese American Zen Buddhist; JUNE: Black Sparrow Press publishes *Just Space: Poems 1979–1989* by **Joanne Kyger**; JULY: **Burroughs** undergoes triple bypass surgery; JULY 1: Cooper Street Publications publishes *Kerouac: Visions of Rocky Mount* by **John J. Dorfner**; SEPT. 15: HarperCollins publishes *The Dream at the End of the World: Paul Bowles and the Literary Renegades in Tangier* by **Michelle Green**; AUG. 1: Black Spring Press (U.K.) and Penguin (U.S.) publish an augmented version of **Carolyn Cassady's** *Heartbeat* titled *Off the Road: My Years with Cassady, Kerouac, and Ginsberg*; OCT. 1: Music and Words/Dig it! releases *From Dream to Dream,* a spoken-word recording by **Herbert Huncke**; OCT.: Paragon House publishes *What's This Cat's Story?: The Best of Seymour Krim*, edited by **Peggy Brooks**; DEC. 27: **David Cronenberg's** film version of *Naked Lunch* (starring **Peter Weller**) is released to mixed reviews; **Gus Van Sant** records a two-minute film of **William S. Burroughs** reciting "A Thanksgiving Prayer" (based on a poem **Burroughs**

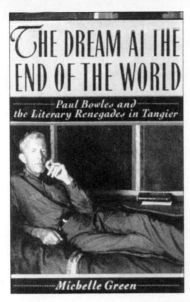

*THE DREAM AT THE
END OF THE WORLD*,
SEPTEMBER 1991

wrote for a 1989 chapbook titled *Tornado Alley*). [DEC.
8: THE SOVIET UNION IS DISSOLVED AFTER SIXTY-NINE
YEARS OF EXISTENCE; THE COLD WAR ENDS AFTER
FORTY-SIX YEARS.]

1992

JAN. 14: Penguin publishes **Ann Charters's** *The
Portable Beat Reader*; JUNE 1: Penguin publishes a
paperback edition of **Kerouac's** *Tristessa*; AUG.: **Henri
Cru**, **Kerouac's** friend from Horace Mann prep school
days, dies at the age of 71; SEPT. 17: **Burroughs** and
factotum **Michael B. Emerton** are involved in a car
accident; **Emerton's** BMW skids off the road near
Lawrence, Kansas in the midst of a fierce rainstorm;
neither person is seriously injured; SEPT. 25:

Burroughs records a spoken version of his story "The 'Priest' They Called Him" at his home in Lawrence, Kansas (later released as an EP with musical accompaniment by **Kurt Cobain**); Virgin (London) publishes **Barry Miles's** *William Burroughs: El Hombre Invisible*; St. Martin's Press publishes **Michael Schumacher's** *Dharma Lion: A Critical Biography of Allen Ginsberg*; [NOV. 3: BILL CLINTON IS ELECTED PRESIDENT, DEFEATING INCUMBENT GEORGE H.W. BUSH.] NOV. 4: **Michael Emerton**, 26, commits suicide by shooting himself; DEC.: The Edinburgh University Collection of Historic Manuscripts publishes *Alexander Trocchi: The Making of the Monster* by **Andrew Murray Scott**; Pantheon publishes *No Nature: New and Selected Poems* by **Gary Snyder**; prompted by **Allen Ginsberg**, **Hiro Yamagata** (a noted Japanese artist) begins giving a monthly stipend to **Gregory Corso**, which allows **Corso** to live comfortably the remaining eight years of his life.

1993

JAN. 25: E.P. Dutton publishes **E. Jean Carroll's** *Hunter: The Stranger and Savage Life of Hunter S. Thompson*; [FEB. 28: THE U.S. MILITARY BEGINS ITS FIFTY-ONE-DAY SIEGE OF THE BRANCH DAVIDIAN COMPOUND IN WACO, TEXAS; THE SIEGE RESULTS IN THE DEATHS OF EIGHTY-TWO CULT MEMBERS AND

OF FOUR AGENTS FROM THE BUREAU OF ALCOHOL, TOBACCO, FIREARMS, AND EXPLOSIVES.] APRIL 15: Arcade publishes *The Adding Machine: Selected Essays* and *The Last Words of Dutch Schultz: A Fiction in the Form of a Film Script*—both by **William S. Burroughs**; MAY 4: HarperCollins releases the audiobook *Run with the Hunted: A Charles Bukowski Reader*, edited by **John Martin**; JUNE: Blast Books publishes *Grace Beats Karma: Letters from Prison, 1958–60* by **Neal Cassady**; Cooper Street Publications releases *Kerouac: Visions of Lowell* by **John J. Dorfner**, with a foreword by **Allen Ginsberg**; AUG. 1–22: A revival of **Jane Bowles's** 1953 play *In the Summer House*, starring **Dianne Wiest**, directed by **JoAnne Akalaitis**, and with music by **Philip Glass**, opens at the Vivian Beaumont Theater (150 West Sixty-Fifth Street Manhattan) and receives good reviews; AUG. 8: Gap launches a series of print ads for khaki pants using photographs of American icons, and **Kerouac** is one of thirteen featured (in a 1957 photo of **Kerouac** and **Joyce Glassman Johnson** taken outside the Kettle of Fish at 59 Christopher Street in Greenwich Village, but **Johnson** is cropped from the photo); AUG. 8: Hyperion publishes a U.S. edition of **Barry Miles's** *William Burroughs: El Hombre Invisible*; SEPT. 1: Rutgers University Press publishes *Venice West: The Beat Generation*

WILLIAM S. BURROUGHS AND KURT COBAIN
AT BURROUGHS' HOME IN LAWRENCE, KANSAS,
OCTOBER 1993

in Southern California by **John Arthur Maynard**;
SEPT.: Grey Fox Press publishes **Jack Kerouac's**
uncollected writings in *Good Blonde & Others*; SEPT.
7: Pantheon publishes **Gary Snyder's** *No Nature:
New and Selected Poems*; SEPT. 20: Fontana Island
releases *Spare Ass Annie, and Other Tales*, a spoken-
word recording by **William S. Burroughs**; OCT. 1:
Chronicle Books publishes *Snapshot Poetics: Allen
Ginsberg's Photographic Memoir of the Beat Era*;
OCT.: **Kurt Cobain** travels to Lawrence, Kansas, to
visit **William S. Burroughs**; **Frankie Edith "Edie"
Parker**, **Kerouac's** first wife, dies at the age of 71;
After forty-seven years on the job, **Lucien Carr** retires
as assistant managing editor for National News at
United Press International (UPI); **Allen Ginsberg** is

awarded the medal of Chevalier de l'ordre des Arts et Lettres by the French minister of culture; DEC.: **William S. Burroughs's** "musical fable" *The Black Rider: The Casting of the Magic Bullets* (directed by **Robert Wilson** with songs by **Tom Waits**) opens at the Brooklyn Academy of Music; DEC. 30: Inanout Press (New York) publishes *Chocolate Creams and Dollars*, a quasi-autobiographical novel by Moroccan storyteller **Mohammed Mrabet (Mohammed ben Chaib el Hajjem)**, translated from the Moghrebi by **Paul Bowles** and illustrated by **Philip Taaffe**.

1994

JAN. 20: **Ginsberg** performs "Howl" with the Kronos Quartet at Carnegie Hall; FEB. 15: Ginsberg appears on *The Charlie Rose Show*; FEB. 18: **Jerry Aronson's** documentary film, *The Life and Times of Allen Ginsberg*, premieres in New York City; MARCH: Pottersfield Press publishes *Visions of Kerouac: A Novel* by **Ken McGoogan**; MARCH 9: **Charles Bukowski**, 73, dies of leukemia in San Pedro, California; MARCH 16: Muse releases *Kerouac: Then and Now*, a forty-seven-minute, ten-track music CD by **Mark Murphy**; APRIL 5: **Kurt Cobain**, 27, commits suicide at his home in Seattle by shooting himself; MAY 18–21: New York University (NYU) sponsors *The Beat Legacy and Celebration*, a four-day literary

HUNTER S. THOMPSON SIGNING BOOKS IN
WASHINGTON SQUARE PARK DURING THE NYU
BEATS CONFERENCE, MAY 1994

conference featuring talks by **David Amram**, **Carolyn
Cassady**, **Gregory Corso**, **Lawrence Ferlinghetti**,
Joyce Johnson, **Hettie Jones**, **Jan Kerouac**, **Joanne
Kyger**, **Ray Manzarek**, **Michael McClure**, **Ed Sanders**,
Cecil Taylor, **Hunter S. Thompson**, and **Anne
Waldman**; at the behest of **Allen Ginsberg**, police
eject **Jan Kerouac** and **Gerald Nicosia,** from the NYU
Conference; **Jan Kerouac**, **Gerald Nicosia** and **Buddha
(John Paul Pirolli**) stage a street protest outside the
conference; MAY 16: **Jan Kerouac** begins a legal action
in Florida's state courts; she alleges that the signature
on **Gabrielle Kerouac's** will is a forgery; JUNE: Farrar,
Straus & Giroux publishes *In Touch: The Letters of
Paul Bowles*, edited by **Jeffrey Miller**; the University
Press of Mississippi publishes *Conversations with
Paul Bowles*, edited by **Gena Dagel Caponi**; Scalo
Publishers/DAP publishes *Paul Bowles Photographs*,

edited by **Simon Bischoff** in collaboration with the Swiss Foundation for Photography; JUNE 6: **Herbert Huncke's** longtime companion, **Louis Cartwright**, 47, is murdered on Second Avenue, Manhattan, by a knife-wielding assailant; JUNE 8: "An Evening with **Jack Kerouac**: Poetry and Prose with Music at Town Hall" (123 W. Forty-Third Street, New York City) features **Kerouac's** work, read by **Allen Ginsberg**, **Lawrence Ferlinghetti**, **Lee Ranaldo**, **Kysia Bostic**, **Gregory Corso**, **Ed Sanders**, **David Henderson**, **Graham Parker**, **David Amram**, **Odetta**, **Anne Waldman**, **Ray Bremser**, and **Andy Clausen**; AUG. 1: Penguin publishes *The Portable Paul and Jane Bowles*, edited by **Millicent Dillon**; SEPT. 6: Rhino releases *Holy Soul Jelly Roll*, a four-CD, fifty-two-track box set of **Allen Ginsberg's** poetry; SEPT. 7: First Run Features releases *Paul Bowles: The Complete Outsider*, a fifty-seven-minute documentary film by **Catherine Warnow** and **Regina Weinreich**; SEPT. 7: Stanford University announces that it has acquired the papers of **Allen Ginsberg**; the purchase terms are not revealed publicly, but the sale is for one million dollars; after taxes and other fees, **Ginsberg** is left with $290,000, which he uses to buy a new loft apartment in a building with an elevator on E. Thirteenth Street, New York City; OCT. 29: To celebrate the release of *Holy Soul Jelly Roll*, **Ginsberg** and record producer

Hal Willner organize a large ensemble performance of "Wichita Vortex Sutra" with musicians **Philip Glass, Art Baron, Stephan Smith, David Mansfield, Arto Lindsay, Marc Ribot, Michael Blair, Elliott Sharp, Lenny Kaye, Lee Ranaldo, Steve Shelley, Lenny Pickett,** and **Christian Marclay**; NOV. 1: Penguin publishes *Scratching the Beat Surface: Essays on New Vision from Blake to Kerouac* by **Michael McClure**; DEC.: New Directions publishes *These Are My Rivers: New and Selected Poems, 1955–1993* by **Lawrence Ferlinghetti**; Alpha Beat Press (New Hope, Pennsylvania) publishes *Madman on the Merrimac* by **John Paul Pirolli**.

1995

JAN. 9: **Allen Ginsberg**, 68, is interviewed by **Jeremy Isaacs** on *Face-to-Face*, a BBC-2 program; JAN. 24: Rhino releases *Call Me Burroughs*, a spoken-word recording by **William S. Burroughs**; FEB. 28: Greenwood Press publishes *The Works of Allen Ginsberg, 1941–1994: A Descriptive Bibliography* by **Bill Morgan**, with a foreword by **Allen Ginsberg**; MARCH 1: Viking publishes **Ann Charters's** *The Viking Portable Kerouac* and *Selected Letters of Jack Kerouac*; [APRIL 19: TIMOTHY MCVEIGH, AN AMERICAN MILITIA MOVEMENT SYMPATHIZER, SETS OFF A MASSIVE TRUCK BOMB IN FRONT OF THE ALFRED P. MURRAH FEDERAL BUILDING IN OKLAHOMA CITY; 168

PEOPLE ARE KILLED AND ANOTHER 680 ARE INJURED;
YOUNG CHILDREN ARE AMONG THE CASUALTIES.]
JUNE 4–6: New York University sponsors the Writings
of Jack Kerouac conference—featured speakers
include **Allen Ginsberg**, **Ann Charters**, **Lawrence
Ferlinghetti**, **David Amram**, **Lee Ranaldo**, **Miguel
Algarin**, **Gregory Corso**, **Ed Sanders**, **Diane di Prima**,
Odetta, **Graham Parker**, **Anne Waldman**, and others;
SEPT.: **Paul Bowles** returns to New York after a long
self-imposed exile in Morocco; SEPT. 26: Premier
Records releases **David Amram's** soundtrack to
Pull My Daisy; OCT. 6: The Eighth Annual Lowell
Celebrates **Kerouac**! Festival presents "**Patti Smith
/ Herbert Huncke**: An Evening of Music & Poetry"
at Smith Baker Auditorium, 400 Merrimack Street,
Lowell, Massachusetts; OCT. 19: **Allen Ginsberg**, 69,
gives his last poetry reading in Britain at Heaven,
a gay nightclub located underneath the Charing
Cross railway station in central London; the event
is filmed and is made available on DVD; OCT. 29:
Terry Southern, 71, dies from respiratory illness at
Saint Luke's Hospital (Amsterdam Avenue and 113th
Street, New York City) after collapsing at Columbia
University, where he taught writing; NOV. 5: "Children
of the Beats," a poignant montage of photographs
and autobiographical vignettes edited by **Joyce
Johnson's** son, **Daniel Pinchbeck**, appears in *The*

BEAT CULTURE
AND THE NEW
AMERICA,
WHITNEY MUSEUM
OF ART

New York Times Magazine; NOV. 9: "Beat Culture and the New America, 1950–1965," a major exhibit, opens at the Whitney Museum of American Art, 945 Madison Avenue at Seventy-Fifth Street, New York City; it runs until February 4, 1996; NOV. 25: *The Charlie Rose Show* features an interview segment with **Allen Ginsberg**, **Steven Watson** (author of *The Birth of the Beat Generation*), **Nat Hentoff** (columnist at *The Village Voice*), and **George Herms**, a California Beat artist.

1996

FEB. 15: Coffee House Press publishes **Bob Kaufman's** *Cranial Guitar: Selected Poems*, edited by **Gerald Nicosia** with an introduction by **David Henderson**; MARCH 1: Penguin publishes *Kerouac: Selected Letters; Volume 1, 1940–1956*, edited by **Ann Charters**; MARCH 14: **Jan Kerouac** is rebuffed in her efforts to have her father's body moved from Lowell to a cemetery in New Hampshire; MARCH 30: Greenwood Press publishes *The Response to Allen Ginsberg, 1926–1994: A Bibliography of Secondary Sources* by **Bill Morgan**, with a foreword by **Allen Ginsberg**; MAY 1: **Timothy Leary**, 76, dies of cancer in California; Conari Press (Berkeley, California) publishes *Women of the Beat Generation: The Writers, Artists and Muses at the Heart of a Revolution*, edited by **Brenda Knight**; MAY 15: The Whitney Museum of American Art publishes *Beat Culture and the New America, 1950–1965*, the catalog of the 1995–96 exhibit; JUNE 1: Penguin publishes **William S. Burroughs's** *My Education: A Book of Dreams*; JUNE 5: **Jan Kerouac**, 44, dies in Albuquerque, New Mexico of liver failure; JULY 18: The Los Angeles County Museum of Art publishes *Ports of Entry: William S. Burroughs and the Arts* by **Robert A. Sobieszek**, with an afterword by **William S. Burroughs**; AUG. 8: **Herbert Huncke**, 81, dies in New York City of congestive heart failure; SEPT. 12–NOV. 30: "The Haight-Ashbury Counterculture, 1964–1968," an exhibit of sixty photographs by **Larry Keenan**, is held at Great Modern Pictures, 48 E. Eighty-Second Street, New York City; SEPT. 20: Greenwillow Books publishes *Beat Voices: An Anthology of Beat Poetry*, edited by **David Kherdian**; OCT. 3–6: The Ninth

Annual Lowell Celebrates **Kerouac**! Festival occurs; NOV.: **Sheri Martinelli**, 88, protégé of **Anais Nin** and friend and/or lover of **H.D.**, **Ezra Pound**, **William Gaddis**, **Allen Ginsberg**, and **Charles Bukowski**, among others, dies of natural causes; [NOV. 5: BILL CLINTON IS REELECTED PRESIDENT.] NOV. 15: St. Martin's Griffin publishes *With William Burroughs: A Report from the Bunker* by **Victor Bockris**; NOV. 26: The Nova Convention (Revisited) is held in Lawrence, Kansas; 1978 Nova Convention alums **Patti Smith**, **Debbie Harry**, **John Giorno**, **Philip Glass**, **Laurie Anderson**, and **Ed Sanders** attend, as does **Michael Stipe** of REM; DEC. 1: Water Row publishes *Beat Speak: An Illustrated Beat Glossary Circa, 1956–1959* by Ashleigh Talbot; DEC. 15: Sun Dog Press publishes **Neeli Cherkovski's** *Elegy for Bob Kaufman*; **Robert Franks's** *Pull My Daisy* is added to the National Film Registry; **Gyula Gazdag's** ninety-six-minute film on **Allen Ginsberg**, *A Poet on the Lower East Side: A Docu-Diary*, is released.

1997

JAN. 1: Charles H. Kerr publishes *From Bughouse Square to the Beat Generation: Selected Ravings of Slim Brundage—Founder & Janitor of The College of Complexes*, edited with an introduction by **Franklin Rosemont**; JAN.: City Lights publishes

1418½ CLOUSER AVENUE, COLLEGE PARK SECTION OF ORLANDO, FLORIDA—KEROUAC'S HOME FROM JULY, 1957 TO MARCH, 1958—WHERE HE WROTE *THE DHARMA BUMS*

Philip Lamantia's *Bed of Sphinxes: Selected Poems*; Viking publishes **Kerouac's** *Some of the Dharma* (forty-three years after it was written); MARCH 1: Lawrence Hills Books publishes *The Autobiography of LeRoi Jones*; MARCH 1: ECW Press publishes *The Buk Book: Musings on Charles Bukowski* by **Jim Christy**, with photos by **Claude Powell**; MARCH: Rebel Inc. publishes *A Life in Pieces: Reflections on Alexander Trocchi*, edited by **Allan Campbell** and **Tim Niel**; MARCH: **Bob Kealing**, a journalist, publishes an article about **Kerouac's** 1957–58 Orlando home at 1418 1/2 Clouser Avenue in the *Orlando Sentinel*; **Jeffrey Cole**, chairman and president of Cole National, donates $100,000 to buy the **Kerouac** house for preservation purposes; MARCH 28: **Allen Ginsberg** is diagnosed with inoperable liver cancer;

APRIL 5: **Allen Ginsberg**, 70, dies peacefully at his loft apartment on E. Thirteenth Street in New York City; APRIL 7: *The Charlie Rose Show* features a brief "Remembrance of **Allen Ginsberg**"; APRIL 28: Judge **Gerard Thomson** of the New Mexico State District Court issues a ruling in favor of **Gerald Nicosia** regarding the **Jan Kerouac–Jack Kerouac** literary estate controversy; JUNE: City Lights publishes **Janine Pommy Vega's** *Tracking the Serpent: Journeys into Four Continents*; JUNE 5: **Jan Kerouac** is interred at Saint Louis de Gonague Cemetery in Nashua, New Hampshire; JUNE 20: **Stephen T. Kay's** *The Last Time I Committed Suicide*, a ninety-two-minute film based on **Neal Cassady's** "Joan Anderson Letter," opens in the U.S.; JULY 1: Serpent's Tail publishes *A Different Beat: Writing by Women of the Beat Generation*, edited by **Richard Peabody**; JULY 15: Southern Illinois University Press publishes *A Tawdry Place of Salvation: The Art of Jane Bowles*, by **Jennie Skerl**; JULY 25: Steerforth Press publishes **Neeli Cherkovski's** *Bukowski: A Life*; AUG. 2: **William Seward Burroughs**, 83, dies of a heart attack in Lawrence, Kansas; AUG. 4: *The Charlie Rose Show* features "A Remembrance of **William Burroughs**" with **Morgan Entrekin** and **Robert Wilson**; AUG. 6: **Burroughs's** memorial service held in Lawrence, Kansas; SEPT. 5: William Morrow publishes *The*

Herbert Huncke Reader, edited by **Ben G. Schafer** with a foreword by **William S. Burroughs** and an introduction by **Raymond Foye**; SEPT. 16: Appleseed Records releases **Ramblin' Jack Elliott's** CD *Kerouac's Last Dream*; SEPT. 17: PBS series *American Masters* airs *The Life and Times of Allen Ginsberg*; OCT. 2–5: The Tenth Annual Lowell Celebrates **Kerouac**! Festival occurs; OCT. 13: Tarcher publishes *Beat Spirit* by **Mel Ash**; OCT. 28: Polygram Records releases *Readings by Jack Kerouac on the Beat Generation*; NOV.: City Lights publishes **Bill Morgan's** *Beat Generation in New York: A Walking Tour of Jack Kerouac's City*; DEC. 19: University of California Press publishes *Collected Prose* by **Charles Olson**, edited by **Donald Allen** and **Benjamin Friedlander** with an introduction by **Robert Creeley**.

1998

JAN. 5: The University of California Press publishes *Wising Up the Marks: The Amodern William Burroughs*, a critical study of **Burroughs** by **Timothy S. Murphy**; FEB. 27: **Jack Micheline** dies on a Bay Area Rapid Transit (BART) train in the East Bay area of San Francisco at the age of 68; MARCH 25: Fantasy releases the CD *Howl, and Other Poems* by **Allen Ginsberg**; APRIL 1: The University of California Press publishes *A Little Original Sin: The*

Life and Work of Jane Bowles by **Millicent Dillon**; Water Row Press publishes *The Conquerors* by **Ray Bremser**; APRIL 17: **Laki Vazakas's** documentary film *Huncke and Louis* is screened at the Cucalorus Film Festival in Wilmington, North Carolina; APRIL: Counterpoint Press publishes *Sleeping Where I Fall: A Chronicle* by **Peter Coyote**; APRIL 30: Scarecrow Press publishes *The Beat Generation: A Bibliographical Teaching Guide* by **William Thomas Lawlor**; *Gargoyle*, no. 41 (Summer 1998), contains "Sheri Martinelli: A Modernist Muse," by **Steven Moore**; JULY 16: Autonomedia publishes *Crimes of the Beats*, a demystification of the Beat mythos by the "Unbearables" (**Bart Plantenga**, **Ron Kolm**, and others); AUG. 1: Penguin publishes a paperback edition of **Diane di Prima's** *Memoirs of a Beatnik*; August 7–9: The Cherry Valley Arts Festival 1998 gives "A Tribute to 30 Years of Beat and Bohemian Influence"; performers include **Ralph Ackerman**, **David Amram**, **Gordon Ball**, **Mary Beach**, **Ray Bremser**, **Andrew Clausen**, **Carol Goss**, **Richard Houff**, **Rochelle Kraut**, **Linda Lerner**, **Catfish McDaris**, **Claude Pelieu**, **Charles Plymell**, **Charles Potts**, **Bob Rosenthal**, **Ed Sanders**, **Danny Shot**, **Herschel Silverman**, **Janine Pommy Vega**, and **Anne Waldman**; AUG.: St. Martin's Press publishes **Ellis Amburn's** controversial biography, *Subterranean*

CHERRY VALLEY
TRIBUTE TO
BEATS FESTIVAL

Kerouac: The Hidden Life of Jack Kerouac; therein,

Amburn alleges that **Kerouac** carefully concealed his

bisexuality to protect his career; SEPT. 1: Mystic Fire

Video releases *William S. Burroughs: Commissioner

of Sewers*, a sixty-minute film on VIIS; SEPT. 1: ECW

Press publishes *The Long Slow Death of Jack Kerouac*

by **Jim Christy**; SEPT. 11: The New Mexico Court of

Appeals rules in favor of **Jan Kerouac's** ex-husband,

which appears to spell defeat for **Gerald Nicosia**

in the **Jan Kerouac–Jack Kerouac** literary estate

controversy; SEPT. 16: Harper/Perennial publishes *The

Herbert Huncke Reader*; SEPT. 29: **Janet Forman's**

documentary film *The Beat Generation: An American

Dream* is released on VHS; OCT. 1–4: The Eleventh

Annual Lowell Celebrates **Kerouac**! Festival occurs;

OCT. 24: **Jerry Aronson's** documentary film *The

Life and Times of Allen Ginsberg* is screened at the

United Nations Association Film Festival at Stanford University; OCT. 30: The New Mexico Supreme Court rules favorably on a motion by **Gerald Nicosia** in the **Jan Kerouac–Jack Kerouac** literary estate controversy; Southern Illinois University Press publishes **David Sterritt's** *Mad to Be Saved: The Beats, the '50s, and Film*; NOV. 3: **Ray Bremser** dies of lung cancer in Utica, New York at the age of 65; NOV.: Rebel Inc. publishes *Charles Bukowski: Locked in the Arms of a Crazy Life: Biography of Charles Bukowski* by **Howard Sounes**; NOV. 29: Simon and Schuster publishes **Hunter S. Thompson's** early novel (written in 1959) *The Rum Diary*; DEC. 16: **William Gaddis**, 75, dies of prostate cancer.

1999

JAN. 23: **Chuck Workman's** *The Source*, a documentary film about **Burroughs**, **Kerouac**, and **Ginsberg** at Columbia University in the 1940s, is screened at the Sundance Film Festival and nominated for the Grand Jury Prize; [FEB. 12: BILL CLINTON, IMPEACHED BY THE HOUSE OF REPRESENTATIVES ON DECEMBER 19, 1998, FOR THE LEWINSKY AFFAIR, IS ACQUITTED BY THE SENATE.] FEB. 16: Modern Library publishes *Beat Writers at Work*, edited by **George Plimpton** with an introduction by **Rick Moody**; FEB. 23: **Gershon**

Legman, 81, dies in France a week after suffering a major stroke; MARCH: ECW Press publishes *Use My Name: Jack Kerouac's Forgotten Families* by **James T. "Jim" Jones**; APRIL 1: The Robert Briggs Association releases *Poetry and the 1950's: Homage to the Beat Generation*, a spoken-word CD by **Robert Briggs**; [APRIL 20: THE COLUMBINE HIGH SCHOOL MASSACRE—ERIC HARRIS, 18, AND DYLAN KLEBOLD, 17, SHOOT AND KILL TWELVE STUDENTS, ONE TEACHER, AND THEMSELVES.] MAY 1: Penguin publishes *Huge Dreams: San Francisco and Beat Poems* by **Michael McClure**; MAY 1: Penguin publishes *Overtime: Selected Poems* by **Philip Whalen**; The University of Delaware's Hugh M. Morris Library obtains **Paul Bowles's** papers; The VU University Press publishes *Beat Culture: The 1950s and Beyond* by **C. Van Minnen** et al.; Penguin publishes *Overtime: Selected Poems* by **Philip Whalen**, edited by **Michael Rothenberg** with an introduction by **Leslie Scalapino**; JULY: Steerforth Press publishes **Neeli Cherkovski's** *Whitman's Wild Children: Portraits of Twelve Poets*; the twelve poets are **Michael McClure, Charles Bukowski, John Wieners, James Broughton, Philip Lamantia, Bob Kaufman, Allen Ginsberg, William Everson, Gregory Corso, Harold Norse,** and **Lawrence Ferlinghetti**; JULY 1: Penguin publishes a paperback edition of **Joyce Johnson's** *Minor*

MOONDOG2 ALBUM COVER

Characters; SEPT. 8: **Moondog**, 83, dies in New York City; SEPT. 11: The New Mexico Court of Appeals upholds the ruling that **John Lash** as "general personal representative" has control over **Jan Kerouac's** estate and not **Gerald Nicosia**, her "personal literary representative"; SEPT. 14: Rykodisc releases a rediscovered, remixed, and augmented recording, *Jack Kerouac / Tom Waits & Primus—Jack Kerouac Reads "On the Road"*; SEPT. 22: **Gerald Nicosia** resigns as literary personal representative of **Jan Kerouac's** estate; SEPT. 30–OCT. 3: The Twelfth Annual Lowell Celebrates **Kerouac**! Festival occurs; OCT. 1: Water Row Press publishes *The Dying of Children* by **Ray Bremser** (written in 1957); OCT.: Chicago Review Press publishes **David Sandison's** *Jack Kerouac: An Illustrated Biography*; OCT. 7: An auction of Beat memorabilia at Sotheby's (New York City) called "**Allen Ginsberg** and Friends" surpasses expectations by netting $674,466; OCT. 20: Southern Illinois University Press publishes *Jack Kerouac's Duluoz Legend: The Mythic Form of An Autobiographical Fiction* by **James T. Jones**; NOV. 1: Penguin publishes a new edition of **Jack Kerouac's** *Some of the Dharma* (written between 1953 and 1956); NOV. 15: Basic Books publishes *The Outlaw Bible of American Poetry*, edited by **Alan Kaufman** and **S.A. Griffin**; NOV. 18: **Paul Bowles**, 89, dies of heart failure in Tangier, Morocco; NOV.: Greenwich Exchange publishes *Liar! Liar! Jack Kerouac—Novelist* by **R.J. Ellis**; DEC. 10: **Ed Dorn**, 70, dies of pancreatic cancer in Denver, Colorado.

2000

JAN. 1: St. Martin's Press publishes *You Can't Catch Death* by **Ianthe Brautigan**, a memoir that explores her father's 1984 suicide; JAN. 29: **Gary Walkow's** (historically inaccurate) film *Beat* (starring **Kiefer Sutherland** as a young **William S. Burroughs** and **Courtney Love** as **Joan Vollmer**) premieres at the Sundance Film Festival; APRIL 1: Sun & Moon Press publishes *The Journal of John Wieners is to be Called 707 Scott Street for Billie Holiday*; APRIL 4: Counterpoint publishes *The Gary Snyder Reader: Prose, Poetry, and Translations*; APRIL: McFarland

& Co. publishes *The Beat Generation and the Popular Novel in the United States, 1945–1970* by **Thomas Newhouse**; MAY 4: North Atlantic Books publishes *Charles Olson: The Allegory of a Poet's Life* by **Tom Clark**; MAY: Viking Press publishes *Recollections of My Life as a Woman: The New York Years—A Memoir* by **Diane di Prima**; MAY 14: **Darren Aronofsky's** critically acclaimed film version of **Hubert Selby Jr.'s** *Requiem for a Dream*—starring **Ellen Burstyn**, **Jared Leto**, **Jennifer Connelly**, **Marlon Wayans**, and **Christopher McDonald**—premiers at the Cannes Film Festival; JUNE 22: Grove Press publishes *Word Virus: The William S. Burroughs Reader*, edited by **James Grauerholz** and **Ira Silverberg**; JULY: **Edward Sanders's** *The Poetry and Life of Allen Ginsberg: A Narrative Poem* is published by Overlook Press; JULY 12: A reprint edition of *The Rolling Stone Book of the Beats: The Beat Generation and American Culture*, by **Holly George-Warren**, is published by Hyperion; AUG.: Creative Arts publishes **Joan Haverty's** memoir, *Nobody's Wife: The Smart Aleck and the King of the Beats*, with an introduction by **Jan Kerouac**; SEPT. 15: North Atlantic Books publishes **Joanne Kyger's** *Strange Big Moon: The Japan and India Journals, 1960–1964* (which reveals that **Gary Snyder— Kyger's** husband at the time—was often surly and even physically abusive); OCT. 5–9: The Thirteenth

Annual Lowell Celebrates **Kerouac**! Festival occurs;
NOV. 1: Penguin publishes *Kerouac: Selected Letters, Volume 2, 1957–1969*, edited by **Ann Charters**; NOV. 14: Da Capo Press publishes *Beat Punks* by **Victor Bockris**; NOV.: **Omar Swartz's** *The View from "On the Road": The Rhetorical Vision of Jack Kerouac* is published by Southern Illinois University Press;
DEC. 1: Semiotext(e) publishes *Burroughs Live: The Collected Interviews of William S. Burroughs, 1960–1997*, edited by **Sylvère Lotringer**; [DEC. 12: BUSH V. GORE—THE REPUBLICAN-DOMINATED U.S. SUPREME COURT RULES IN FAVOR OF **GEORGE W. BUSH** AND EFFECTIVELY DECIDES THE ELECTION; **BUSH** "WINS" THE PRESIDENCY BY JUDICIAL FIAT MORE THAN A MONTH AFTER THE NOVEMBER 7 ELECTION.]
DEC. 22: Schirmer Trade Books publishes *Beat Generation: Glory Days in Greenwich Village* by **Fred W. McDarrah** and **Gloria S. McDarrah**.

2001

JAN. 1: Grey Fox Press simultaneously publishes four **Lew Welch** books: (1) *Selected Poems*, (2) *How I Work as a Poet*, (3) *How I Read Gertrude Stein*, and (4) *Trip Trap: Haiku on the Road* (by **Jack Kerouac**, **Lew Welch**, and **Albert Saijo** about their cross-country trip in 1959); City Lights publishes a revised and expanded edition of *The First Third* by **Neal Cassady** and *Postcards from the Underground: Portraits of the Beat Era* by **Larry Keenan**; JAN. 17: **Gregory Corso**, 69, dies of cancer at his daughter's house near Minneapolis, Minnesota; FEB. 1: Peter Lang Publishing publishes **Rod Phillips's** *"Forest Beatniks" and "Urban Thoreaus": Gary Snyder, Jack Kerouac, Lew Welch, and Michael McClure*; MARCH 30: Grove Press publishes *Last Words: The Final Journals of William S. Burroughs*, edited by **James Grauerholz**; MARCH 7–12: Lowell Celebrates **Kerouac**! sponsors the **Jack Kerouac** Birthday Celebration in Lowell; APRIL 11: *Queer*, a chamber opera adapted by **Erling Wold** from **Burroughs's** eponymous novel, premiers in San Francisco to rave reviews; MAY 1: City Lights publishes *San Francisco Beat: Talking with the Poets*, edited by **David Meltzer**; MAY 4: Picador publishes a paperback edition of *Cities of the Red Night* by **William Burroughs**; MAY 5: The remains of **Gregory Corso** are buried next to **Percy Bysshe Shelley** in the protestant cemetery of Via Caio Cestio, Rome, Italy; MAY 11: Black Sparrow Press publishes *Beerspit Night and Cursing: The Correspondence of Charles Bukowski and Sheri Martinelli, 1960–1967*, edited by **Steven Moore**; MAY 23: **Jim Irsay** (owner of the Indianapolis Colts) purchases the one-hundred-twenty-page first draft of *On the Road* (written in APRIL–MAY 1951) at auction for $2.43 million—the

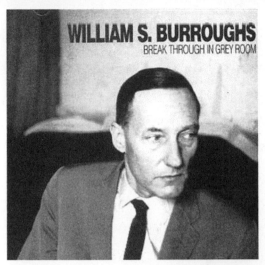

WILLIAM S. BURROUGHS, *BREAK THROUGH IN GREY ROOM*

most money ever paid for a literary manuscript;
JUNE 1: Penguin publishes **Joyce Johnson's** *Door Wide Open: A Beat Love Affair in Letters, 1957–1958*;
JUNE 1: Coffee House Press publishes *Beats at Naropa*, edited by **Anne Waldman** and **Laura Wright**;
JUNE 5: Penguin publishes **Ann Charters's** *Beat Down to Your Soul: What Was the Beat Generation?*;
JULY 3: Sub Rosa (U.K.) releases *Break Through in Grey Room*, a spoken-word recording of **William S. Burroughs's** collaborations with **Brion Gysin**;
JULY 10: St. Martin's Griffin posthumously publishes **Richard Brautigan's** last and quasi-autobiographical novel, *An Unfortunate Woman: A Journey*, which he wrote just prior to his suicide in 1984; JULY 10: Grove Press publishes **Barry Miles's** *The Beat Hotel:*

Ginsberg, Burroughs, and Corso in Paris, 1957–1963; JULY 20: Palgrave publishes **Jamie Russell's** *Queer Burroughs*; AUG. 22: **John Sampas**, executor of the **Kerouac** estate, sells **Kerouac's** literary and personal archive to the New York Public Library's Berg Collection for an undisclosed sum (probably in excess of $10 million); AUG. 31: Da Capo Press publishes a third edition of **Tom Clark's** *Jack Kerouac: A Biography*; [SEPT. 11: NINETEEN ISLAMIC FUNDAMENTALIST TERRORISTS, MOSTLY FROM SAUDI ARABIA, HIGHJACK FOUR U.S. COMMERCIAL AIRLINERS AND DESTROY THE WORLD TRADE CENTER TOWERS IN NEW YORK CITY AND BADLY DAMAGE THE PENTAGON IN WASHINGTON, D.C.; MORE THAN 3,000 AMERICANS ARE KILLED.] SEPT. 12: **Victor Wong**, 74, dies in Locke, California; OCT. 3–8: The Fourteenth Annual Lowell Celebrates **Kerouac**! Festival occurs; The University of Illinois Press publishes **John Lardas's** *Bop Apocalypse: The Religious Visions of Kerouac, Ginsberg, and Burroughs*; Gale Group publishes *The Beats: A Literary Reference*, edited by **Matt Theado**; NOV. 1: Cityfull Press publishes *Jack Kerouac's Nine Lives: Essays* by **James T. "Jim" Jones**; NOV. 10: **Ken Kesey** dies of liver cancer at the age of 66; DEC.: McGill-Queen's University Press publishes *Robert Creeley: A Biography* by **Ekbert Faas**; DEC. 4: **Henry Ferrini's** twenty-seven-minute film, *Lowell Blues: The Words of Jack Kerouac* (narrated by **Robert Creeley**, **Johnny Depp**, **Carolyn Cassady**, **Gregory Corso**, and others), wins the Grand Festival Award for Documentary at the Eighth Annual Film and Video Festival in Berkeley, California; Bloomsbury publishes *Family Business: Selected Letters Between a Father and Son* (**Allen Ginsberg** and **Louis Ginsberg**), edited by **Michael Schumacher**.

2002

JAN. 1: Rebel Inc. publishes a new edition of **Alexander Trocchi's** erotic novel *Helen and Desire*; JAN. 9: Thunder's Mouth Press publishes *Offbeat: Collaborating with Kerouac* by **David Amram**; JAN. 15: Wesleyan Press publishes *Back in No Time: The Brion Gysin Reader*, edited by **Jason Weiss**; JAN. 29: Penguin publishes a reprint edition of *The Cat Inside* (1986) by **William S. Burroughs**; MARCH 5: I Books publishes *Orpheus Emerged* (1945), **Kerouac's** first novel; MARCH 26: Harper Perennial publishes *Allen Ginsberg: Spontaneous Mind; Selected Interviews, 1958–1996*, edited by **David Carter** with a preface by **Václav Havel** and an introduction by **Edmund White**; MARCH 29: Venice West Beat poet **John Thomas**, 71, dies of congestive heart failure in Los Angeles; APRIL 1: Sun Dog Press publishes **Jean-François Duval's** *Bukowski and the Beats: A Commentary on the Beat Generation*; APRIL 16: Counterpoint publishes **John**

Suiter's *Poets on the Peaks: Gary Snyder, Philip Whalen & Jack Kerouac in the Cascades*; APRIL 17: Thunder's Mouth Press publishes a paperback edition of **Regina Weinreich's** *Kerouac's Spontaneous Poetics: A Study of the Fiction* (1987); APRIL 30: Thunder's Mouth Press publishes a new paperback edition of *Memoirs of a Bastard Angel: A Fifty-Year Literary and Erotic Odyssey* by **Harold Norse**; MAY: Southern Illinois University Press publishes **Benedict Giamo's** *Kerouac, the Word and the Way: Prose Artist as Spiritual Quester*; MAY: **Gary Snyder** retires from his teaching post at the University of California, Davis, after sixteen years; JUNE 1: Ecco publishes a reprint edition of *Beerspit Night and Cursing: The Correspondence of Charles Bukowski and Sheri Martinelli, 1960–1967*, edited by **Steven Moore**; JUNE 26: **Philip Whalen** dies at the age of 78 in San Francisco; JULY 1: Rutgers University Press publishes *Girls Who Wore Black: Women Writing the Beat Generation*, edited by **Ronna C. Johnson** and **Nancy M. Grace** with a foreword by **Ann Charters**; JULY 1: Cherry Red (U.K.) releases *Final Academy Documents,* starring **William S. Burroughs**, on DVD; JULY 5: *L.A. Weekly* publishes "Hitting the Beats," an exposé of the late **John Thomas** by his adult daughter, **Gabrielle Idlet**, which discloses that **Thomas** was a deadbeat dad, a Benzedrine addict, the country's

GIRLS WHO WORE
BLACK BOOK COVER

leading perpetrator of mail-order fraud, and was, at
the time of his death, serving a one-hundred-twenty-
day sentence in Los Angeles County Jail for sexually
molesting his fifteen-year-old daughter (**Idlet's** half
sister), Susan, in 1972. JULY 30: Penguin publishes *As
Ever: Selected Poems* by **Joanne Kyger**, edited with a
foreword by **Michael Rothenberg** and an introduction
by **David Meltzer**; SEPT. 1: SAF Publishing Ltd.
publishes *AsEverWas: Memoirs of a Beat Survivor* by
Hammond Guthrie; SEPT. 4: Thunder's Mouth Press
publishes a new edition of **John Clellon Holmes's**
Go: A Novel (with afterwords by **Seymour Krim** and
Ann Charters); SEPT. 19: At the 2002 Geraldine
R. Dodge Poetry Festival at Waterloo Village in
Stanhope, New Jersey, **Amiri Baraka** reads his poem
"Somebody Blew Up America," which alleges that the

9/11 terrorist attacks were orchestrated by the U.S. and Israel; a media uproar ensues; SEPT. 26: **David Mackenzie's** film adaptation of **Alexander Trocchi's** 1957 novel, *Young Adam*, premiers in the U.K.; **Ewan McGregor** plays the lead role; OCT. 15: The Fifteenth Annual Lowell Celebrates **Kerouac**! Festival occurs; DEC. 9: The University of California Press publishes **James Campbell's** *This Is the Beat Generation: New York, San Francisco, Paris*; DEC. 17: Da Capo Press publishes a paperback edition of **Matt Theado's** *The Beats: A Literary Reference*; Peter Lang publishes *The Beat Generation: Critical Essays*, edited by **Kostas Myrsiades**; **Paul Blake Jr.**, **Jack Kerouac's** nephew, reopens the case over **Gabrielle Kerouac's** allegedly forged will.

2003

MARCH 13–15: The University of Michigan's Special Collections Library presents a symposium: "Makeup on Empty Space: A Celebration of **Anne Waldman**" in honor of the acquisition of the **Anne Waldman** archive; MARCH 18: Da Capo Press publishes a new edition of *Desolate Angel: Jack Kerouac, the Beat Generation, and America* (1979) by **Dennis McNally**; [MARCH 20–MAY 1: THE SECOND PERSIAN GULF WAR DEPOSES IRAQI DICTATOR SADDAM HUSSEIN; HE IS EVENTUALLY HANGED FOR WAR CRIMES.]

APRIL: New Directions publishes *An Accidental Biography: The Selected Letters of Gregory Corso* by **Bill Morgan**, with a foreword by **Patti Smith**; APRIL 1: Penguin publishes **Jack Kerouac's** *Book of Haikus* and **William S. Burroughs's** *Junky* (the fiftieth anniversary edition, with the "definitive" text); APRIL 14: **Kirby Doyle** dies at the age of 70; **Jerry Cimino** opens the Beat Museum in Monterey, California; APRIL 15: Southern Illinois University Press publishes *William Burroughs and the Secret of Fascination* by **Oliver Harris**; APRIL 20: **Jack Shea's** controversial documentary *Who Owns Jack Kerouac?* debuts at Artist's Television Access, San Francisco; MAY 1: City Lights publishes **Bill Morgan's** *The Beat Generation in San Francisco: A Literary Tour*; MAY 16: Gale publishes *The Beat Generation: A Gale Critical Companion*, edited by **Lynn M. Zott**; JUNE 15: **Joyce Johnson's** *Door Wide Open* is dramatized by Sanctuary Theater Workshop at the Bowery Poetry Club in New York City's East Village; it garners good reviews; AUG. 21: A "**Jack Kerouac** Bobblehead Doll" is given to the first one thousand fans attending a game between the Lowell Spinners and Williamsport Crosscutters of the Class A New York–Penn Baseball League; OCT. 2–5: The Sixteenth Annual Lowell Celebrates **Kerouac**! Festival occurs; NOV. 24: Counterpoint

JACK KEROUAC
BOBBLEHEAD

publishes **Gary Snyder's** *The Practice of the Wild: Essays*; NOV. 24: Thames & Hudson publishes *Brion Gysin: Tuning In to the Multimedia Age*, edited by **José Férez Kuri** with contributions by **Guy Brett, William S. Burroughs, Mohammed Choukri, Gregory Corso, Gladys C. Fabre, John Grigsby Geiger, John Giorno, Bruce Grenville, Bernard Heidsieck, Felicity Mason, Barry Miles**, and **Nicholas Zurbrugg**; DEC. 2: Mystic Fire Video releases a DVD version of *William S. Burroughs: Commissioner of Sewers*; DEC. 17: At Christie's "Playboy at 50" auction, an original thirty-three-page typescript section of *Visions of Cody* (written in 1951, first published as "Before the Road" in the December 1959 issue of *Playboy* magazine, and appraised at $20,000–$30,000) is sold for $71,700; DEC. 17: Soft Skull Press publishes *Chapel of Extreme*

Experience: A Short History of Stroboscopic Light and the Dream Machine by **John Geiger**; DEC. 29: Da Capo Press publishes *In the Hub of the Fiery Force: Collected Poems of Harold Norse 1934–2003*.

2004

JAN. 23: Southern Illinois University Press publishes **David Sterritt's** *Screening the Beats: Media Culture and the Beat Sensibility*; JAN. 26: Grove Press publishes **Burroughs's** *Naked Lunch: The Restored Text*, edited by **James Grauerholz**; FEB. 1: HarperCollins publishes **Sam Kashner's** *When I Was Cool: My Life at the Jack Kerouac School, A Memoir*; MARCH 4: Palgrave Macmillan publishes **Jennie Skerl's** *Reconstructing the Beats*; MARCH 24–JULY 15: The Rare Book Collection at the Wilson Library, University of North Carolina at Chapel Hill, displays the exhibit "Lines Drawn in the Sand: The Life and Writings of **Allen Ginsberg**"; MARCH 28: Thunder's Mouth Press publishes a second edition of **William Plummer's** *The Holy Goof: A Biography of Neal Cassady* (1981); APRIL 2–3: The University of North Carolina at Chapel Hill's library marks a decade of collecting Beat and American avant-garde literature by sponsoring a conference titled "The Beats in America: Alternative Visions, Then and Now"; guest speakers are **Bill Morgan** (freelance archivist and bibliographer of **Lawrence Ferlinghetti** and **Allen Ginsberg**), **Ann Charters**, **Hilary Holladay** (director of the biennial Kerouac Conference on Beat Literature sponsored by the University of Massachusetts Lowell), **Jennie Skerl** (coeditor with **Robin Lydenberg** of the 1985 critical collection *William S. Burroughs at the Front: Critical Reception, 1959–1989* and author of *Reconstructing the Beats*, published in 2004), **Tim Hunt** (author of *Kerouac's Crooked Road: Development of a Fiction*), **Gordon Ball** (friend and associate of **Allen Ginsberg** and editor of **Ginsberg's** early journals and other writings), **Matt Theado** (author of *The Beats: A Documentary Volume* and *Understanding Jack Kerouac*); **Nancy Peters** (codirector of City Lights), **Barney Rosset** (founder of Grove Press); **Robert Wilson** (owner of the Phoenix Book Shop in New York during the 1960s), **John Cohen** (still a photographer for *Pull My Daisy*), **David Amram**, **Michael McClure**, and **Steven Clay** (publisher of Granary Books in New York); APRIL 5: *Beat Angel* premieres at the Method Fest Independent Film Festival, Calabasas, California; APRIL 7: University of California Press publishes **Jonah Raskin's** *American Scream: Allen Ginsberg's "Howl" and the Making of the Beat Generation*; APRIL 26: **Hubert Selby Jr.**, 75, dies in Highland Park, Los Angeles, from chronic obstructive pulmonary lung disease; MAY: The University Press of Mississippi publishes *Breaking the Rule of Cool: Interviewing and Reading Women Beat Writers*, edited by **Nancy M. Grace** and **Ronna C. Johnson**; MAY 20: Pluto Press publishes *Retaking the Universe: William S. Burroughs in the Age of Globalization* by **Davis Schneiderman** and **Philip Walsh**; MAY 28: **John Dullaghan's** *Bukowski: Born into This*, a documentary on **Charles Bukowski**, is released to excellent reviews; JULY 24: *Beat Angel* is screened at the Wine Country Film Festival, Sequoia Grove Winery, Napa, California; JULY 5: Penguin publishes **Joyce Johnson's** *Missing Men: A Memoir*; JULY 27: Harvard University Press publishes *Blows like a Horn: Beat Writing, Jazz, Style, and Markets in the Transformation of U.S. Culture* by **Preston Whaley Jr.**; AUG. 30: Greenwood Press publishes **Michael J. Dittman's** *Jack Kerouac: A Biography*; SEPT. 29–OCT. 3: The Seventeenth Annual Lowell Celebrates Kerouac! Festival occurs; OCT. 7: Viking Press publishes *Windblown World: The Journals of Jack Kerouac 1947–1954*, edited by **Douglas Brinkley**; OCT. 31–NOV. 4: The Spirituality of the Beat Generation conference is held at Esalen Institute, Big Sur, California; [NOV. 2: GEORGE W. BUSH IS REELECTED PRESIDENT.] NOV.: Shoemaker and Hoard publish **Gary Snyder's** *Danger on Peaks: Poems*; NOV. 4:

R.L. Crow publishes *Leaning against Time* (poems) by **Neeli Cherkovski**; NOV. 24: Da Capo publishes *Departed Angels: The Lost Paintings*, with artwork by **Jack Kerouac** and text by **Ed Adler**.

2005

JAN. 25: Penguin publishes *Neal Cassady: Collected Letters, 1944–1967*, edited by **Dave Moore** with an introduction by **Carolyn Cassady**; Jan 28: **Lucien Carr**, 79, dies of bone cancer in Washington, D.C.; FEB. 20: **Hunter S. Thompson**, 67, commits suicide by shooting himself at his home in Woody Creek, Colorado; MARCH 4: A tribute to **Lucien Carr** is held at the National Press Club in Washington, D.C.; 164 friends and United Press International associates attend; MARCH 7: **Philip Lamantia**, 77, dies of heart failure in San Francisco; MARCH 12: The first official celebration of **Jack Kerouac** Day is observed throughout Massachusetts; MARCH 30: **Robert Creeley**, 78, dies in Odessa, Texas; APRIL 12: *Factotum*, the film version (directed by **Bent Hamer** and starring **Matt Dillon** as Hank Chinaski and **Lili Taylor** as Jan) of the eponymous 1975 **Charles Bukowski** novel, premiers at the First Trondheim Kosmorama International Film Festival, Trondheim, Norway; APRIL 22: **William Kirkley's** eighty-nine-minute documentary, *Excavating Taylor Mead*, premiers

ROBERT CREELEY,
1926-2005

to good reviews at the fourth annual Tribeca Film Festival, New York City; APRIL 29: The University Press of Mississippi publishes *Conversations with Kerouac*, edited by **Kevin J. Hayes**; MAY 20: ABC-Clio publishes *Beat Culture: Lifestyles, Icons, and Impact*, edited by **William Thomas Lawlor**; JUNE 1: The Disinformation Company publishes *Nothing Is True—Everything Is Permitted: The Life of Brion Gysin* by John Geiger; JULY 18–AUG. 7: *The Girls Who Wore Black*, "a fusion of poetry & drama" based on the book by **Ronna Johnson** and **Nancy Grace**, runs for six performances at the Jewel Box Theater, 312 W. Thirty-Sixth Street, New York City; AUG. 1: **Al Aronowitz**, 77, dies of cancer in New York City; AUG. 25: Farrar, Straus & Giroux publishes a new edition of *My Sister's Hand in Mine: The Collected*

Works of Jane Bowles, with a preface by **Joy Williams**;
OCT. 6–9: The Eighteenth Annual Lowell Celebrates
Kerouac! Festival features the theme "Jack's Roots";
OCT. 12: Da Capo Press publishes *Empty Phantoms:*
Interviews and Encounters with Jack Kerouac by **Paul**
Maher Jr.; the Jack and Stella **Kerouac** Center for
American Studies (at the University of Massachusetts
Lowell) is founded with generous support provided
by **Kerouac** Estate Executor **John Sampas**; OCT. 17:
Virtualbookworm.com Publishing releases *Drugs and*
the "Beats": The Role of Drugs in the Lives and Writings
of Kerouac, Burroughs and Ginsberg by **John Long**;
NOV. 15: Photology publishes *Allen Ginsberg: Beat &*
Pieces; A Complete Story of the Beat Generation in the
Words of Fernanda Pivano with Photographs by Allen
Ginsberg; NOV. 29: Overlook Press publishes a reprint
edition of *The Process* by **Brion Gysin**.

2006

JAN.: City Lights publishes *The Yage Letters Redux*,
edited by **Oliver Harris**; JAN. 26: **Allan Temko**, 81,
dies of congestive heart failure in Orinda, California;
MARCH 1: The New York Public Library's Berg
Collection purchases **William S. Burroughs's** eleven-
thousand-page personal archive for an undisclosed
sum; MARCH 21: Farrar, Straus & Giroux publishes
The Poem That Changed America: "Howl" Fifty Years

THE BEAT MUSEUM: AN UNAVOIDABLE
CONTRADICTION IN TERMS?

Later, edited by **Jason Shinder**; APRIL 4: Penguin

publishes a paperback edition of *Windblown World:*

The Journals of Jack Kerouac, 1947–1954, edited by

Douglas G. Brinkley, and *Book of Sketches* by **Jack**

Kerouac; APRIL 15: The University of Iowa Press

publishes *Gary Snyder and the Pacific Rim: Creating*

Countercultural Community by **Timothy Gray**;

APRIL 30: Aldine Transaction publishes a revised and

expanded edition of *Hustlers, Beats and Others* (1969)

by **Ned Polsky**; MAY: Texas A&M University Press

publishes **Rob Johnson's** *The Lost Years of William S.*

Burroughs: Beats in South Texas; JUNE 28: Southern

Illinois University Press publishes **Michael Hrebeniak's**

Action Writing: Jack Kerouac's Wild Form; JUNE

29: **Gary Snyder's** third wife, **Carole Lynn Koda**, 58,

dies of cancer; JULY 6: BookSurge publishes *The Beat*

Face of God: The Beat Generation as Spirit Guides

by **Stephen D. Edington**; AUG. 17: Southern Illinois

University Press publishes *William Burroughs and*

CURSED FROM BIRTH
BOOK COVER

the Secret of Fascination by **Oliver Harris**; SEPT. 1: Chicago Review Press publishes *Neal Cassady: The Fast Life of a Beat Hero* by **David Sandison** and **Graham Vickers**; SEPT. 27: **Jerry Cimino's** Beat Museum (540 Broadway, San Francisco) has its gala opening (**Michael McClure**, **John Cassady** [**Neal Cassady's** son], **Wavy Gravy**, **Al Hinkle**, and **Stanley Mouse** attend); OCT. 1: Soft Skull Press publishes *Cursed from Birth: The Short, Unhappy Life of William S. Burroughs, Jr.*, edited by **David Ohle**; OCT. 5: Viking Press publishes **Bill Morgan's** *I Celebrate Myself: The Somewhat Private Life of Allen Ginsberg*; OCT. 5: Da Capo publishes *Beat Generation: The Lost Work*, a play written in 1957 by **Jack Kerouac**; OCT. 5–8: The Nineteenth Annual Lowell Celebrates **Kerouac**! Festival occurs; OCT.

21: *Beat Angel* is released on DVD; OCT. 31: Harper
Perennial publishes a new paperback edition of
Let It Come Down, a 1952 novel by **Paul Bowles**;
Penguin publishes a "deluxe edition" of **Kerouac's**
The Dharma Bums; NOV. 1: City Lights publishes
Howl on Trial: The Battle for Free Expression,
edited by **Bill Morgan** and **Nancy Peters**; NOV.
12: **Alan Ansen**, 84, dies in Athens, Greece; NOV.
21: Screen Edge releases *Destroy All Rational
Thought: Celebrating William Burroughs and
Brion Gysin in Ireland* on DVD; NOV. 21: Kultur
Video releases a DVD version of **Colin Still's** fifty-
minute documentary, *No More to Say & Nothing to
Weep For: An Elegy for Allen Ginsberg 1926–1997*;
DEC.: Facts on File publishes *Encyclopedia of Beat
Literature* by **Kurt Hemmer**; DEC. 30: Greenwood
Press publishes *Masterpieces of Beat Literature*,
edited by **Michael J. Dittman**.

2007

JAN.: Canongate Books publishes *Charles Bukowski:
Locked in the Arms of a Crazy Life* by **Howard
Sounes**; FEB. 28: Last Gasp publishes a new edition
of *Revolutionary Letters* by **Diane di Prima**; JUNE 23:
BNpublishing.com releases a mass market paperback
edition of **Jack Black's** *You Can't Win* (1926); JULY:
David S. Wills, a Dundee University (Scotland)

graduate, founds *Beatdom*, an online literary journal; JULY 10: Shambhala publishes *The Beat Book: Writings from the Beat Generation*, edited by **Anne Waldman**; JULY 17: New Yorker Video releases **Jerry Aronson's** 1994 film *The Life and Times of Allen Ginsberg* in a deluxe two-disc DVD set; JULY 24: Facets Video releases **Gyula Gázdag's** film on **Allen Ginsberg**, *A Poet on the Lower East Side: A Docu-Diary*; AUG. 16: Viking simultaneously publishes (1) a fiftieth anniversary edition of **Kerouac's** *On the Road*, (2) *On the Road: The Original Scroll*, and (3) **John Leland's** *Why Kerouac Matters: The Lessons of On the Road (They're Not What You Think)*; AUG. 28: Penguin publishes *The Portable Jack Kerouac*, edited by **Ann Charters**; SEPT. 1: Library of America publishes *Jack Kerouac: Road Novels 1957–1960; On the Road, The Dharma Bums, The Subterraneans, Tristessa, Lonesome Traveler, Journal Selections*, edited by **Douglas G. Brinkley**; City Lights publishes **Edie Parker's** *You'll Be Okay: My Life with Jack Kerouac*; AUG. 21: **Philomene Long**, 67, Beat poet and filmmaker, dies of heart failure in Venice, California; SEPT. 25: Axios Press publishes *Bohemia: Where Art, Angst, Love and Strong Coffee Meet* by **Herbert Gold**; SEPT. 30: Dundurn publishes *Ecstasy of the Beats: On the Road to Understanding* by **David Creighton**; OCT. 1: Running Press publishes *The Beats: From Kerouac to Kesey, an Illustrated*

Journey through the Beat Generation by **Mike Evans**;
OCT.: 4–5: The Twentieth Annual Lowell Celebrates
Kerouac! Festival occurs; OCT. 9: Harper Perennial
Modern Classics publishes *Collected Poems, 1947–1997*
by **Allen Ginsberg**; OCT. 11: **Noah Buschel's** eighty-
minute biopic, *Neal Cassady*, which focuses on
Cassady's alleged entrapment in the Dean Moriarty
myth, premieres at the Woodstock and Austin Film
Festivals simultaneously (**Tate Donovan** plays **Neal
Cassady**, **Glenn Fitzgerald** plays **Jack Kerouac**, **Amy
Ryan** plays **Caroline Cassady**, **Chris Bauer** plays **Ken
Kesey**); **Cassady** family members find the film highly
inaccurate; OCT. 11: The first issue of *Beatdom*, a
journal about the Beats, is published in the U.K. by
David S. Wills; NOV. 2: Da Capo Press publishes **Paul
Maher's** *Jack Kerouac's American Journey: The Real-
Life Odyssey of On the Road*; NOV. 10: **Norman Mailer**,
84, dies of acute renal failure at Mount Sinai Hospital
in New York City; DEC. 17: The Ohio State University
Press publishes *Everything Lost: The Latin American
Notebook of William S. Burroughs*, assembled in
facsimile and transcribed by **Geoffrey D. Smith**, **John
M. Bennett**, and **Oliver Harris**.

2008

JAN. 8: Harper Perennial publishes **Robert Stone's**
Prime Green: Remembering the Sixties; JAN. 28:

Counterpoint publishes **Gary Snyder's** *Back on the Fire: Essays*; JAN. 28: The University of California Press publishes *Selected Poems, 1945–2005* by **Robert Creeley**, edited by **Benjamin Friedlander**; MARCH 3: Counterpoint publishes **Gary Snyder's** epic poem *Mountains and Rivers without End*; APRIL 1: City Lights publishes *Tau & Journey to the End* by **Philip Lamantia** and **John Hoffman**; APRIL 10: Penguin publishes **Deborah Baker's** *A Blue Hand: The Tragicomic, Mind-Altering Odyssey of Allen Ginsberg, a Holy Fool, a Lost Muse, a Dharma Bum, and His Prickly Bride in India*; APRIL: The MIT Press publishes *Andy Warhol: "Blow Job,"* an in-depth examination of the 1964 film by **Peter Gidal**; APRIL: D&E Entertainment releases **Curt Worden's** documentary film *One Fast Move or I'm Gone: Kerouac's Big Sur*; APRIL 23: *Flicker*, **Nik Sheehan**'s seventy-five-minute documentary film about **Brion Gysin** and his Dreamachine, premiers at the Fifteenth Annual Hot Docs Film Festival in Toronto; MAY 1: **Gary Snyder** wins the ($100,000) 2008 Ruth Lily Poetry Prize; MAY: The University of California San Diego Libraries acquire the letters of **Gary Snyder**; JUNE 16: Greater Midwest Publishing publishes *681 Lexington Avenue: A Beat Education in New York City 1947–1954* by **Elizabeth Von Vogt** (sister of **John Clellon Holmes**); JUNE 21: The ZBS Foundation releases an audio CD version of *Jack's Last Call: Say Goodbye to Kerouac*; JUNE 23: Olympia Press publishes a new edition of **Gregory Corso's** only novel, *The American Express*; JUNE 25: Oneworld Publications releases *The Beat Generation: A Beginner's Guide* by **Christopher Gair**; JUNE 27: New Directions publishes *We Meet* by **Kenneth Patchen**; JUNE 28: Counterpoint publishes a revised edition of **Gary Snyder's** *A Place in Space: Ethics, Aesthetics, and Watersheds*; JULY 7: The University of California Press publishes *Syncopations: Beats, New Yorkers, and Writers in the Dark* by **James Campbell**; JULY 9: Arcade Publishing releases *Still Alive: A Temporary Condition* by **Herbert Gold**; JULY 17: New Directions publishes a new illustrated edition of *The Walking-Away World* by **Kenneth Patchen**; AUG. 7: Southern Illinois University Press publishes **Michael Hrebeniak's** *Action Writing: Jack Kerouac's Wild Form*; AUG. 19: Picador publishes a new edition of **Tom Wolfe's** *The Electric Kool-Aid Acid Test*; AUG. 26: Penguin publishes a new paperback edition of **Kerouac's** *On the Road: The Original Scroll*; SEPT. 8: Da Capo Press publishes *The Letters of Allen Ginsberg*, edited by **Bill Morgan**; SEPT. 13: BookSurge Publishing releases *The Beat Handbook: 100 Days of Kerouactions* by **Rick Dale**; SEPT. 18: Viking publishes **Jack Kerouac's** *Wake Up: A Life of the Buddha* (written in 1955); SEPT. 28: Gunther's

Jack's Last Call: *Say Goodbye to Kerouac*

A new Audio Play for Public Radio by Patrick Fenton

JACK'S LAST CALL

Taproom, 84 Main Street, Northport, Long Island, hosts a daylong tribute to **Jack Kerouac** near the time of the thirty-ninth anniversary of his death; the celebration and tribute begins at 3 PM with the return performance of an original one-act play, *Jack's Last Call: Say Goodbye to Kerouac*, written by Massapequa playwright **Patrick Fenton**, directed by **Ed Dennehy**, and featuring Long Island actors **Drew Keil** as **Jack Kerouac**, **Jack O'Connell** as **Leo Kerouac**, **Sonya Tannenbaum** as **Memere (Gabrielle) Kerouac**, **Derek McLaughlin** as **Neal Cassady**, **Suzanne Guacci** as **Jan Kerouac**, and **Steve Ryan** as the *Newsday* reporter who narrates the story; OCT. 3–5: The Twenty-First Annual Lowell Celebrates **Kerouac**! Festival occurs; OCT. 10–11: The Beat Generation Symposium is held at Columbia College, Chicago; OCT. 3–NOV. 26: The Center for Book and Paper Arts (1104 S.

Wabash Avenue, Columbia College, Chicago) shows the exhibit "**Jack Kerouac**—*On the Road* around the World: 66 International Book Covers from the Collection of **Horst Spandler**"; OCT. 11: *Neal Cassady*, a biopic by **Noah Buschel**, opens simultaneously at the Woodstock and Austin Film Festivals; OCT. 14: NYRB Classics publishes a new edition of **Emmett Grogan's** *Ringolevio: A Life Played for Keeps* (with an introduction by **Peter Coyote**); NOV. 1: Grove Press publishes *And the Hippos Were Boiled in Their Tanks*, the 1945 novel about the Kammerer slaying, cowritten by **Kerouac** and **Burroughs**; [NOV. 4: BARACK OBAMA IS ELECTED FORTY-FOURTH PRESIDENT OF THE U.S.] NOV. 19: Southern Illinois University Press publishes *What's Your Road, Man? Critical Essays on Jack Kerouac's "On the Road,"* edited by **Hilary Holladay** and **Robert Holton**; NOV. 19: IUniverse publishes *The Twilight of Romanticism: Lives and Literature in French Bohemian Culture and the Beat Generation* by **John Wells**; NOV. 25: Counterpoint publishes *The Selected Letters of Allen Ginsberg and Gary Snyder, 1956–1991*, edited by **Bill Morgan**; DEC. 3, 2008–JAN. 28, 2009: The Barber Institute of Fine Arts, University of Birmingham, United Kingdom, hosts "**Jack Kerouac**: Back 'On the Road,'" an exhibit of the 1951 scroll manuscript of *On the Road* and accompanying events (see below).

2009

JAN. 1: Soft Skull Press publishes a revised edition of **Jack Sargeant's** *Naked Lens: Beat Cinema*; JAN. 7: Penguin publishes a paperback reprint edition of **Deborah Baker's** *A Blue Hand: The Tragicomic, Mind-Altering Odyssey of Allen Ginsberg, a Holy Fool, a Lost Muse, a Dharma Bum, and His Prickly Bride in India*; JAN. 8: **Richard Ellis**, curator of the exhibition "**Jack Kerouac**: Back 'On the Road'" at the Barber Institute of Fine Arts, University of Birmingham, U.K., leads a panel discussion titled "What Exactly Is 'Beat'?"; the panel is chaired by **Ann Sumner**; JAN. 21: A poetry reading with original work by **Ian McMillan**, **David Tipton**, **Jim Burns**, and **Dick McBride** is held at the Underground Bar, Guild of Students, University of Birmingham, U.K.; MARCH 13: Pocket Essentials publishes a Kindle edition of *The Beat Generation: The Pocket Essential Guide* by **Jamie Russell**; MARCH 17: Hill and Wang publishes *The Beats: A Graphic History*, edited by **Paul Buhle**; APRIL: *Ferlinghetti: A City Light*, a seventy-three-minute documentary by **Christopher Felver**, premiers at the San Francisco International Film Festival; MAY 1: Counterpoint publishes the first trade paperback edition of **Gary Snyder's** *Passage through India: An Expanded and Illustrated Edition* and *Tamalpais Walking: Poetry, History, and Prints* by **Tom Killian** and **Gary Snyder**; MAY 1: Peter Lang Publishing

releases *The Beat Generation and Counterculture:*

Paul Bowles, William S. Burroughs, Jack Kerouac

by **Raj Chandarlapaty**; JUNE 1: Coffee House Press

publishes *Beats at Naropa*, edited by **Anne Waldman**

and **Laura Wright**; JUNE 8: **Harold Norse**, 92, dies of

natural causes in San Francisco; JUNE 25: Southern

Illinois University Press publishes *The Daybreak*

Boys: Essays on the Literature of the Beat Generation

by **Gregory Stephenson**; JULY 24: Seven years after

the case was reopened by **Jack Kerouac's** nephew,

Paul Blake Jr., Judge **George W. Greer** rules that

Gabrielle Kerouac's signature on the 1973 will is a

forgery; the ruling vindicates **Gerald Nicosia** and the

late **Jan Kerouac**; AUG. 2: SueMedia Productions

hosts a special Theatre on the Vine performance

of *Jack's Last Call: Say Goodbye to Kerouac* at

Castello di Borghese Vineyard and Winery, Route 48,

Cutchogue, Long Island, New York; AUG. 13: Olympia

Press publishes **Alexander Trocchi's** *The Carnal Days*

of Helen Seferis; AUG. 18: **Fernanda Pivano**, **Allen**

Ginsberg's Italian translator, 92, dies in Milan, Italy;

AUG. 28: A celebration of the fiftieth anniversary of

Naked Lunch and a fundraiser for **Jonathan Leyser's**

film *William S. Burroughs: A Man Within* are held

in Chicago; SEPT. 1: *The Road to Interzone: Reading*

William S. Burroughs Reading by **Michael Stevens**

JAN KEROUAC: A LIFE IN MEMORY BOOK COVER

is published by Suicide Press; SEPT. 9: Chronicle
Books publishes **Jack Kerouac's** *You're a Genius All
the Time* (with a foreword by **Regina Weinreich**);
SEPT. 11: **Jim Carroll**, 60, dies of a heart attack in
New York City; OCT. 1–4: The Twenty-Second Annual
Lowell Celebrates **Kerouac**! Festival occurs; SEPT.
22, 2009–Jan 3, 2010: "Looking In: **Robert Frank's**
The Americans," a fiftieth anniversary exhibition,
is held at the Metropolitan Museum of Art, Fifth
Avenue at Eightieth to Eighty-Forth Streets; New York
City; OCT. 7: City Lights holds *Jan Kerouac: A Life
in Memory*, hosted by **Gerald Nicosia** with special
guest appearances by **Adiel Gorel**, **Brenda Knight**,
John Cassady, **Carl Macki**, and **Phil Cousineau**, to
mark the City Lights publication of *Jan Kerouac:
A Life in Memory*, edited by **Gerald Nicosia**; OCT.

18: **Lenore Kandel**, 77, dies of lung cancer in San Francisco; NOV. 1: Oneworld Classics publishes a new edition of **Alexander Trocchi's** *Man at Leisure* (with an introduction by **William S. Burroughs**); SEPT. 15: Counterpoint publishes an anniversary edition of **Gary Snyder's** *Riprap and Cold Mountain Poems*; OCT. 8: *Corso: The Last Beat*, an eighty-seven-minute documentary film by **Gustave Reininger**, premieres at the Seventeeth Annual Hamptons International Film Festival; OCT. 27: Penguin publishes a paperback edition of **Jack Kerouac's** *Wake Up: A Life of the Buddha* (with an introduction by **Robert Thurman**); NOV. 1: City Lights publishes **Helen Weaver's** *The Awakener: A Memoir of Kerouac and the Fifties*; DEC. 29–30: In Philadelphia, the 2009 Modern Language Association's annual convention features two panels on the Beats: (1) "Understanding the Beats Globally" with **Jennie Skerl** (panel chair), **Todd Thorpe** ("**Bob Kaufman**: Genealogical Drift"), **Hassan Melehy** ("**Jack Kerouac** and the Nomadic Cartographies of Exile"), **Timothy S. Murphy** ("Seduced across the Border: Globalizing **William Burroughs**"), and **Ronna Catherine Johnson** ("Beat Transnationalism under Gender: **Bonnie Bremser's** *Troia*") and (2) "Recasting Minor Characters: Beat Women" with **Mary Paniccia Carden** (panel chair), **Nancy McCampbell Grace** ("**Diane di Prima** and the Beat

HOWL
MOVIE POSTER

Fairy Tale"), **Ronna Catherine Johnson** ("**Diane di Prima**'s Anarchist Heritage and *Revolutionary Letters 1971–2007*: Global Radical Chic"), **Mary Paniccia Carden** ("Intertextual Identity in **Joyce Johnson's** *Minor Characters*"), and **Jennie Skerl** ("Mid-Century Bohemia Redefined: Portraits by Beat Women").

2010

JAN. 14: Canongate Books publishes a new edition of *Charles Bukowski: Locked in the Arms of a Crazy Life* by **Howard Sounes**; JAN. 21: *Howl*, a docudrama by **Rob Epstein** and **Jeffrey Friedman** about the 1957 *Howl* obscenity trial, debuts at the Sundance Film Festival to negative reviews; MARCH 11–13: Lowell Celebrates **Kerouac**! weekend and birthday celebration occurs; APRIL 30: Syracuse University Press publishes *Missing a Beat: The Rants and Regrets of Seymour Krim*, edited by **Mark Cohen**; MAY 10: *Beat Memories: The Photographs of Allen Ginsberg* by **Sarah Greenough** is published by Prestel USA; MAY 11: Free Press publishes *The Typewriter Is Holy: The Complete, Uncensored History of the Beat Generation* by **William Morgan**; MAY 30: **Peter Orlovsky**, 76, dies of lung cancer in Williston, Vermont; JUNE 22: Merrell Publishers releases *Brion Gysin: Dream Machine*, edited by **Laura Hoptman**. JULY 8: Viking publishes *Jack Kerouac and Allen Ginsberg: The Letters*, edited by **Bill Morgan** and **David Stanford**; AUG. 2: Virgin Books publishes *Jack Kerouac: King of the Beats*, and *Allen Ginsberg: Beat Poet*, new biographies by **Barry Miles**; AUG. 20: Southern Illinois University Press publishes *A Map of Mexico City Blues: Jack Kerouac as Poet* by **James T. Jones**; Aug. 31: Harper Perennial publishes a graphic novel version of Allen Ginsberg's *Howl* by **Eric Drooker**; SEPT. 1: University Press of Mississippi publishes *Brother-Souls: John Clellon Holmes, Jack Kerouac, and the Beat Generation* by **Ann & Samuel Charters**; OCT 1: Counterpoint Press publishes *The Etiquette of Freedom: Gary Snyder, Jim Harrison, and the Practice of the Wild* by **Gary Snyder & Jim Harrison**, edited by **Paul Ebenkamp**; NOV. 1:

Degrees Books publishes *Howl: A Look Inside the Beat Generation's Writers and the New Movie About Allen Ginsberg* by **Courtney Hutton**; NOV. 2: Southern Illinois University Press publishes *Capturing the Beat Moment: Cultural and Politics and the Poets of Presence*; NOV. 23: City Lights publishes *White Hand Society: The Psychedleic Partnership of Timothy Leary & Allen Ginsberg* by **Peter Connors**. DEC. 21: Manchester University Press publishes *Beat Sound, Beat Vision: The Beat Spirit and Popular Song* by **Laurence Coupe**; New Pacific Press publishes *Beat Attitudes: On the Roads to Beatitude for Post-Beat Writers, Dharma Bums, and Cultural-Political Activists* by **Rob Sean Wilson**.

PHOTO CREDITS

INDEX

ABOUT THE AUTHOR

Robert Niemi is a Professor of English and American Studies at St. Michael's College in Colchester, Vermont. He is the author of several previous nonfiction and reference works including *History in the Media: Film & Television* and a biography of Russell Banks. He lives in Vermont.